# YOUR PLAY TO CALL

# YOUR PLAY TO CALL

RACHEL LABERGE

Paperback ISBN: 979-8-9891308-2-5



Editing (developmental, line, copy) and proofreading by Sophie Fitzpatrick with Wonder and Wander Editing Co.

Cover design by Love Lee Creative.

*This is for anyone who has a song or album that feels like it's part of your bones and has altered your chemical makeup.*

*And, to my dad, for letting me watch sports with him when I was a kid, and teaching me how therapeutic it is to yell at the tv...*

*Lastly, to the younger version of myself who would record songs from the radio onto a cassette in her room: you dreamed of writing songs, and you did it. You also one-upped yourself with the whole songs-in-a-book-you-wrote thing.*

# PLAYLIST

**Champagne Supernova |** Oasis

**Call It What You Want |** Taylor Swift

**Running From Lions |** All Time Low

**An Encounter |** The 1975

**Don't Take The Money |** Bleachers

**Kiss Me |** Ed Sheeran

**Feels Like |** Gracie Abrams

**I Think I'm In Love |** Taylor Acorn

**Remember When |** Wallows

**Out of My League |** Fitz and The Tantrums

**The Weatherman |** The Gaslight Anthem

**The Alchemy |** Taylor Swift

**American Baby |** Tyler Ward

**Sidelines |** Phoebe Bridgers

**A Movie Script Ending |** Death Cab for Cutie

**Hands Down |** Dashboard Confessional

**Our Secret Cove |** Beò (Custom Song) 

# Chapter 1
## Willow

I'M CURRENTLY INSIDE AN empty beer cooler as they wheel me to the back of the stage. It wasn't plugged in, but the metal interior still chills my skin. The glass door is covered with an *out of order* sign; no one knows someone is inside. Well, no one besides the people wheeling it. I can't believe I'm about to play the Super Bowl halftime show and no one knows. The league is going for the ultimate shock factor and I know it's going to land.

That's why I agreed to it. Since I'm near the end of my largest tour to date, no one expected me to say yes. It's best to keep everyone on their toes; that's my motto.

*Bang! Bang! Bang*! The knocking on the cooler startles me and I'd jump if there was room. Muffled laughs and someone making jokes about needing a beer are faint on the other side.

When this idea of a completely surprise halftime show was made public, everyone thought it would flop. Between the logistics of rehearsing, schedules, and the inability of people to keep a secret, they thought there was no way it would work.

That's where I come in.

To be honest, I think Claire, my manager, and I are some of the only people who could realistically pull this off, considering even some of my closest people are in the dark. My parents, and boyfriend, Dexter, think I'm in Los Angeles doing costume alterations for my final tour dates. No one suspects I'm in Arizona, about to pull off one of the biggest surprises of my career.

I can't *wait* to see their faces.

But most of all, I can't wait to hear the fans. Feel them.

The theories are my favorite. Currently, I think the top contender is "the performer won't even be human but a hologram, or some sort of AI-generated mashup of the top artists of the year." And then you always have the "my sister's boyfriend's aunt works at the stadium and confirmed it's fill-in-the-blank."

Do you know who isn't on the surprise half-time theory list? The only female artist to sell out *every* NFL stadium in a single tour.

In other words—me. Willow.

The teams playing are also in the dark on the halftime show performer. Similar to how I only found out who was playing in the championship game this morning when I was doing last-minute prep with the technical crew.

A few months ago, the NFL sent me an address that was nothing more than an abandoned warehouse with a practice stage. It may have been compact and left little room for imagination, but it would get the job done. They didn't want to give anything away, and that's something I can respect.

Claire, the human version of a vault, helped me put together the short setlist. I wanted to do my part to keep it a secret, which meant Claire and my head of security were the only people I told. Plus, if I included Claire, my security wouldn't completely lose their minds.

Someone taps on the top of the cooler, in a predetermined pattern, indicating it's almost time. I'm wearing a black cloak with my single outfit underneath. The black bodysuit hugs me in all the right places, adorned with lace and crystals. I wear something similar on tour, but this is a fresh piece I've held onto for a special occasion. I think the Super Bowl counts, right?

The stage is in one of the end zones, fifteen feet tall, and close to a tunnel. That way, they can wheel me right underneath it.

The cooler stops moving.

Here we go.

The door swings open, and I pull myself out and keep my hood up and face down. If anyone is around, I don't want them to get even a quick glimpse of who I am. Not even a minute early.

I go to my starting spot—a five-foot square that will rise through the center. My hand trembles for a few seconds, so I grip the microphone tighter. Flutters take over my stomach and chest like I'm a hollow shell. I'm a little light-headed but in a way that feels right, like something big is coming. I've had my fair share of accomplishments, but this is a dream of mine about to come true. One of the biggest stages in the world and it's all mine.

The lights go out—by design. Screams and cheers from the crowd flood my ears. The platform starts moving. My heartbeat picks up to match the crowd response.

I keep my chin to my chest, my hood still up, and feel the stage lock into place. I take a single, slow breath. Hold. One. Two. Three. Four. Exhale.

The sound team is waiting for my cue. I do my best to be patient and stand razor-sharp for a few seconds and each moment that passes feels agonizingly long, but they're filled with screams and delicious anticipation.

I let the energy from the crowd run through me before I snap with my right hand. I slowly grab the side of my hood while the other holds my microphone. Tight.

The hood comes down.

The first note of one of my most popular songs drops and I come in—vocals strong—a second later. I picked this song because it has the quickest start, and the crowd won't even have a chance to register what's happening.

Until it's already underway.

# Chapter 2
## Tripp

Down by seven at halftime is not where you want to be when playing in the Super Bowl. Having only two catches and eighteen yards is also not what you're hoping for as a starting wide receiver either. The opposing team's defense has stopped everything before my quarterback even has a chance to read the coverage. There's no time for plays to develop.

The veins bulging in my offensive coordinator's neck are starting to freak me out; it's hard not to stare. I know everyone with the Seattle Serpents, from the owner down, has felt the pressure as we prepared for the game.

We weren't supposed to play in the Super Bowl. We started the season 0-4, and if our start wasn't rough enough, we lost our top three wide receivers in week four. The reality of playing in the championship game was not on any of our minds, but when you win nine straight games at the end of the regular season, anything is possible.

We're supposed to be home, watching this game on TV, and certainly not getting our asses handed to us by the entire coaching staff.

You'd think we were down by thirty. Coach is going through the adjustments we need to make if we "want a shot at winning this thing".

Man, I want to win this game.

This is the first season I've been WR1 out of the seven I've been in the league. I'm the top receiver on our depth chart which means I'm targeted the most. Honestly, I'm the main target because of the injuries to my teammates. There literally is no one else.

Everyone was worried about me crumbling under the pressure. I was a consistent athlete, in college and the NFL; one you could rely on. I always played well enough to be included in a few play packages, but I was never the guy you immediately wanted to get involved.

I felt the pressure but did my best to have fun. And you know what? It fucking worked.

There's nothing like scoring your first touchdown and getting up from the turf in the end zone after. The sound from the crowd reaches your bones. Teammates pick you up, eyes surprised and relieved. Making eye contact with fans, giving them high-fives, and jumping up into the first-row seats. Going back to the sideline to have your coach pat you on the back.

I was always the one hyping up my teammates when they did something worth celebrating. Being on the receiving end was different and felt much better than I ever imagined—a rush that I'll chase and do almost anything to feel.

If I want that intoxicating rush, something has to give. It's kind of ridiculous that this is only a one-score game. We're *technically* still in it thanks to our defense and definitely not our offense. My quarterback threw three interceptions in the first half. Hell, that's more than the last three games combined. Adrenaline is kicking his ass, and every time I look at him, I swear he's going to throw up. If he can't settle in and loosen up, we've got no shot, and I won't get that hit of dopamine I crave from scoring a touchdown.

He's next to me, looking like his shoulders are glued to his ears. I hit him with my elbow, flashing him a quick look, and jumping up and down. Hoping he'll do the same.

Just as Coach is getting into the details of how we're going to "get our heads out of our asses" and "play like we've seen a football field before," the crowd goes absolutely wild. The halftime performer must've revealed themselves—sounds like someone worth seeing.

The crowd keeps getting louder, almost feral, and I'm not the only one who notices. My teammates break their concentration from Coach and look toward the locker room door. We're all wondering the same thing: who could possibly be on stage to warrant this reaction?

"Can y'all pretend you're interested in winning this game?" Coach spits, clearly annoyed.

I try to tuck the adrenaline and curiosity away.

When it's time to head back to the field, the crowd's noise hasn't lessened at all. I'm a few steps out of the tunnel when I see the stage, and my eyes flash up to the Jumbotron.

It all makes sense.

Willow is playing the halftime show. *The* Willow. The woman is a genius. How the hell did the NFL pull this off? She's wrapping up a record-shattering tour, and she's arguably the best artist to ever do it.

She's also gorgeous.

I own every one of her albums, on vinyl, and know probably every damn word. Some may call it a guilty pleasure, but the woman is remarkable. I stand by that. No guilt here.

I can't help but smile and practically dance to the warmup area. I jump up and down when I get close to my quarterback, trying to hype him up. He looks at me and laughs when he sees me singing along.

"Tripp!" my quarterback yells out. "Is the second half going to get in the way of your dance party?"

His laugh is all it takes, and other guys start singing along with me. With Willow. I dance, doing some of her tour choreography, because I know it. At this point, I'd do anything to help my guys relax and make them feel like we belong.

"Guys, it's like this." I start doing the moves, slow, in a way that they can catch on. The entire team has slowed or come to a stop. I do the moves, in order, one more time while Willow is wrapping up the verse. "Ready?" I yell to my guys. My team.

Willow hits the chorus and does the same choreography I just showed a group of professional athletes. Some of them hoot and holler and start doing the dance alongside me, mimicking the popstar. The fans near us laugh, point their smartphones, getting the video they didn't they know needed.

"Tripp Owens, get your ass moving and warm up," Coach says, playfully hitting my back and jostling my shoulders. He smiles and shakes his head.

Stress and anxiety are heavy, but it feels like it lifts just enough for us to focus.

For the first time tonight, it feels like we can win this game.

# **Chapter 3**
## Willow

I BET THIS IS what flying feels like. I practically float back to my dressing room, no longer heavily guarded to keep my identity a secret. Since the secret was so critical, I was heavily encouraged to use security provided by the venue and not my own.

I knew my parents wouldn't like it. Or Dexter. *Ah, I need to call Dexter.* My stomach flips when I think of him. Lately, I've been contemplating big picture things. Like, marriage things. Dexter hasn't proposed but there have been so many moments where I felt like he might, and like I would say yes.

I thought about letting him in on the secret, but ultimately decided against it. I wanted it to be a surprise. My brain goes back to one of our earliest dates...

*"What's one venue you'd give anything to play?" Dexter asks, taking a sip of his coffee. We're hanging out at a studio I'm recording in later today. "Like, a limb. You'd give a limb."*

*"That's easy. The Super Bowl."*

*"Interesting. Not really a venue though." He winks and sets his mug down.*

*"Fine, wherever the Super Bowl is the year they ask me to play it." I feel silly saying it like this but it's something Claire and I have been working on. She's on a manifestation kick. We have affirmations, mood boards, and are trying to speak things into existence.*

*"When they ask you, huh?" He smirks in a way that brings me to my knees. "Confident. I like it."*

*I didn't have the heart to tell him that the confidence was just a fluke. No matter how many albums I sell or tours I go on, I still feel like a fraud.*

*"I can't wait for the day you get to make that dream come true." He sweetly reaches and grabs a hold of my hand on top of the table.*

I can't wait to remind him of that day. Clutching my phone to my chest, I spin in my dressing room. It buzzes with notifications from what looks like every friend and family member reaching out about my performance. A smile spreads even further across my face. I wish I could grab hold of this feeling and bottle it to keep forever.

I dial Dexter's number, not bothering to look and see if he reached out.

"Will—" He says my nickname like I'm being scolded. "Have you lost your mind?" Dexter's voice is rough and hurried. It immediately brings me down a notch.

"Got you! Wasn't it awesome?" I skip right over the agitation.

"I mean, yeah, but it's awfully reckless. How could you not tell me? Do you at least have your security team with you?" Concern drips from his words, but it's not enough to lessen my annoyance. This isn't what I expected.

"Dex. Come on. Are you really going to give me a single 'yeah'? I pulled off one of the most prolific halftime shows ever, *and* I was able to do it with practically no one knowing. The crowd was wild. I loved it."

"Willow, you know you're good at this. You just heard 70,000 people tell you that. You don't need me to." He sounds like he's trying to be compassionate, but it falls flat. So incredibly flat. "Your security team. Who is with you?"

Where's the guy who praised me for confidence? Who acted like this is something I could accomplish? Who wanted to cheer me on?

"Actually, it's a team provided by the NFL. Don't worry. Everything is fine."

"I bet that place is crawling with paparazzi and crazy fans. How are you going to get out of there?!"

To be honest, I knew this would be a difficult piece of the logistical puzzle. But, in all honesty, this isn't unusual. I wanted to play the half-time show, and I wanted it to be a secret. I figured I'd deal with this later.

"I'm not even in the same state as you. I can't help," Dexter says. My brain is still trying to think of the next steps.

"Dex. Take a breath. I'm sure I'll be able to get out of here safely. Everything's going to be fine. My plane leaves tomorrow morning. I'll be home for lunch," I say, hoping that if I focus on the future and what happens after I figure out the issue at hand, he'll relax.

Dexter exhales into the phone.

"You're right. It was very surprising," he says. I can hear the smallest trace of a smile. I know I've won him over, even just enough for him to loosen the reins. He's not always this overly protective but he does worry about my safety. Usually, it's something I love about him.

Dexter never entertains the paparazzi or anything of the sort. It's a rare occurrence for people to see us out together. Fans know we're still a couple—three years and counting—mostly because of my publicist.

He'll do almost anything to stay out of the public eye except when it's band related. Dexter is in an indie band that never entertained signing with a label. They tour every year but we're talking ten to fifteen dates. The venues are small and are usually filled with die-hard fans or someone who thought a $20 cover would be worth something to do.

I've never told him but sometimes I'm jealous. I'd love it if I could play smaller venues and do things like invite fans on stage to sing with me. My label, and security team, would never go for it.

"Let me know when you get back to your hotel. *Wherever* you're staying," Dexter says, getting in his jab at me for being left out.

"You got it. I'm just going to do a quick visit with the winning team, congratulate them, and then be on my way. I'll text you."

"Love." Dexter says our parting greeting. I'm not sure how it started but it's our thing.

"Love." I end the call and put my phone face down on the vanity.

It stings that he didn't recognize I just made one of my dreams come true. Something people only wish they could do.

"How did *that* go?" Claire asks while fixing her hair in my mirror. She looks like she walked right out of a corporate meeting in an onyx Valentino pantsuit.

"He's worried, that's all." I know I'm minimizing his reaction. How much it hurt. How I'm holding back tears.

"Oh, the sting of fragile masculinity," Claire says, wearing a saccharine grin.

Instead of spiraling about Dex's reaction, or having Claire launch into a rant, I reach for the blank thank-you cards—including matching 'W' stickers to seal the envelopes—on the vanity. I grab my favorite pen, one that will not smear as I write left-handed, and take a deep breath. This is one of my favorite parts about my performance routine.

I make it a point to write out a few thank-you notes at each venue or event, and hand them out before I leave. It started when I played at a small local coffee shop with one of my friends playing guitar. A young fan gave me the note on my way out, and it's something that has stuck with me. For ten years.

There's just something special about a handwritten thank-you note.

While there's nothing I can do about Dex right now, I can express my gratitude and hopefully make someone smile.

# **Chapter 4**
## Tripp

THIS IS FUCKING INCREDIBLE. I'm a Super Bowl Champion. I've never been "the guy" when it comes to winning big games. This season, this game specifically, I was key. Me. Tripp Owens. It wasn't just me hyping up the guys on the sideline but making plays.

Black and green Seattle Serpent confetti falls on the field. The same field where I caught two touchdowns in the second half. We trailed the entire game, except for the last three minutes of the fourth quarter. I scored the touchdown that put us on top and it feels fucking great.

Un-fucking-real.

The field is now full of families—wives, girlfriends, kids, parents. Everyone is looking for their player. I've got my eyes looking for the only person I had a ticket for.

"Tripp!" Someone puts their hand on my shoulder, lightly turning me. I can tell by voice alone it's my mom. Exactly who I was looking for.

I face her and envelop her in a massive hug. The woman who constantly drove me to practices, tutoring sessions, and never missed a college home game. I've never been the golden boy on any roster, but I always was on hers.

"I can't believe *you*." She kisses both of my cheeks. "Two touchdowns! TWO." She is yelling and jumping up and down, holding my hands. "129 yards!" She wraps me up in hug.

All I can do is cry. It's more than football at this point. It's always been me and her ever since my dad left when I was a kid. He never looked back but neither did she. In this moment, I'm so fucking thankful she didn't.

I set her down and she puts both of her hands on the sides of my face. "Tripp. You did it. Your team did it." Tears trickle down her face. "I'm so proud of you!" she yells.

I hear the clicks of cameras around me and hope someone is capturing this moment. This is one I'll want to relive repeatedly—celebrating with the person who always put me and my dreams first.

"*We* did it. I love you, Mom." I hug her again, dipping down so I can put my head in the crook of her neck and shoulder. She squeezes as tight as she can. A few stray tears of excitement, gratitude, and adrenaline fall down my face.

Someone pulls me away to the makeshift stage where my coach, quarterback, and general manager gather. The rest of the team is close behind. Friends and family surround the stage; I find my mom right away. Someone hands me a Seattle Serpent Super Bowl Champion hat, and my mouth hangs open.

I've watched the Super Bowl every year for as long as I can remember. Logically, I know what happens next, but knowing and experiencing it are two wildly different things.

"Wouldn't be a Super Bowl without an MVP," the NFL commissioner says. It's surreal being on the same stage as him. My brain can barely make sense of it.

He pauses as the crowd claps. I'm shoulder to shoulder with my guys, and this smile is fucking glued to my face at this point.

"And your Super Bowl most valuable player is…" The commissioner pauses again just as my head coach makes eye contact with me and winks. "Tripp Owens!"

My mom's face is the only thing I see. Her hand covers her mouth as she jumps up and down. Hands clap me on the back. Coach makes his way over to me, reaches out a hand, and shakes mine before pulling me in for a hug. I can't hear anything he says. The crowd. My teammates. Clicks of cameras. Everyone trying to get closer.

I don't know how it happened but I'm the MVP.

Fuck.

Adrenaline and bliss wash over me. It's like I'm twelve years old, watching my favorite player win a Super Bowl, nose almost touching the TV screen. Except, this time, it's me.

THE LOCKER ROOM IS in complete chaos. The field was almost like a shock to the system, and now, letting it soak in, the locker room is crazier. It's bottles of Champagne and goggles—no one likes to get blasted in the eyes with bubbly. Teammates and coaching staff scream, clap each other on the back, and there are even some chest bumps. Music blares from somewhere as we dance in a circle. A laugh bursts from my chest when Coach gets in the middle.

A security guard asks if we mind an interruption. None of us object because we don't give a fuck. It doesn't matter who walks through that door with the high we're on.

She steps into the locker-room, cautious, knowing there's a Champagne party happening. A pair of goggles dangles from her hand.

Willow is wearing a Seattle Serpents jersey, black leggings—which hug all of her curves, and white sneakers. It's simple but ridiculously attractive. In a room full of mostly professional athletes she looks short, but I'm guessing she's around 5'4". When she turns to talk to someone, I see her name on the back of the jersey.

Fuck. She looks good.

"Hey!" she says, louder than I expected. "Super Bowl champs!" she shouts and starts clapping. The rest of the locker room follows suit and claps along, hooting and hollering.

"Just wanted to say amazing job. I didn't get to watch the first half but sounds like the second half is where it was at anyways." The guys don't even let her finish before they're yelling, hitting hands with teammates, and letting another wave of excitement wash over the room.

It's hard for me to look anywhere else. Her hair, pinned back from her face, and rich like chocolate, is short enough that it doesn't touch her shoulders. Her cheeks are pink, and it doesn't look like she's wearing any makeup. Fresh faced, her features glow. Fucking gorgeous.

We line up and take a photo with her. She stands in the middle of our team huddle, arms around the guys next to her like she knows all of us. I wish I was next to her.

"I don't want to take up any more of your time but congrats and have some fun tonight!" Everyone yells as she waves and leaves the locker room.

I stand there smiling. In awe. Like an idiot. I'm the Super Bowl MVP, and I'm star struck.

⚬

AFTER ABOUT ANOTHER HOUR in the locker room, the guys are packing up to head to the airport. It sounds like we're going to Vegas because according to my Coach, that's where you go after you "win a fucking championship".

I can't believe this is my life.

I forgot something in my locker so I'm one of the last ones to leave the stadium. I'm about to head out when I see Willow at the end of the hallway. She's on the phone, pacing back and forth.

Gone is the cool and collected woman in a rowdy locker room. Her chin is folded into her chest, and she's twirling her dark hair nervously.

Three security guards stand near the doors, peering out the window. They seem unsure of the next step. I can hear the maniacal shuffle of the paparazzi from here.

Willow's voice is short and low while she paces, staring at the floor. I don't catch much of her conversation, but I do hear, "Dex, I know how you feel about me being here without my standard team, but there's nothing I can do about that now. If you let me hang up, I could try to figure this out."

She pulls the phone from her ear. It appears that Dex, whoever that is, hung up on her. Tucking the short dark strands behind her ears she clasps her hands in front of her chest, still pacing. "Miss... ugh... Willow. What do you want to do?" one of the guards asks her, instilling zero confidence.

"I can't believe how bad you are at this," a woman wearing a black pantsuit snaps.

Before I know what I'm doing, I interject myself into a situation I have nothing to do with. Sounds like me—impulsive as fuck.

"What seems to be the issue?" I ask. Willow's eyes snap to mine, and I see a moment of clarity when she realizes I'm one of the players.

"I'm trying to get to my car, but the paparazzi have blocked every single door. It keeps getting worse the longer I wait."

Immediately, I go into problem-solving mode.

"Is the car still safe? Like, if you got there, it'd be fine?" I don't step into the line of sight of the window. I'm not as popular as Willow, but I don't need to make it worse.

"Yes. My driver says no one is there. It's around the corner."

"Sounds like you need a distraction." A small smirk reaches my lips.

Willow laughs. "Yeah, I guess you could say that." Her hands are on her hips, and she puts weight on one of her legs.

An idea pops into my brain. My mom, publicist, and maybe even my coach probably won't love it but I feel like I get a pass after winning a Super Bowl. Sometimes you go for it and ask for forgiveness later. If you're me, you do this *most* of the time.

"I can get them away from the door. Long enough for you to get to the car."

I run back to the locker room and see exactly what I need: a bottle of unopened Champagne. Not just any bottle but a magnum. Perfect.

While jogging back to the end of the hallway, I'm smiling and love that I'm going to be able to help her out.

"What are you going to do?" She's hesitant but inquisitive.

"Don't worry about it." I turn to the three security guards. "Can you get her out of here safely? You've done a piss poor job so far." Willow grins behind them.

"Yes. We just need a little space to get her to the vehicle."

I nod. "You better."

"Now that is what I'm talking about!" The woman in black claps her hands and points at me.

"Be ready to run, okay?" I make eye contact with Willow. She trades her look of annoyance with one of determination and nods her head in understanding.

I take a deep breath and stretch my neck from side to side. I run my hands through my hair, messing it up and making it even more disheveled.

Before I open the door, I look at Willow a final time and give her a wink. I hope it makes me seem much more confident than I feel. If this doesn't work, I'll look like a major jackass.

The second the door opens, it's nothing but flashes and clicks of cameras. People scream my name, trying to get me to look at them. I fake stumble out of the hallway, into the mob, and continue to move forward. They move away from the door, trying to see what I'm doing.

"Super Bowl champs, baby!" I scream as I pop the cork of the Champagne. It's a mix of screaming fans and whooping paparazzi. They're getting the shot they were hoping for: the drunk MVP overindulging and making a fool of himself.

As soon as I've moved the mob from the door, and I can feel the attention on me, I spray everyone with Champagne.

Just like I planned. Out of my peripheral vision, the door opens, and four figures run toward the car as I spray the rest of the magnum bottle. Someone yells about their equipment, but I act like the drunk football player who can't control themselves.

And because I am stone-cold sober, I know they buy it.

The only thing I wish was different? Telling her my name.

# Chapter 5
## Willow

*5 Months Later*

No one has seen me for months, but strangely, it's exactly what I needed.

After the Super Bowl performance and the final leg of my tour, Dexter and I couldn't bounce back. The paparazzi, always a pain point in our relationship, were relentless afterward. They served as a reminder of him being in the dark—the secret I kept from him.

It hurt that this was the thing we couldn't get past. One of my dreams coming true and the man I loved couldn't co-exist. How screwed up is that?

Did I tell him I thought we could end up happily ever after? That he was the only person I ever thought about marrying? That this was a bump, but we could get over it? No. I didn't say anything like that.

At the end of the day, Dexter left me, on the day before my thirtieth birthday, and I let him. He packed up his things in our apartment in SoHo, and when he shut the door for the last time, I sat in the living room, silently crying, staring out the window at a day that was too bright for my mood. My heart broke open in our empty bedroom.

Part of me wishes I would've asked him to stay but the part being too scared to say the words won.

The press had a field day considering Dexter's departure from our apartment was far from graceful. Despite his aversion to the paparazzi, he didn't hold back, shouting about our breakup while they snapped photos. ***Another One Bites the Dust: Dexter Has Enough! Indie Musician Leaves Willow!*** was the first headline I saw, paired with a picture of Dexter, red-faced and annoyed.

Critics always come out in full force during times like this, but this time, the noise was deafening. Everywhere I turned, there was a tabloid asking ***When Will Enough Be Enough for Willow?*** or ***Has Willow Run Out of Men to date?***

Whether it was magazines, blogs, or people shouting the same questions whenever I stepped outside, I couldn't escape it. Mentally, I needed a break. I needed to spend time with myself to figure out if I was worth staying for.

So, I did something Dexter would've been proud of. I hid. I desperately needed to do some soul searching.

I retreated to the first house I ever bought. It's nestled in the woods, about an hour from the city. The tree line serves as a much-needed, makeshift fence before the actual security perimeter. I was only 18 when I purchased this place, and we took every precaution to conceal my identity. Right from the beginning, I knew I needed a place that was just for me.

I wanted the ability to be somewhere no one knew about. I craved writing new music in peace, without anyone charting my every move in and out of the studios in the city. It's been a saving grace these last five months.

As soon as Dexter left his key and closed our apartment door for the last time, I packed my bags, and snuck out the back. The paparazzi had no idea I'd left.

I hired a new assistant, Emilie, to help me day to day. She brings groceries and anything I need from the city. Since there's no previous business tying us together, the press has no idea she's part of my team—she's one of my favorite parts of this whole thing.

Emilie, twenty-five and an ambitious college graduate from Michigan, took an unconventional path to graduate—she lived a little and did it on her own timeline. During the interview, I asked where she was from, and she showed me with her hands. Believe it or not, Michigan is legit shaped like a mitten. It was then and there I knew I wanted to hire her. She was the perfect pick to help me pull this off.

I needed to process this loss. The stability and comfort I knew—gone. The hope and promise of the future—non-existent.

Emilie and I hit it off right away, just like I knew we would. We have this way of bouncing between being friends and being professionals. Her knack of knowing what I want, before I want it, makes it easy.

Well, except for now.

"Dress is steamed and ready," Emilie says, standing between the patio chair, which I'm lounging in, and the pool. It's the end of July and it feels like summer has just started.

"Won't be necessary. Not going." I shimmy my shoulders, tipping my face to the sun.

I did commit to attend tonight's award show, but things change.

Emilie launches into her spiel, one that sounds like she practiced, similar to what I heard from Claire.

I hope it looks like I'm paying enough attention, but I've zoned all the way out. Instead, I watch the sun glimmer off the pool.

"Are you even listening?" Emilie cuts in, tossing a patio pillow towards me.

"I mean, sort of." I laugh and put the pillow in my lap. "Listen, it has nothing to do with you. I just don't want to go." I'm smiling and careful enough. I aim to be gentle because she's only trying to do her job.

Emilie throws her hands up before putting them on her hips, shifting her weight to one leg. "Can I say something? Something borderline unprofessional?" she presses.

I lean forward, definitely interested, and give her a nod—the green light to continue.

"I hate to be the one to call this out, but this, this right here—" She uses her hands to point to me and the empty house behind her. "—is *exactly* what Dexter wanted."

Ouch.

When I don't react, she continues. "You'd be perfect for him now. Locked up in your big house. The public is a thing of the past. You don't go anywhere or do anything. I don't understand it."

Part of me wants to tell her the truth. How the thought of getting close to anyone else makes me almost physically ill. How I'm sick of being left behind. How I can't take another hit.

I'm surprised it took her this long to bring this up. It's no secret I'm doing what Dexter wanted me to do, even though it was out of the question when we were together. I had hoped his love for me would outweigh the discomfort of dealing with the paparazzi and life in the public eye. It hurts that it didn't.

Even if I've thought this, it's always different hearing it from someone else.

In this moment, like so many these last few months, I'm thankful for her. I like how she gives me the occasional push.

"I didn't know you when you were with him, but I know enough to know you're letting him win," she says, going for the jugular.

My head jolts back in response. I press my lips together, trying to gather my thoughts, the ones that tell me, in my bones, she's right. Tucking my hair behind my ears, longer than it's been in years, I clap my hands under my chin.

"Fine." Emilie eyebrows raise as her eyes go wide. She freezes like she's a statue on my patio. "But you have to come with me." She gives me a thumbs up before running inside to get ready.

This wasn't on my agenda for today. Or this month. But here's something about me...

I *hate* to lose.

# Chapter 6
## Tripp

LEARNING YOUR TEAM CHOSE not to protect you in an expansion draft blows. It's even worse when your name gets picked, on national television, and you know it's time to pack your bags and relocate. After winning a Super Bowl, being named the MVP, you sort of think your spot is cemented into the roster.

Guess not.

The Seattle Serpents had the chance to "protect" me from the expansion draft which would keep my name out of the pool of players available to be picked. They chose to take the risk and include my name. Lucky me, I was the first one picked.

Fuck me.

Here I am: wide receiver for the Upstate Cosmos. Cosmos like stars and space. Not the flower. Upstate, not like true upstate New York, but on the outskirts of the city, and idiotically close enough to still be crippled by city traffic. Just what the NFL needs, another team in New York.

The Serpents' general manager and coaching staff said they were sad to see me go. I believed them. Still, they were the only NFL team I've known, and it fucking stung. It's a business, which I get, but it's also piss-poor luck.

I could've done without the whole "this is a good move for you" framing. They made it seem like since I had such a successful year, I'd have the opportunity for a massive long-term deal with the Cosmos.

Here's what I know: I'm a thirty-year-old wide receiver. There's never a guarantee about how many years someone has left to play, but I know I'd be lucky to get a few more. Football has always been my identity—not just the thing I did, but the thing I am. Knowing I can't play forever has been creeping into my brain and it scares the shit out of me.

Plus, after getting a taste of winning, as a critical part of the team, it's like everything clicked—how much I depend on the sport.

When I got drafted to the new team, the panic attacks came roaring back. I hate the unknown, and this new team plus what happens after football both fall in that category. I've seen a sports psychologist on and off throughout my life and made sure to get a good recommendation for one in New York.

Not only is this a new team for me but it's literally new for everyone. There's no previous roster, established relationships with coaching staff, or existing fan base. It's like we've been plucked and jammed together for some weird sports experiment. There's nothing wrong with the guys here but it's just fucking weird.

The locker rooms and training facilities are shiny-new, but the culture is non-existent. I didn't love my previous team because we figured out how to win, but because we were friends. Everyone had everyone else's backs. It was more than football, and we had a fucking blast.

Needless to say, moving across the country to a brand-new franchise made for a crazy off-season. Plus, the Champagne stunt definitely made its rounds—I built up a touch of a wild card reputation. Some people love it, some people hate it, and I have no idea how to feel about the strong reactions and opinions. I pretended to be drunk, spraying paparazzi with Champagne, only so Willow could get to her car. She needed some help. I helped.

During my first meeting with the Cosmos front office, the general manager asked me to keep the Champagne events to a minimum, unless we're winning a Super Bowl.

I've always been a little spontaneous. That's no secret. The only difference is the stunt was on a bigger stage and people sort of knew who I was this time.

Now, the press follows me incessantly, whether I'm going for a run, doing dinner with friends, or trying to get groceries. I don't think I'm that exciting, but sure, go ahead and watch me pick out kale for my juicer.

Before being named Super Bowl MVP, people may have known who I was, but not everyone. And no one cared enough to say anything, that's for sure.

My mom moves into her new apartment today and my heart squeezes with relief. She'll finally be in the same city as me. I'm browsing bouquets from a farmers market stand a few blocks from my apartment, picking one out for my mom's new place. I breathe in and the sweet smell of lilacs reminds me of her.

I can feel someone lurking. They pull something out of their pocket. Not unusual. People ask me to sign stuff all the time.

"Tripp?" The voice is quiet and comes from a man I'm guessing is probably fifty years old.

"Didn't know people could recognize me out of the pads." It's the same joke I'm prepared with whenever I'm approached. "Want me to sign something?"

"No, nothing like that. Just wanted to give you this." He hands me a card—information for Alcoholics Anonymous. My jaw drops and my eyes feel like they don't fit my face. By the time I look back up at him, he's already turned and on his way.

Put this on the list for potential public interactions. I've had every-thing from screaming, crying, and awkward selfies. Don't forget about the occasional, "Why did you leave the Seattle Serpents?" coated with anger, like it was my choice.

I also get invited to a lot of shit. Like tonight, I got roped into going to an awards show. Not usually my sort of vibe, but some of my old teammates will be there, and it seems like it could be fun.

I settle on an arrangement of flowers and get back to my apartment.

Before I get in the shower, I turn on music that plays throughout my entire penthouse. A song by Willow is on.

*Willow.*

What I'd do to just spend some time with her. The rumor mill says she went through a nasty breakup and is off the grid. She wrapped up a massive tour and sort of disappeared into thin air. And not just any tour, but the most successful and lucrative tour of any artist. Ever.

You can't blame someone for wanting to take a break.

I step into the shower and start singing along—no shame in knowing these lyrics.

# **Chapter 7**
## Willow

WHEN MY HEELS SINK into the red carpet, gasps ripple through the crowd before I'm met with the typical shouts and pose requests. Cameras click and flash. It's impossible to make out anyone's face.

My backless Chanel dress slinks down, grazing the red carpet as I take my first few steps. The front has a decent plunge, nothing too scandalous, but shows just enough of my skin for me to feel sexy. With a slit that hits the top of my thigh, my muscular legs are on display with each step. I'm wearing one of my favorite pairs of Christian Louboutin heels; the pair Dexter would throw a fit over if I wore them. He didn't want me to be near his height. And definitely not taller than him. That was tough when he was only 5'8", even though I'm only 5'4" on a good day.

The satin top of the dress clings snugly to my skin, its fabric shimmering subtly under the lights and camera flashes. As I run my hands down the sides, I feel the structured boning of the dress, highlighting my curves. This type of top is perfect for my shape and I know it. I've never fallen into the too-skinny-popstar stereotype. I've always been all thick thighs and, as Claire says, "tits that don't quit".

With each second, I feel more and more rejuvenated. I move through poses—grateful for muscle memory. It's only a matter of time before the barrage of questions hit me like a wave: "Where have you been?" "Is your heart still broken?" "Did you go to rehab?" "Are you still in contact with

Dexter?" The lack of boundaries at events like this is staggering, which is something I definitely didn't miss.

I'm almost near the end of the walk when the energy and focus shifts from the carpet to a black car pulling up. Sometimes, the paparazzi feels like a living thing, a monster with a camera trying to capture their prey.

I slowly turn my head to see who it is.

My stomach drops.

Tripp Owens—I'd know that face anywhere. The night of the Super Bowl comes roaring back. I still can't believe he jumped in and helped me when I didn't even know his name.

The media was all over Tripp Owens after that night.

First, it was the most adorable photo of him and his mom right after his team won the Super Bowl. They're both crying and he leans into her like he needs her to help him stand. She pulls at his jersey. It's the sort of picture you couldn't stage if you tried.

Second, it was him being the Super Bowl MVP. The tears on his face when he held up the trophy.

Third, it was the video coverage, and photos, of him going wild with Champagne for me to make my exit. Something he absolutely didn't have to do.

I know there was speculation about Tripp being an alcoholic after the Champagne incident. Who knows what shrew started that rumor. Here's the thing, I remember him in the locker room. He was having a good time, but he had it under control. I'd put money on him being sober but one hell of an actor, all in the name of helping a complete stranger.

I never got to thank him.

I pause for my last set of photographs, still looking in his direction. He catches my eyes with his, flipping my stomach again, and I smirk in response. When I offer a tiny wave, I swear his cheeks get a little pink, deepening his olive complexion. He nods to me in recognition, wearing a full smile, before turning back to the cameras because we both know if we have too long of a moment, it will be all over every single website and trash magazine tomorrow.

Smart.

Ridiculously hot.

He's wearing a dark gray suit. And I mean *wearing*. His tailor deserves some sort of award. Do they have those? This suit is a perfect fit, showing off his muscular build in a way that I'd love to see him take that jacket off, roll up his sleeves...

*Wow. That escalated quickly.*

Tripp pulls on the front of his suit jacket before putting a hand in his pants pocket. From here, I can tell he's much taller than me, even as I wear my highest heels. His chest is broad, and there's no way this man can buy a jacket off the rack. He lifts his face towards the cameras, his jawline is strong, and his lips pull into a coy smirk before he winks at me.

Before the wide smile, and my flushed cheeks, are caught, I slink into the awards show, leaving the paparazzi with Tripp.

○○○

TONIGHT IS WHAT YOU'D expect: excellent wine, solid food, and truly decadent desserts. And I'm never one to turn down dessert, no matter how many times the tabloids get a photo of me enjoying one and pair it with a disgusting headline about my weight and lack of discipline.

I'm thankful everything was pretty lowkey as I sat with some industry friends and acquaintances. We've kept in touch while I've been out of the public eye, but I'm relieved when no one asks about Dexter.

Now's the time when everyone goes their separate ways or to the after-party.

Dexter would never entertain the idea of going to the after-party, and that was *if* he even accompanied me to the event. When my tablemates ask if I'm going to join them, my cheeks flush a bit when I say yes. I'm excited to do something I haven't done in what feels like years.

Emilie joins me and I can tell she is absolutely beside herself. She smooths her dark red hair in the car and fixes her lipstick. This is the first real event I have brought her to, given the whole season of hiding away. I can tell she's trying to keep it together, and I love her for it.

We get a few steps inside the after-party before I see a band I know Emilie loves. I practically know all their music considering how much she plays it at my place. When I introduce her, I laugh as her mouth is doing everything it can to not be on the floor. I throw a wink her way.

I giggle when I hear someone ask where she's from. She looks down at her hands, wondering if she does the hand thing to pay homage to her home state of Michigan.

I feel like the air is different here; it's exciting and refreshing. I think I've missed events like this. I look around and take in the room but don't get farther than the bar when I see him. Tripp. Smirking at me in all that dark-gray-suit glory. Ironically, he's all alone.

I make a split-second decision before my brain can talk me out of it. As I approach the bar, it's hard not to stare at his smile. It's contagious. I feel my own lips pulling up. My legs strut, and I tip my chin up.

"We were never formally introduced," he says while putting out his hand. "I'm—"

"Tripp. Tripp Owens," I interrupt, putting my hand in his. "Super Bowl MVP. Recently traded to the bright and shiny-new Upstate Cosmos." With each word, his stare gets a little more intense. But in a good way. He bites his lip and tilts his head as he listens and shakes my hand.

He. Bites. His. Lip. I am a puddle on the floor.

"Wow. Not even going to try and lie. I fucking love that you know who I am." He laughs to himself as he runs a hand through his hair, which looks almost black in the dim light. "My turn." He shakes his shoulders and pretends to crack his neck. "You're Willow. Ten albums. Possibly the driving force behind cassettes making a comeback. The first artist to sell out every NFL stadium during a single tour." His hands are on his hips as he takes me in.

His eyes on me make my skin prick and burn. I realize I'm holding my breath.

"Want to know a secret?" he asks, leaning into me, close enough that his voice is barely above a whisper. I move in, closing the rest of the distance. "I was fucking pissed I missed your halftime show. Well, I did catch the end of the last song." His voice is low, and I can hear the smirk in the way he speaks.

I remember the clip of him dancing out of the tunnel—he knew some of my tour choreography. It made me laugh but I was mostly envious of him. How he was unapologetically himself even during one of the most important games of his career. Clearly, doing what he wanted on what's arguably the biggest stage he'll ever touch.

"You seemed to be having your own fun, you know, winning a championship and all."

"You're right. I was. And it was a fucking blast."

Instead of doing the thing where he awkwardly plays down the accomplishment, he soaks in the compliment. I love it.

"What can I get you to drink?"

"Sauvignon blanc, please."

"Want to find a spot?" His voice is smooth like velvet as he gestures to the array of sitting areas around the after-party. This is one of the safest places in the sense of being able to have real conversations. No cameras allowed. Of course, there will be people lined up when everyone makes their exit, but for now, we're all safe.

This gorgeous man, who put himself in a precarious position to help me out, seems like a worthwhile way to spend my time this evening. Didn't see this coming.

I grin at him before I turn and walk towards a booth in the corner. I wonder if he's watching me. The venue is all dark fabrics, velvet, and the lights are dim. As I sink into the booth, my heart catches me off guard.

Quick. For the first time in months.

Honest excitement.

There's no part of my brain trying to come up with a way to win a fight. Or begging someone to go out or stay out a little longer. And if we were out, Dexter would be so concerned about how we were going to end up getting out of there.

My brain feels quiet. The only thing I feel is my heart beat picking up.

And it feels good.

# Chapter 8
## Tripp

I CAN'T BELIEVE THIS is happening.

Willow walks to the booth and it's like my eyes have finally adjusted. The dress she's wearing is inky black and has some sort of glitter effect in the fabric—moving like rippling water on her body. The back is so low it demands that you glance all the way down where the fabric meets the top of her lower back.

I wonder what it'd be like to take my knuckles from the nape of her neck down to the end of that dress.

*Rein it in, Tripp.*

While I wait for our drinks, I pretend not to freak out. Not because I was talking with Willow, but because she's currently waiting for me to bring drinks over, in a dark corner of a dimly lit room. Because she knew exactly who I was. What team I played for. Because of the way she smiled at me on the red carpet, even if it was just for a second.

I knew, right then, I'd be making an after-party appearance. Thank God my buddies called it a night. I can't remember the last time they skipped one of these.

It's like the stars have aligned.

This is a perfect example of something I should "soak in"—my psychologist's favorite phrase. The goal is to be more mindful of experiences and moments like this since there will be a time when there are no award shows or after parties to attend.

With a knowing look, the bartender sets our drinks in front of me, like he's telling me "good luck". When my hands tremble just enough for him to see it as I reach for the glasses, he mimics taking a deep breath. I immediately take his advice.

*Tripp, you're such a sucker.*

I carry our drinks, careful not to spill because that would be fucking embarrassing. Willow sits, hands in her lap, in an odd corner booth. We're sort of next to each other and across at the same time. I set our drinks down and sit.

"Cheers," she says while clinking her wine with my Old Fashioned. I take a long sip, welcoming the burn of the bourbon.

"I never got a chance to thank you," she says, eyes peering down at her wine before she looks up. "You didn't have to help me, and you did. Thank you." Her voice is level and sincere.

"Come on, it was nothing. Just took the party outside." I shrug my shoulders and lean back.

She takes a sip of her wine, her pink lips bright against the clear glass. "Right. I have to say, that was one of the most *unique* distractions I've seen."

"I'll take that as a compliment." I feel my cheeks getting warm. Luckily, it's dark in here. It'd be nice if I could get a grip. "Is it always like that? The press?" I reach for anything to divert my thoughts.

"Yes. It's not always *that* wild but it does seem like anytime I go anywhere someone is trying to get a picture of me. Doesn't matter what I'm doing," she says matter-of-factly. "My boyfriend hated it."

"Hated?" I ask, like I don't fucking know that I read about the breakup for months. Not willingly, it was just everywhere.

"Yes. Now ex-boyfriend," she confirms, like I knew she would. "It was a lot for him. It felt like I was a lot for him..." She takes a long drink of her wine. "I don't know why I said that." She looks intently at her fingers wrapped around the long-stemmed wine glass.

I choose not to dwell on the last comment since it doesn't feel like she wants to keep talking about it. I pivot.

"Ironically, no one really cared who I was before the Champagne incident. You sort of put me on the map," I joke, trying to bring up the mood.

Willow laughs. A quick type of laugh which is a bit loud at first, but it's genuine. "I think it was the championship. I'm betting the 129 yards and two touchdowns helped." She peers at me over her wine glass.

She knows my stat line. Recited it like it was something she typically talks about.

*Fuck.*

Her hair is longer than the last time I saw her. She always seemed to have this shorter haircut, always above her shoulders, but it's grown out. If, for some reason, any of my friends could listen in on my thoughts right now, I'd be getting so much shit. How is it that this woman's haircut is burned in my memory?

While I'm stuck in my head trying to keep track of all Willow's details, someone practically falls into our booth. They land awkwardly next to and partially on top of Willow, nudging her closer to me. It's instinct when my arm reaches around, lightly grabbing her side, feeling her rib cage under the soft fabric of the dress. Her arm holding the wine reaches across me and spills a little on my suit.

A small price to pay for this woman practically being in my lap. We both realize how close we are and pay no attention to the drunk man who just fell into her. I'm holding my breath. My eyes trail to her lips and back again. She's leaning in.

And then her glass of wine splashes me in the face.

# Chapter 9
## Willow

OH. MY. GOD. NOT only am I practically in Tripp's lap, but someone hit my arm just right and made me throw my wine in his face. Wine currently drips from his eyelashes. This can't be happening.

He shakes his head, causing the white wine to trickle down his face, in an attempt to clear his eyes.

"Buddy, you good?" He asks the man who fell into me. Tripp's eyes are wide, but he's not angry, or irritated, it looks like he's trying not to laugh. His voice stays calm and almost feels playful.

This is *not* the reaction I anticipated.

Tripp dabs his face with his suit sleeve and lightly pushes me to an upright position. I already miss his hands on me. The guy who fell into us stands, clearly embarrassed. He calls Tripp by his first name, obviously recognizing him, but he goes eerily still when he sees me.

I know the look. The one that says, *I know who you are* or *I can't believe it's you.* The one that makes me feel guilty—like I don't belong.

"It's no big deal. Don't worry about it," I say as I stand up. I set the empty wine glass on the table, smooth my dress, and reach for the drunk guy's hand to shake. I know him too. He's an up-and-coming actor; I like his work so far.

"Are you sure?! Do you need anything? I'm such a big fan. Of you. Of both of you." It's painful to watch but he can't stop. "I'm sorry. I didn't mean—" He's borderline panicking. That's when Tripp claps him on the back and does the unthinkable.

"Want to take a selfie? This is my first afterparty where someone threw their drink in my face. Kind of want to commemorate it," he says, giving me a quick wink.

Part of me melts.

"Let's do it!" I play up the excitement because I really don't want him feeling any worse. It was an accident. The secondhand embarrassment is already too much.

We group together as Tripp pulls his phone out of his wet jacket pocket and reaches his arm out. Our faces are close like we've all known each other forever. Tripp takes a few pictures and then asks for the guy's number to text them.

My eyebrows are raised. He texts this stranger like it's no big deal. It's not, *give me your number and my publicist will send it or even share it via email.* He doesn't seem to have a care in the world about sharing his real number.

Who is this guy?

The drunk man goes back to his group, looking back at us and waving, a smile taking over his entire face. He and his group of friends huddle together to relive his brief encounter with us.

"Wow." It's all I can muster. Tripp is still dabbing parts of his face with his suit, seemingly unbothered.

"I hope you were okay with the selfie thing. I didn't even think—"

"Totally okay. I'm sorry I spilled my wine on you." I laugh and lightly touch his shoulder, wiping at stray droplets.

"You could've just said you weren't having a good time." He smirks. "It's all good," Tripp says in a way that is totally believable. No second-guessing if there's a sub-conscious meaning. It's refreshing.

My phone vibrates. Emilie is in the car, ready to go whenever I am. I told her I wanted to come out for a single drink. I kind of wish she would've seen that whole thing transpire.

"That's my cue." I shake my phone at him. "My car's ready." I don't have to rush out, but I always feel weird having anyone wait on me.

"I'll walk you out. Which door?" And because I know there's no use arguing with him and pleading I can handle it without any help, I lead him to the door my security team discussed earlier.

He puts his hand on my lower back as we walk together. Goosebumps flood my skin, and my stomach drops, just a bit. Enough to know that I wish our time wasn't ending.

We get to the door, and it's complete chaos. Looks like people have been camping out, waiting for celebrities to leave the afterparty. I'm guessing some are fans, but many of them are press, hoping to get a solid shot for the evening.

"Is this okay? Or do you want to try something else?" Tripp asks as I am gauging the situation outside.

"It should be fine. It's not a secret I'm here. I'm not bothered if people get some pictures. Unless you have another idea for a distraction." I grin and catch his eyes. I'm a bit surprised by how "cool girl" I sound when I know I'm about to question every piece of this interaction.

He greets me with a full-blown smile. My stomach drops, and I feel my own lips pull up.

"Let me walk you to the car. Maybe they'll be so surprised seeing us together that they'll be in awe and click that camera a little slower," he says, and I can't tell if he's joking. "It's that one, right?" He points correctly to my driver. Emilie sits in the front seat, making it easy for me to find my black car.

My face must give me away because he puts one hand on the door handle and the other on my lower back.

"Come on, Lo." He winks and then leads me out the door.

*Lo.* No one has ever called me that.

The door opens and people are indeed shocked to see us walking out together. Tripp's suit is still wet, especially the white button up shirt. People shout and gasp while taking as many pictures as they can. I don't hear anything super clear but it's hard not to hear the "ARE YOU TOGETHER?" screams.

Tripp throws on his 1000-watt smile and walks me to my car. I don't rush or cover my face. When we get to the car, he opens the door and gives me his hand as he helps me in.  Once I'm safely inside, he stands in front of the door opening and smiles.

"See you around, hopefully," he says with a wink and shuts the car door.

I glance to the front to see Emilie wide-eyed and mouth hanging open. "What the hell did you get into during the afterparty?!" she shrieks.

"He called me Lo," I say, more as a question than a statement. Emilie whips to the back looking at me as I put a hand on my chest, feeling the quick heartbeat under my fingers.

"Is that a good thing?" she asks.

"I'm not sure."

All I know is I can still feel the place where his hand rested on my lower back.

# **Chapter 10**
## Tripp

My phone buzzes obnoxiously, even though it's barely 6 a.m.

What the hell? I grab it from the nightstand and see 54 unread text messages and even more notifications

My stomach drops. The last time something like this happened, it was the fallout from being re-drafted. All the roots I tried to put down, gone. I'll never forget the way my phone buzzed as I talked to the Seattle Serpents general manager, wishing me luck.

Before I have a chance to investigate, my phone rings: Mom.

I yawn into the phone before I say, "It's so early."

"That is no way to greet your mother," my mom lovingly snaps.

"Good morning, Mom," I sweetly croon.

"Is there something you want to tell me?" she pokes. It's not condescending or accusatory.

"Why do I feel like I'm in trouble?"

"It looks like you had a good time at the afterparty last night..." Her voice trails off and my brain tries to catch up.

"I did have a good time. *But* I think I know what you're referring to and I just walked her to the car, like a gentleman."

"Ah, I was thinking about the pictures of where she's in your lap in what looks like a dark, dark corner where you couldn't be bothered, but what do I know? I don't have my glasses on."

"Huh?"

"Google yourself or something. Let's get on the same page."

I put my mom on speaker phone and Google my name, which is always weird.

And there it is, a blurry but clear enough picture where Willow looks to be draped all over me, my arm around her, and our noses so close they could be touching. It was the moment that guy fell into her but whoever sent this photo in deviously cut that man out of the picture. Before I have a chance to click into anything, I know everyone is eating this up.

Fuck. *I'm* eating this up.

"Oh, wow," is all I can muster while I'm taking in the photo and headlines.

"Are you seeing Willow? You know I love her music." My mom sounds excited.

"No, I'm not seeing her. I mean, I saw her, but you know what I mean."

My mom snickers, "I wish you believed in fate because I'm really questioning the coincidence of your first meeting and now this one."

"We were just talking, and someone fell into her. If you would've seen five seconds later, you'd see me wearing that glass of wine that's in the photo."

"Did she throw it at you?" she asks, her voice concerned but also living for these details.

"No, she didn't throw the wine at me." I give her a tiny laugh. "Someone caught her arm and it ended up going all over. Complete accident."

"Well, I thought maybe you'd dipped your foot in the dating pool. Guess not." She sounds a little disappointed now. "Have you heard from Bailey? She called me last week."

Bailey. The closest thing I had to a girlfriend in college. Really, we were more like long-term friends with benefits. Sometimes we went to events and things together, but most of the time we didn't.

Being with Bailey was easy and comfortable but then we graduated and went our separate ways. I was sad to not see her as frequently, but it didn't hurt like it would to lose someone you love.

We're still in touch. She gets tickets whenever she wants and sometimes she'll ask me to go to something, and it's always a blast to see people react to her bringing an NFL player to a wedding or work event.

My mom adores Bailey and doesn't quite understand our connection. We were in a situationship long before the kids had coined the term.

"Haven't heard from her. She texted when I got re-drafted but that was it." It was nice for her to reach out and we exchanged a few texts, but nothing more than that.

My mom sighs. I know she wishes Bailey and I were a thing.

"I'm going to go back to my morning. Seems like you'll have a wild few days." I can hear her smiling on the other line.

"Love you, Mom." I hang up the phone and start looking at the long list of notifications.

MY MOM WAS RIGHT, but I don't know if the word "wild" cuts it. The Cosmos had to add extra security to the practice facility since Willow's fans and the press were camping out, trying to get any bit of information. My teammates found it hilarious and would only give answers that weren't really answers and would just leave the person asking them to spin their wheels. Like when they were asked, "Is Tripp Owens dating Willow" the answer was, "I don't even think Tripp Owens is on this team".

I was getting so much shit in the locker-room. Even Coach had some jabs for me when I dropped a couple easy passes while we were running routes.

It sort of brought us together. Now, I wish it was at someone else's expense, but you win some and you lose some.

I took it. It's part of the gig. I knew something would happen when I walked her to the car, but I didn't expect this kind of response. It's especially surprising considering I haven't been in a serious relationship since I made it in the league.

My manager called to let me know they hired more security for my apartment and shared new routes for arriving and departing.

This is insane. And a tad annoying.

Doesn't help that today was brutal. Not only has practice been kicking my ass but it's been hard to get quality sleep at my place. When I finally got home last night, it took hours for people to stop shouting.  Things are clearly not letting up. The line of paparazzi is longer than any other day this week. My shoulders fall and I tip my head up in exasperation. Teammates snicker and playfully hit my back when they walk out in front me.

"I thought they'd be sick of you by now." Zack shakes one of my shoulders. "It's been two weeks." He's our long snapper and the guy I've meshed with the easiest. Weird considering he's part of special teams and we don't practice a ton together. It's not that I don't get along with the other guys, but it's like Zack and I have known each other forever.

"I was being a gentleman," I reason with him.

"That's all it was?" He smirks at me while the rest of the team leaves the locker room. He knows all about the Champagne distraction at the Super Bowl.

"Right." I don't even convince myself.

"Why don't you find a way to get a hold of her? I'm sure you've got some strings to pull."

"That's rich coming from you. You have a line of people waiting for dates, longer than that." I point towards the window. Zack has a different woman what feels like every week.

"Some of us are lucky." Zack shrugs his shoulders. He was named a finalist for some sexiest guy alive title. The man is good-looking, that's for sure.

It would be annoying if he wasn't so genuine. Zack is truly a good guy—he'd do anything for you.

"And don't act like you date." He claps me on the back before heading for the doors.

I follow my teammates and it's like someone turns the sound up full blast when the paparazzi see me. Fuck. I just want to go home.

I take a deep breath, trying to gather myself, and open the door.

Complete chaos never gets any easier. It's a mix of people yelling, handing me things to sign, trying to take photos with everything from iPhones to massive professional cameras.

It's exhausting.

Per my manager, I've not made any sort of statement—the plan was to be quiet and let this blow over. Well, so far that hasn't happened.

Maybe it's time to say something. Before the thought is fully formed, I can already hear my manager, mom, and my new coach scolding me.

Just when I think I'm in the clear, that I'm going to be a good boy and follow instructions, the least threatening of reporters grabs my attention. She's clearly a journalist, with a professional microphone branded with her network. Maybe it's because she talks to me at a normal level but when we make eye contact, I know I'm going to answer her question.

"Tripp, is it true you're dating Willow? Care to make a comment?"

She tips the microphone to me, and I take a step forward. It feels like everything pauses, for a single second, when they realize I'm about to say something. The world feels like it's moving in slow motion.

I did not think this through. What am I supposed to say?

*Tripp, you fucking idiot.*

Fuck.

The reporter looks at me and her eyebrows keep rising the longer I don't say anything. I go with my gut and tell the truth.

"No, I'm not dating Willow." The reporter goes to pull back the microphone and the chaos starts to rise again. I lightly pull the microphone to me.

"But I wish I was. If anyone can get a hold of her and pass that message along, I'd appreciate it."

I smile into the camera as everyone's mouth hangs open. They did not expect that.

To be honest, neither did I.

# Chapter 11
## Willow

I'M SUPPOSED TO BE working on new music, not thinking about Tripp Owens. But he's such a pleasant distraction.

I just finished the verse for a new song I've been playing with and the second the pen comes off the paper, my phone is in my hands. I'm a woman obsessed, unable to watch anything besides the clip. Clearly, I'm not the only one. It's gone viral and has been posted on every entertainment and news outlet that has any interest in football or music.

Tripp. Trying to leave practice. Cheeks red from what I'm guessing was a shower. He's in a simple gray athletic t-shirt and black athleisure shorts. The shorts have that *good* inseam.

The first time I saw it, I couldn't believe it. I'm not sure I believe it now.

Celebrities don't do this. It's all about keeping everything quiet, under the radar, even fake dating in public to throw the scent off your real partner.

Nonetheless, here's one of the most popular NFL players, asking me out, and it's been seen by millions of people.

My public relations team isn't quite sure what to do. I told them to do nothing until I had a chance to think about it. They aren't even allowed to say "no comment" until I wrap my brain around this.

The fire crackles and pops. The air is cold for an August night, and I have a thick blanket wrapped around my shoulders. My laptop sits on my lap with a discarded journal to the side of it.

Since my tour has ended, it's always *what comes next?* I have a ton of music and songs written, but I'm a little nervous about getting my label on board. I usually share new music direction with them when I'm wrapping up the end of a tour, but I've kept all of these songs and pieces to myself. For the first time, I asked for a break.

"How many times have you watched that?" Emilie asks as she walks toward me, holding a beautiful arrangement of flowers.

"What's all that?" I reference the bouquet and sidestep her question.

"I'm guessing *loverboy* has some connections." She sets them down on the patio table. "The envelope is sealed and there were instructions to leave it that way until this was in your possession. Security signed off so they know what's going on."

"I'll leave you to it," she says, wearing a massive grin like we're in middle school and I'm about to read a love note that was left in my locker.

"You don't have to," I protest.

"I know I don't, but I want to." She says it in a way that's final and compassionate. "So much of your life is available to others. Sometimes it's nice to find little pieces you can keep to yourself." She turns to head back to the house like she didn't say the most enlightened thing I've heard in a while.

I make sure my mouth isn't hanging open and make a mental note to give her a raise. The flowers—pink and white peonies—stare at me. My favorite flowers. Someone's been doing their homework.

I pluck the envelope from the bouquet. It's heavy, substantial in my hand. Willow Scott is written on the front; he *full-named* me. I carefully open it and pull out a note on cream paper with black handwriting.

*Willow – Sorry if your week has been crazy.*

*Meant what I said. I'd love to take you out. The number on the bottom is new and you're the only one I'm giving it to.*

*--Tripp*

At the bottom of the note is a phone number, tiny but legible. I'm guessing this is why he didn't want anyone to read it.

I press my lips together, trying to fight the smile. The flowers are lovely but the handwritten note? Swoon.

I sit back in my chair, the blanket hugging my shoulders, moving the note between my fingers—contemplating what to do next. My brain snags on the wildness of it but my heart chases into the *Isn't this exciting?* territory.

Most of the men I've dated have been weird about being in public. If they weren't, it's usually because they had some sort of ulterior motive, like a mediocre music career they're trying to get off the ground or wanting me to connect them with so-and-so. It's hard not to feel like people aren't always looking for something I can give them.

If they didn't want a connection or an introduction, they wanted me to be smaller or "more normal". It's cliché but it's always tricky trying to gauge someone's true intentions.

I know if I was saying this out loud it would sound ridiculous. Poor Willow. She's so popular and really hit her stride with her music but she doesn't know how to pick a man.

A dramatic sigh escapes my lips, even though I'm the only one around to hear it.

Then there's Tripp. I know almost nothing about him. I'd be lying if I said I hadn't done some Googling after our latest interaction.

Interesting because he doesn't seem to have any public relationships, or at least any that the press has gotten their hands on. Besides his antics at the game last season, there really isn't much besides actual updates, a few charities he's tied to, typical professional athlete things.

Most celebrities have those terrible articles showing their dating history in excruciating detail. Not Tripp. Gone is the compilation of any person he may, or may not have, dated served with a side of dramatic contemplation from whoever wrote it.

I once sat next to a stranger at a coffee shop while I was waiting for my order. Something fell out of my bag and this sweet gentleman grabbed it and handed it back to me. That was the entirety of the interaction. However, in the next twelve hours, the press knew everything about him, and we were rumored to be dating. Outrageous.

Nothing like that for Tripp. Which makes me think back to those silver eyes and his boyish but ridiculously sexy grin. And If I think about it long enough, it's like I can feel his hand on my lower back and see that wink he left me with.

My cheeks pinch when I realize I've been sitting here smiling, all alone. I grab my phone and dial the number on the card before I can change my mind.

"You called," Tripp says, and I swear I can hear him smiling on the other line.

# Chapter 12
## Tripp

THIS NEW PHONE HAS become the equivalent to an additional limb. Ever since the flowers got cleared by her security team, this thing hasn't left my side.

Flowers are one of my go-to gestures. When I was little and my dad was still in the picture, he brought flowers home one night. They were from the supermarket, still had the price tag on them, wrapped in the patterned cellophane. My mom didn't care. The way her eyes lit up and her shoulders relaxed. It was like I could feel her mood shift.

That might be the only good thing my dad ever did for me. But I'll take it.

I send a lot of flowers. My mom gets a bouquet every month and I use them as my key thank-you gift. And If I'm being honest, one of the saddest parts about leaving my original team and city was the flower shop. Everyone who worked there was so kind, and they made me feel like we were friends.

This is a secret I keep to myself. And my mom—she knows everything. She's the one who helped me find a new flower spot when I ended up on the Cosmos roster.

I take the phone out of my pocket and stare at the blank screen. Kind of like it's teasing me with its silence.

Until it rings. *Holy shit.*

I can't help but wear a smile like it's my fucking job. If anything, I expected a text message, not a phone call. Willow is the type of person who calls. Noted.

My heart beats too fast.

"You called," I answer, probably too quickly, but I don't care how excited I sound. It's the truth.

"Thank you for the peonies. They're my--"

"Favorite. I know." I feel borderline smug, but it is what it is.

"How do you know that?" Her voice is sly and inquisitive.

"I have my ways." I've seen almost every interview she's done and probably have read the ones in print. She does *not* need to know that I'm a bigger fan than I'm letting on. "So, are you going to let me take you out?"

"You're for real?" She sounds like she's trying to figure something out.

"Are you kidding? Yes. I'm for real. Just like I declared to many reporters yesterday." I lightly laugh at the end.

The line is quiet. I know she heard me. Maybe I read this whole thing wrong. My stomach dips.

"If I overstepped—I'm sorry. I saw a chance and I took it."

"A chance?" she asks.

My mind runs over itself. I know how much I've thought of her since the night we first met and the way my body felt pulled to her at the awards show. But this isn't something you blurt out. The opposite of cool.

"I told myself if I ever had the opportunity to spend more time with you, I'd take it. I saw you at the awards show and I couldn't help myself."

"You didn't. Overstep, I mean. I'm just surprised."

"I'm going to need more than that..."

She takes a big breath and sighs. I give her all the time she needs.

"Don't worry about it because… I'm in." The tone of her voice shifts at the end. I thought she was going to tell me "no" right up until the last moment. My heart rattles in my chest, beating fast.

"Yeah?" My voice a bit higher pitched than I intended.

"Yes. It sounds fun." Her voice is sweet and makes me want to curl up on the couch and talk for much too long.

"Are you free tomorrow night? Dinner?"

"As long as we can run everything through my head of security—"

"I already have their information. For the flowers. I'll give them a call and get it figured out."

"Right. How did you even get their info in the first place?" she jokingly presses.

"Told you, I have my ways. Is eight a good time to pick you up?"

"You can't just pick me up," she scoffs. "I don't think that will fly—"

"I'll handle security. Just be ready at eight. And bring a jacket."

"Whatever you say, Tripp." She chuckles as she hangs up the phone. I know in this moment she doesn't believe me.

My hand shakes as I'm dialing the number for the head of her security team. I bite my lip as my brain runs through the to-do list of how to make this happen. It's also pointing out the time I'll be missing out on some sort of training activity on the calendar. There's always an extra workout, film session, or something completely outside of the team but football focused.

Tough, but I'm hoping also worth it. There's something about her that's pulling me in.

I have no idea if I played it cool or if I'm going about this all wrong. It doesn't matter. I have a date with Willow.

After I clear the details with Seth, I google *Tesla dealership*. I know her privacy is important. Looks like I need to get a new car.

I call the only person who I know will answer and encourage this behavior.

"Zack, want to help me pick out a new car?"

"Obviously. I'll be at your place in fifteen minutes."

# Chapter 13
## Willow

THE DOORBELL RINGS AT 7:50. I sent Emilie back to Michigan for the weekend. Some of her friends were back in her hometown, and she was debating making the trip. I bought her a plane ticket and sent her on her way.

I have no group of friends who contact me when they're back home. Which means no reason to go back for Thanksgiving or Christmas. My parents always come to me, whether I'm in New York or in between tour dates and cities. My dad always complains about the traffic; he says he prefers the business of our small hometown in Virginia.

It's always been the three of us. I'm an only child, and we've never been close with any of my extended family. Sometimes people get weird when it comes to money and success, or that's what I tell myself to make it sting less. There's nothing quite like landing your first major record deal and cousins you haven't had a real conversation with in years start needing something. Another reason for the armor I've crafted.

My heart squeezes when I think about Emilie still having people back home. I'm a little jealous but I know I won't let her miss weekends like this. No Emilie means I have the house to myself. Well, me and some of the security detail who do a good job of staying out of sight unless necessary.

Somehow, Tripp did handle getting everything organized. All I had to do was confirm I indeed wanted to go out with Tripp Owens; what an easy "yes".

I don't know the full plan but know Tripp requested to drive and asked if the security team would follow. Tripp must've passed all the required checks because everyone seems very chill about this whole thing.

Almost like a professional football player didn't ask me out via paparazzi.

My heart rate picks up as I walk to the door, heels clicking on the hardwood floors. There's nothing like a healthy dose of nerves on top of already existing anxiety.

I slowly open the door and am greeted with a casual Tripp. He's wearing dark jeans and an olive-green Henley shirt. The type that looks so soft you immediately want to touch it. Run your hands down it.

It's also the kind of green that brings out the tan tone of his skin. He's running a hand through his hair and his other is in his pocket. Some of his dark hair falls back and rests on his forehead. His gray, almost blue eyes are bright, catching mine right away.

And then he smiles at me. An actual smile.

I slowly exhale and let my shoulders fall a little from my ears.

"Sorry. I didn't expect you to answer the door," he says, while putting his other hand in his pocket and rocking back on his heels.

"Who else would answer my door?" I smirk.

"Definitely thought I'd be meeting the third line of security at your door. These people do not play, do they? Have you seen any of them smile or blink?" Tripp asks, his cheeks flushed.

A laugh escapes my mouth, a little louder than I'd hoped for. "Yes, they smile. Seth and his team are all right." My hands are on my hips and I put weight on one foot. "He's been with me since the beginning. One of the good ones."

"Well, he knows everything about me, including my blood type, allergies, and middle school locker combination." Tripp laughs and stops when his eyes meet mine.

"What?" I ask looking down at my outfit, seeing if there's something on my top. "What's wrong?"

"Wrong? Nothing. Your eyes, in the sunlight, they're like gold. You're just... stunning." He looks at me, his shoulders up near his ears.

The compliment hits me harder than it should. The words, his reaction, the sincerity of his voice. It's almost like broken pieces of me are coming back together.

I can't show him that, so instead, I smile in appreciation.

"Are you ready?" He steps to the side, giving me room to fall in step beside him.

"I think so," I say as we walk toward his black Tesla.

And then this man does the unthinkable—he opens my door. My face must give me away.

"What? Is this weird?" he asks, still holding the door open.

"No. Just caught me off guard." His hand lightly touches my lower back before I sink into the leather seat. It's hard not to fixate on those strong hands.

I can't remember the last time Dexter, or any of my dates did something like this. I'm used to a mad dash to get in the car, trying to minimize the number of people who would see. If they weren't rushing, they'd be waving to whoever was trying to get our photo. When was the last time someone drove me that wasn't my security detail?

"You still with me?" Tripp clicks his seatbelt in.

"Sorry. Yes. Still here." I smile, trying to hide the embarrassment of taking a somewhat depressing, short trip down memory lane.

"No need to apologize. Thought we could do dinner somewhere low-key. I'm sure you already know that Seth—my new best friend—and all his security buds, will be a few cars back."

He starts the car, a quick message about Bluetooth being connected flashes on the display, and loud music starts to play. My music. Not only my music but a decently obscure live version of one of my earliest albums.

I press my lips together and look down at my hands in my lap. Tripp tries to turn the music down and off at the same time. It takes him a few seconds, and when the music stops, the tips of his ears are pink. He stares ahead.

"That is not ideal," he says too quickly as he puts the car in drive. "Let's pretend that didn't happen." He smirks at me, his face crimson. I nod in agreement even though I know this is something I won't forget.

When he realizes I'm not going to say anything about it, he says, "It sounds like no one knows you're staying here… I'm guessing from the lack of activity." He quickly glances at me before we're out of the security gate and on the road.

I must look at him with just a teeny bit of panic.

"Don't worry. Your secret's safe with me." His smile reassures me. "I only brought it up because I'm thinking we'll be able to fly under the radar tonight. Not that I don't want to be seen with you. It's just…" Tripp is rambling at this point. I press my lips together and look at him. "If you can't tell, I'm nervous. Like really fucking nervous." He chuckles alongside his confession.

"The big bad football player, who asked me out in one of those most public ways possible, is nervous?" I jab him in a way that lets him know I'm joking.

"I'm a fraud. I used all my confidence in that moment and then anything that was left went to Seth and the security check and now I'm—"

"Nervous," I interrupt him, hopefully to give the poor guy a break. There's a little sweat on his forehead.

"Did you hate that I did that? The thing with the paparazzi? I don't know what came over me and I thought, hell, take your shot, but—"

"Definitely didn't hate it," I interrupt again, trying to help him chill out. With everything up to this point, Tripp has been nothing but cool, calm, and collected.

To be honest, I like that he's nervous because that makes two of us.

WE'RE IN A NEIGHBORHOOD thirty minutes outside the city. Tripp pulls into a pretty sketchy-looking driveway. It looks like it's meant for deliveries but there's no discernible business nearby.

He opens my car door and says, "Promise. I cleared this with your security entourage."

Tripp offers his hand, and I instinctively take it. What is it about a man wanting to hold your hand? As our fingers intertwine, I'm reminded of how strong he is. I mean, I know he's a professional athlete, but you don't really think about how powerful someone's hands can be.

Once I'm out of the car, he doesn't let go. Instead, he leads me to an odd-looking side door. It's locked, but he enters a numerical code and the door pops open. We step in, and I still can't tell where we are.

"This way," Tripp says while leading me up some stairs. It's clear he knows his way around.

We reach another door which opens to the roof. It takes just a few steps to see the table, set for two, with candles, twinkly lights, and complete seclusion.

Swoon.

"What's all this?" I ask as we walk towards the table.

"I know the owner and when he saw my little stint with the press, he offered a place for us to get away."

He's thought this out.

Tripp pulls my chair out, grinning while he does it. "Hope you're hungry. This place has some of the best Italian food in the city."

I open the menu sitting in front of me, and my mouth starts to water. The way to my heart starts with fresh pasta and all things cheese.

Before I get too far in, our server greets our table with a bottle of red wine.

"Wine for the table?" the server asks.

Tripp looks at me, waiting for me to make the call.

"Please."

# Chapter 14
## Tripp

THE WINE'S BEEN POURED and our orders placed: chicken piccata for me and pasta Bolognese for Willow. I usually don't drink when I have practice the next day but I figure tonight is the perfect exception.

Asking her to bring a jacket was the move. Wind blows through the rooftop, making Willow's hair a bit wild, dark strands flying around. Her cheeks are tinged pink from the cold, bringing out the pink of her lipstick.

"I'm impressed. I have to say this is a first for me... a first date on a rooftop," she says.

I'd be lying if I hadn't agonized about what we should do tonight. I landed on a classic. Hearing her say "impressed" and "first date" in the same sentence feels like a win.

"I thought this was a safe bet. Far enough outside of the city and not anywhere too busy. Plus, I'm sure you're always going to all the newest restaurants and things... thought you might like something different." She doesn't respond right away, which immediately makes me want to fill the silence.

"Still public enough in case you want to run..." I take a long drink of wine. There's nothing about her that makes me think she might *actually* want to escape but sometimes we all need some validation.

"I don't want to run. Not yet at least," she says playfully. "You've put some thought into this."

"Definitely have. I knew what I was getting myself into, sort of, when I opened my mouth after practice." The look on her face, cheeks pinched with a smile, her eye contact, it makes it impossible to look away.

"You also seem to know quite a bit about me. Like my favorite flower."

I knew this was going to come up. Just didn't know when.

"I remember an interview you did a while back." I try to sound cool and collected. "And to just get this out of the way, I've been a fan for as long as I can remember. I played your first CD in the first car I bought. I can probably sing most of your songs, word for word, and I'm not at all embarrassed." I clap my hands and rub them together.

This might be the fucking worst thing to say. It's not like I date a lot, especially not someone like Willow. Is it gross to admit to being a fan? No clue. I already said it and can't take it back.

I can't tell if it's the candles reflecting in her eyes or if she's processing what I said. She tips her chin a little closer to her chest and runs her tongue over her lip.

"You like my music?" she quietly responds, smiling—not what I was expecting. My stomach flips because I have no chill. Plus, I'm still thinking of her tongue on her lip.

"You're sweet for pretending I wasn't blaring a live version, one that I had to scrounge the internet for, when you got in my car."

Willow's cheeks blush, and she looks down at her hands in her lap. She slowly blinks and shakes her head, still grinning.

"What, like you didn't google me?" I joke and give her space to bypass my confession of being a legitimate fan.

Her chestnut eyes snap up. Busted. And she knows it.

"Guilty." She jokingly puts a hand up, like she's claiming responsibility. "In all fairness, there wasn't much to find. Your record seems to be squeaky clean... minus a rowdy post-championship Champagne incident a few months back." She takes a slow sip of her wine, not losing eye contact. "Not a mention of a single girlfriend. You really threw the paparazzi for a loop with your after-practice shenanigans."

"To be fair, there really hasn't ever been a girlfriend, besides someone back in college." I lean back in my chair. Willow skeptically tilts her chin up, wanting more. "Bailey. She's great." I smile as I share details. "We were close friends and would throw in the benefits when it was needed. She always had my back, and in all transparency, we're still friends. I know it sounds like a line, but it's the truth—there wasn't anyone besides her."

"Or you're just very good at keeping secrets." Her voice drifts.

"That isn't it. Too many people would use the word impulsive to describe me. I don't have the capacity to keep things like that under wraps, and I'd never want to make anyone feel like they were being hidden."

The second the dumb words are out of my idiotic mouth I know there are things she works hard to keep quiet. For example, the home where I picked her up. This was a key mention from her security team. Also, I don't want to feel like I'm giving her shit for her ex.

"But I can keep a secret when it counts. I had one of my assistants take my car for the night. They pulled out of the parking garage first, and when I knew all the paps followed them, I got into my new car. The one no one has seen me in. The one I bought yesterday." The words fall out too fast in a panic.

Willow pauses and nods her head up and down in understanding.

"Are you serious? There's no way you bought a new car for this," she asks with a small giggle, light bouncing from her eyes.

"One hundred percent. I knew it was important to you. So, it was important to me. It was time for an upgrade anyways." The last part is complete bullshit, but she doesn't know that.

The dealership was thrilled to get me in a car, especially because I had to take what they had. It was a done deal before Zack and I walked in the door. I usually prefer white cars but the only Tesla they had, ready to go, was black. Nothing like a little spontaneity paired with a substantial signing bonus from the Cosmos.

"Wow. Thank you." She fidgets her hands in her lap. "Let's get back to the zero-dating history. I feel like there's more to this..." She leaves the door open. Not sure if this is approved for first date territory but we're jumping right in.

She's right. And if I want this to go anywhere, I need to give her something.

"It's always been football. When it wasn't football, it was me and my mom. Making it to the NFL wasn't supposed to happen for someone like me. But I did it and I want to show up and be my best every day."

"What do you mean someone like you?" she asks.

There it is.

"I wasn't a high school phenom. I barely had any scholarship offers. Graduating from college was always part of my plan because I was prepared to have to give up football. There was nothing about me that screamed success. And then, good things happened and continued to happen. I knew I had to pour myself into this if I wanted to do it."

"Your parents must be proud." She smiles and it makes me smile right back.

"My mom is proud. My dad isn't in the picture."

"Oh, Tripp. I'm sorry." She reaches her hand over and grabs mine that's resting on the table near my wine glass. Her touch is warm.

"Don't be. He left one day and never came back. That's on him. He tried to get a hold of me for Super Bowl tickets, and that's the extent of our relationship."

"His loss," she says with a snap.

"That's what my mom always told me."

We're both leaning forward on the table. Willow holds my hand and rubs my palm with her thumb. It's like we're magnets, and I want to pull her into my chest across the table. Hold her to me.

Before I have another second to think about it, the door opens to the stairwell and our server heads to the table with a tray full of food.

# Chapter 15
## Willow

THERE'S NOTHING QUITE LIKE waiting for something to go wrong. But nothing comes. Being with Tripp is easy. Easy in the way that I want to be closer, want to touch him. I don't think I'm the only one when I think about all the errant grazes and excuses to touch.

I'm thankful the cold is hiding my flushed cheeks.

While I'm laughing at something Tripp said, our server drops off a piece of tiramisu.

"This one's on us." He claps his hands and rubs them together before putting one on Tripp's shoulder. "Tripp, so good to see you. Thanks for swinging by."

Tripp's smile is familiar and warm, our server matches it with his own—a smile only friends would share.

I take one bite of the tiramisu, fall back in my chair, and groan. It's heavenly.

"Why do none of my friends work at an Italian spot like this? Amazing."

"I went to college with the owner's son." Tripp pulls up the sleeves of his shirt, his forearms strong and defined. Muscles move and flex as he reaches across the table for a bite of dessert. I can't help but think of those arms around my body.

"He walked on at our college team and probably could've gone to the NFL, but he wanted to take care of this place," Tripp continues as if he didn't show me some of the most delicious arm-candy I've encountered.

*Interesting. What it would be like to have two dreams to chase?* I think to myself while taking my fair share of the lady fingers.

"What'd you study at college?"

"Public administration. When I thought football wouldn't work out, I wanted to work for a non-profit. Find ways to support single-parent families and kids." He bounces his leg under the table.

Meanwhile, I'm trying to put this puzzle together. Is it possible that he has all the pieces?

"That's kind of amazing. Are you still friends?"

"Yeah. We're still close," he continues. "His family used to invite us over for the holidays. It's nice to be in the same area again. We didn't see much of each other when I was in Seattle."

"That sounds lovely." My silverware lightly clinks on the plate as I set it down.

"I bet you have tons of friends all over the world," Tripp says while finishing his wine, his eyes still gazing into mine through the empty glass.

"Not really." I laugh to make it sound less pathetic than it really is.

"What's that mean?" Tripp presses.

"Friends are hard. They've always been hard for me, at least. When I was in high school, I had a group of friends, but we fell out, like girls do. We never fell back together." I clasp my hands together to explain. "And I didn't even consider going to college. It was always music. I know I'm lucky. I was talking with major labels when I was seventeen. Gosh, I sound like a brat."

Embarrassment washes over me. Why did I say that?

"No, you don't. I get it. Being successful at a young age, it's hard. Being young is hard enough. I don't know how you handled it."

Honestly, not well, but I don't tell Tripp that. Sometimes I'm sad thinking about the friendships I had and how they fizzled. There are times when I dread going home. It's either people acting like we were best friends when they were horrible to me or seeing people I was friends with at one time being completely content to never speaking to me again.

I might tour the world but that doesn't leave much room for close friends. I'm thankful for Claire. And Emilie. They're the closest I get to true girlfriends, but they're on my payroll so I'm not sure they even count.

"I did my best. Sometimes it was good enough. A lot of times it wasn't."

"I think you could say that about anyone. Anything." His voice is light but also commanding. Like I shouldn't argue that my best wasn't good enough. It catches me off guard. I have to swallow past the lump in my throat.

Tripp grins and leans across the table. He slowly takes my chin in his hand, and I lean into the touch. His eyes hold contact, piercing blue, but then they're looking at my lip. He uses his thumb to lightly wipe something from the corner of my lip. Neither of us move.

It's almost like the moment is paused. I can feel his chest, rising and falling. His hand stays on my chin and it tilts it up just enough for me to gaze up into him. My brain short-circuits, and my skin starts to itch in a way that makes me need to fidget. I want to lean further into him. I want my mouth on his. My breath halts in my lungs.

The door to the stairway closes, and Tripp sits back in his seat. Our server awkwardly leaves us our to-go boxes with some extras for "a good lunch tomorrow".

I can't help but be a little disappointed.

Before we leave, I grab a thank you note and pen from my purse.

"What's that?" Tripp asks.

"It's this thing I do. I try to leave a thank-you note whenever I'm out."

"You carry those in your bag? At all times?"

"Pretty much." I laugh as I write our server's name at the top of the card. "I had a fan write me a thank-you note, and she handed it to me when I was walking by, when I was out for drinks. She chose a private moment, and it seems like nothing, but I'll never forget the way I felt when I read it." I place a hand on my chest, thinking back to that moment, how grateful I felt. "I've kept it, even after all this time."

"That's sort of amazing," Tripp says, crossing his arms, grinning at me.

I smile back while I finish writing out the note.

TRIPP PULLS INTO MY driveway. The light illuminates my front steps.

"Let me walk you," he says, too fast, as he practically jumps out and opens my door.

He sweetly grabs my hand, and we walk to my door. The wind runs through the trees, rustling the branches and leaves. Night has completely fallen, and the stars are putting on a show. That's one of my favorite parts of being out of the SoHo apartment. Here, the stars have a chance.

Tonight feels new. There were never early dates with sweet hellos or goodbyes. It was dodging being seen or something else chaotic. Or finding somewhere "neutral" to meet.

I melt a little. Like I'm having an out-of-body experience and I'm a normal woman wrapping up a date with someone she randomly met. Almost like a fortunate fluke. I've been in the industry ever since I've been old enough to date. It's always been complicated.

This is easy.

"What's that smile for?" Tripp scoffs and nudges my shoulder with his. He matches my smile.

"This is all so… normal. Nice. It's refreshing."

"Nice?" Tripp teases. "Did you have a *nice* time?" He raises his eyebrows as he turns toward me.

"I did. Everything was lovely," I say as I look down at the hand he's still holding.

This man turns, scoffs, and bites his lip before turning back to me. A deadly combination. I'm no longer thinking about him holding my hand.

"I'm not that sweet…" His voice drifts as he takes a small step towards me.

"No?" I don't know if I've had too much wine or tiramisu, but I bait him. "Prove it." My words come out breathy, and Tripp's eyes go wide, just long enough for me to register. He takes the hand he was holding and pushes it up, near my head, hitting the back of my door while he moves my back to the same place.

His free hand comes to my chin, like it did at dinner. This time, he tilts it up and greets me with a deadly smirk—the type that could make me tell him all my secrets.

Tripp's mouth crashes to mine. His lips press in a way that screams *hot hot hot,* even though he tastes sweet from the tiramisu. I hear, and feel him, loud and clear. Consider the message delivered.

His body presses into mine. Muscles meet me and demand to be felt. He lets the arm above me go, and I run a hand over his chest, the soft shirt a stark contrast to his firm muscles. He nudges into me, and bites at my lip. I moan when I can't help it and that urges him on. I throw my arms around his neck doing all I can to get closer.

Tripp picks me up, my back up against the wall, and I wrap my legs around his waist.

Damn, I know he's a football player, but he picks me up and throws me around like I'm nothing. And I love it.

He envelops me. His skin smells like the forest after a rain. He tastes sweet thanks to the tiramisu.

All I can think of is his touch. Wanting more of it. How good it feels. Tripp's hands go from the sides of my face to the nape of my neck until they're in my hair. He peppers my neck with teasing licks and the lightest of bites. His lips are forceful but still soft.

Want builds and pulls, low in my core. The pulls rapidly turn to throbs.

He's careful not to leave a mark. His arms, muscular and determined, wrap around my back, pulling me even closer to him. I tip my head back, and he kisses the tops of my breasts.

A car door slams.

"Ugh, shit. Sorry, Willow. I had something to check in the house." Seth scrambles and has no idea what to do with himself.

Tripp sets me down, and my legs immediately miss his waist.

"All good, my man." Tripp turns and waves to my security team like he didn't have me pressed up against my front door. He's full of surprises. I like that he took control.

He tugs at the crotch of his jeans, and I cover a laugh with my hand.

"Goodnight, Lo," Tripp says as he tucks a piece of hair behind my ear and kisses my lips a final time.

*Lo.* It takes everything I have not to wrap myself up in him.

Tripp walks back to his car and waves to the security team before he pulls out of the driveway. Seth meets me at the door, and his cheeks are crimson.

"I can't believe that happened. And we're *never* talking about it again," I say, a finger in his chest, before opening the door and going inside.

# Chapter 16
## Tripp

THERE'S SOME UNWRITTEN RULE about not texting or calling someone after a date. I don't know who wrote it or decided it was the move, but I think they're idiots. As soon as I get home, I'm texting Willow. I can't help myself.

Me

would you judge me if I told you I've already started snacking on my leftovers

Willow

that little piece of tiramisu was gone ten minutes after you left lol

my kind of girl

Why do I say shit like this? I groan and fall back onto the couch. I shake my head, picturing Willow reading that and cringing. Rolling her eyes. My phone buzzes.

:) sorry about Seth

not ideal but he didn't hurt me. I'll take that as a win

he would never

he's not used to nights like tonight

what the hell did your other dates do?

schedule a car to pick me up, plan with my driver, ask me to meet them somewhere

if my mom found out that I asked you to MEET me somewhere

I don't even want to think about it

to be fair, I let it slip to my dad once, that dexter would ask me to meet him and I had to beg him to not call him.

I get it

and I think I'd like your mom

Everything I've read about Dexter seems douchey. Plus, anytime Willow brings him up it's like the blueprint of what *not* to do. Guess I can thank him for setting the bar so low.

oh, she's a fan

the morning after the after-party, she was the first person to call me

she was bummed I wasn't secretly dating you

does she know we went out tonight?

She doesn't know. No one knows. I don't know how that will look to her. Fuck. Maybe she didn't want this to be a secret?

no

I don't know what the protocol is for this

and if it was a disaster I didn't want to have to tell her

it's okay

I like the idea of it being between us for now

and far from disastrous

The way I'm holding my phone right in front of my face. I need to get a grip.

whew

is that your way of saying you had a good time?

thought me pinning you against your front door was a clue

but I had a fucking great time

good isn't the right word

:) what's on the mvp's schedule for tomorrow?

team meetings, practice, agility coach, dinner with my mom, and yoga

always try to get to yoga on Thursdays

what's the difference between practice and agility?

practice is with the team

agility coach is my own thing. I have some training I do outside of official team stuff

mvp things

don't want to lose my starting spot things

I get that. Trying to stay a step ahead

I feel like you're 1000 steps ahead

ha! Wish it was true

We go back and forth until a yawn catches me off guard. The clock tells me it's almost 2 AM. How is that possible?

I had no idea I was keeping you up

I didn't know it was that late

or early

better let you get to bed.

goodnight Lo

night mvp

When she calls me MVP, fuck. Why is that the hottest but also the sweetest thing ever? I know tomorrow is going to feel extra long. But you know what? It's worth it.

ANOTHER DAY, ANOTHER PRACTICE. I'm standing in front of my locker, towel around my waist, and my bonus phone is vibrating in my bag. I reach for it and see more texts from Willow. Couldn't be from anyone else; no one has this number. It's been a week since our date and I love the rush I get when there's messages waiting for me.

"Why are you smiling like that?" Zack says, skeptically looking over at me.

"Jesus. You scared me."

"Why do you look like you got caught with your dick out?" He laughs.

Fun fact, I'm a terrible liar. No one has any idea about my date with Willow. We successfully kept the press and everyone out of it. I'm about to blow this wide open.

"Nothing. It's nothing." And what wouldn't come at the worst possible time is a notification from my other phone, my real one. Zack doesn't miss a beat.

"Wait. Is that a burner phone?" he gives me shit and peeks into my locker.

"No. Not a burner phone." I try to buy some time because I don't really know what to call the bonus phone. "This is a secure line." I shrug my shoulders with the bonus phone in my hand. I check to see who's left in the locker-room. It's just the two of us.

"Why in the hell would *you* need a secure line." His eyes are bugging out as the words fall out of his big mouth. He reaches for the phone and I let him grab it. As much as I want to keep this to myself, I'm dying to tell someone.

I know he sees her name because his eyes are like fucking saucers.

"Don't make this a big—"

"You fucking did it. You went out with her. How the hell was it?" He punches my shoulder.

"Good. Incredible. I don't know. We've been texting and FaceTiming like high schoolers. I could listen to her talk about anything..." My voice trails off and I feel like a chump. "I feel like I'm out of my league."

"You *play* in the fucking league." He laughs at me before slapping his knees in dramatics. "You've got it bad. When are you seeing her next?"

When I don't say anything, Zack rolls his eyes.

"I can't believe I'm about to say this, but don't fucking fumble this thing with Willow."

"Did you really just use a pun—"

"I did. And it seems like football might be the only thing you grasp in that thick skull of yours." Zack laughs at me before physically knocking on my head. "Go have some fun. Quit being so boring."

"I'm not boring." I straighten at the thought. "Wait, do the guys think I'm boring?"

"Tripp, man, they don't know you. All you do is workout, run drills, show up to practice early, leave late. Maybe it's time to loosen the reins a bit?"

Well, that blows. Not exactly what you want to hear.  It stings but I know Zack is right. I've always been all football. I fill any and all free time with training sessions or recovery. That's how it's been for as long as I can remember.

"I'm aware that this sounds stupid, but I don't know how to do... this." I gesture to the bonus phone.

"You'll figure it out."

I'll figure it out. Maybe. Maybe not.

"Hey, man. Can you not say anything?"

Zack mimics locking his mouth and throwing away the key.

# Chapter 17
## Willow



This is the headline I've been sent, tagged in, and inundated with all morning. Every rendition of the article includes Dexter draped over a gorgeous model. The smile he wears, his hand on her thigh, and her mouth on his neck is lemon juice on the cut you forgot about.

Seems like Dexter has no issue being out with the cover of Sports Illustrated. You'd never find a photo like this of the two of us. The second Dexter thought there was a camera in the vicinity, he'd act like we were middle schoolers at our first "boy-girl" dance. Once, I tried telling him it made me feel weird, but he twisted it into how he was doing what was best for me. To this day, I still can't explain why he didn't want to be seen with me.

"Quit subjecting yourself to those pictures," Emilie says while peeking over my shoulder. "That man is not worth it." Some people might be annoyed at the nosiness, but not me.

"I know," I lie.

"Do you? Because it looks like you were questioning why it's different with her..." She tucks her red hair behind her ears.

"How do you know that?" Emilie always seems to surprise me.

"I'm very intuitive. Also, anyone would be thinking that. Let's go do something." She sits across from me and taps her hands on the table.

"Like what?"

"Something in the city. Anywhere that someone will get a picture of you doing something fun. Being unbothered. See where I'm going?"

This Dexter headline is one where the press will do anything to get a reaction. Maybe I make it easy for them?

"Let's shop! You have an invite to a few boutiques in the city and an old college friend recently opened a lingerie shop I've been dying to go to." Her eyes light up. "That's it! What could be better than casually browsing lingerie? Not giving a fuck about Dexter and his flavor of the week?" She gasps in excitement.

Whenever Emilie is confident about something, there's no stopping her. She's a force. Part of me hopes some of her rubs off on me. It's not that I can't put my foot down, but I have a tough time going for what I want, whenever it's not the logical next step. Sometimes, I don't know what I want, and I stay quiet, terrified of giving the wrong answer.

"You know what? You're right. Let's shop."

○ ✕ ✕ ✕

EMILIE MADE THE RIGHT calls on the way into the city, tipping off a few members of the press. She seems to always know a little bit about everything. Currently, we're browsing some of the most gorgeous lingerie while the press is lined up at the door—I'm happy the tip panned out. Sometimes, they get tips celebrities will be somewhere but it's just to throw them off from their actual destination.

I take my time in the window. Making sure they have a chance to get a shot of me moving from table to table.

The soft lighting casts a warm glow over the displays, highlighting the intricate lace and delicate fabrics. My fingers instinctively reach out to touch the garments, feeling the softness and smoothness of the fabrics against my skin. Lace, chiffon, silk.

I flip the tags, looking at the sizes. A flush of red creeps up my neck to accompany the panic. It's not uncommon for me to struggle to find things in my size. This is not what I, or my ego, need today.

I've always been thick. Substantial. Muscular. Curvy. The words have changed since I've been a kid but it's all the same. I've never been thin.

Lucky for me, I have access to some of the best personal trainers and dieticians. When I booked my first major tour at nineteen years old, I needed a workout regimen that would let me keep up, night after night. I've always liked to cook, and my dietician helped find creative ways to have healthy meals. The things I've learned have stuck but that doesn't mean I don't ever have terrible body image days; I am human.

I've never been one to beat myself up about what I'm eating or go on a crash diet before an event. That doesn't mean the press hasn't made their fair share of comments regarding each of those items.

My phone vibrates. It's a picture of an ice bath from Tripp. I send him a picture of the lingerie table I'm currently swooning over.

Tripp

your plans are much better than mine

good lord where are you

never mind don't tell me

Me

Emilie's friend opened this shop a few weeks back. We're shopping

Shopping, huh? shopping for who

> maybe for my next date? Who knows

> it's a shame Mr. MVP has been so busy

The second I click send my cheeks flush. I don't remember being this playful with anyone. Everything was always so serious. I take a picture of two sets, one red and one black, and send them to Tripp.

> which do you like better?

Black. Always black

> sold. Remember, these are in my possession.

> whenever you're free

Tripp's schedule is always packed. It could be that mine feels light since I'm getting back into album mode, it feels that way. We haven't been successful in making plans. It makes me wonder if he's into me the way I'm into him. The idea of chasing someone who doesn't want me flips my stomach.

tomorrow night? I'll move things

> I'll be around :)

I don't let on how excited I am. If there's one thing I've learned it's to keep your cards close. I don't lay them down unless I like my odds to win.

As I browse the racks, I'm struck by the sheer variety of the designs. There are classic styles that exude elegance and sophistication, as well as more daring pieces that hint at a sense of adventure and allure. Every garment seems to tell a story, each stitch a line and every detail a twist.

It kind of reminds me of music. Every word, beat, instrument a piece of the story. Honestly, it makes me think of why I wanted to get into music in the first place. I wanted to tell stories. I'd spend my days daydreaming before putting pen to paper—getting lost in an empty notebook was an ideal way to spend free time.

Once I figured out I could sing, it was over. I remember putting on little skits and shows for my parents and since I didn't have any siblings, it was always the three of us in the living room. The day I sang a song I wrote, I'll never forget my mom's reaction.

*"Willow Jo. Where did you learn to do that?" Two little tears slid down her face.*

*"Holy shit," my dad says.*

*"Alan!" My mom hits him with a couch pillow. "Don't talk like that."*

*"Kath. Did you hear her?!"*

*"Of course, I heard her." My parents always got along. They sometimes bickered but always made up before things got out of hand.*

*"I don't know. I just tried to do it. Wrote a song and tried to sing it."*

*"You wrote that?!" My mom lightly takes the paper out of my hand, looking at my scribbled lyrics.*

*I nod and my cheeks turn pink.*

*"Honey, this is lovely. Do you want to try singing or music lessons?"*

And that was it. Everything was music after that. My parents never pushed me but always gave me a chance to try new things. Ultimately, I landed on learning the guitar and the piano.

"Tell me this stuff isn't gorgeous," Emilie interrupts my thoughts while her friend stands next to her.

"It's all beautiful. I can't get over the intricate details." I'm holding a few pieces in my size.

"Let me wrap those up for you," the shop owner says. I feel like she's going to try and give them to me for free.

"Thank you but you are not giving these to me. I'm paying full price." I follow her to the register.

EMILIE AND I ARE at dinner. She picked a Thai spot I could never get sick of. We order a bunch of dishes to share and I'm already drooling about the leftovers we haven't even eaten yet.

"That did *not* happen to you." I try to cover my mouth before my laugh disrupts the whole restaurant.

"It totally did. I thought I was showing up for an assistant interview. They thought I was there for the backup dancer audition."

"So, they handed you a black sports bra and spandex shorts and you did what?"

"I put them on and spent the next three hours pretending I knew what I was doing," she says like that was the only logical option.

"Why didn't you tell them you got it wrong?" I can barely get the words out.

"I was nineteen! It was one of my first big opportunities. I had zero backbone then."

"Are you a good dancer? Did you get picked?!" I ask, eyebrows raised, trying not to laugh.

"Willow. Do you think I got picked for one of the largest rap and r&b tours to date? I did hold my own but no. No, I didn't."

Her sarcasm is my favorite. We both laugh, feeding off each other, wiping tears from our eyes. She looks at her phone.

"I may not be a good dancer but damn I'm good at this!" Emilie shows me her screen. It's pictures of me at the lingerie shop. Someone even got a photo of me texting Tripp, judging by my smile. The headline reads ***What's Got Willow All Smiles?***

"You really are."

My smile almost matches the one in the photo. Today turned into a great day and I'm hoping tomorrow is even better. The lingerie bag sits on the bench next to me, the pieces I bought wrapped in blush pink tissue paper. I think of the lace, dark and delicate.

I press my lips together, trying not to blush.

I'm unsuccessful.

# Chapter 18
## Tripp

I'm about to walk out the door to go to Willow's. It's later than I'd hoped, but better late than never. There was an opening for a private session at the Pilates place I like and couldn't pass it up.

Now, all I can think about is that photo she sent of the lingerie. *Fuck.* The smile I'm wearing is only for her. I can't get out of here fast enough.

As I reach for the door, someone knocks.

I swing the door open to see Bailey, with a duffle bag.

"Surprise!" she yells before wrapping her free arm around my neck and kissing me on the lips. A standard Bailey greeting.

"What are you doing here?"

"I'm in town for work. Thought I'd surprise you!" She pushes herself into my apartment. "I called your mom, and she didn't think you had anything going on tonight."

Note to self: revoke my sweet mother's access to my online calendar.

"Are you going somewhere?" She looks at the bag, my sneakers, and the tiramisu I'm holding.

"Umm, no. Just getting home," I lie and shut the door.

"Thank god. I just flew in and I've been stuck in airports all day. I'm going to take a quick shower. Down the hall I'm guessing?" Bailey is walking towards my room before I even have a chance to register what's happening.

The water turns on.

Fuck.

Bailey is in my shower. In my apartment. With an overnight bag. Maybe it's not a hookup thing? Maybe it's a hang out thing? I take my shoes off, put the tiramisu in the fridge, and sit down on the couch.

I did not think this was something I'd have to deal with today. The excitement that flooded my veins is now replaced with anxiety, rugged and choppy. Willow and I have only been on the one date, but I feel like this is bad news, especially because I'm supposed to be going over there tonight. I pull my phone out to text her.

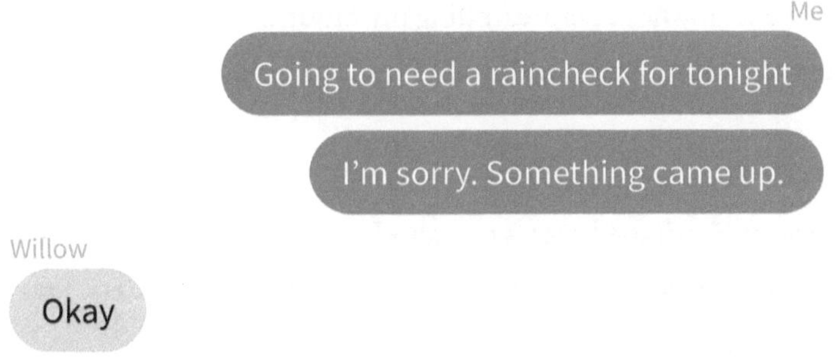


That's it. Nothing else.

I think back to my message and cringe. Why didn't I take a minute and think about it? Nope. That would make too much sense. The dreaded *okay*. No one is ever okay when they text that. She must think I'm blowing her off.

My mind runs and jumps to conclusions. What the hell am I supposed to do? Willow and I aren't exclusive. I didn't ask Bailey to come here.

Maybe this thing with Willow isn't meant to be? I scoff at the thought. Meant to be? Who am I? I don't even believe in that shit.

There's a part of my brain that itches. The part that always wondered if I'd end up with Bailey. We'd both just realize one day that what we had was enough. Maybe we were all we needed?

Before I can spiral any further, Bailey walks out of my bedroom. She's wearing matching pink satin pajamas, her long blonde hair damp. Gorgeous as ever.

"Ahh, so much better." She sighs, standing in front of me on the couch, stretching with her arms above her head, side to side. I smile at her, and she takes that as the greenlight to straddle me before wrapping me into a hug.

"I've missed you. It's been forever," she says into my neck.

"I know." I hug her back. I do miss her. Bailey's one of my only friends from college I still talk to. Hell, she's one of my only friends I made in college. Period.

She kisses my neck before finding my mouth. I kiss her back. Just long enough to realize she's not the one I want to be kissing. Alarms go off in my head.

*STOP. DANGER. ABORT MISSION.*

I look at her draped across me, and I know this isn't what I want.

I move my mouth from hers and lightly grab her shoulders. I push her back a little.

"I'm sort of seeing someone." The words fly out of my mouth.

"What?" She looks at me, questioning what I said. Probably because in all the years we've known each other I've never said those words to her.

"I'm sorry. I didn't know if you just wanted to hang out or catch up."

"Why are you apologizing? I'm the one who just threw myself at you without asking." Her cheeks flush with heat as she looks away, which only makes me feel worse.

"Bailey. You know it's not like that," I plead.

"Why didn't your mom say anything?"

"Well..." I don't know how much I want to share.

"She doesn't know." She sits back further on her heels wearing a look of understanding.

"It's new, okay? And I don't ever fucking do this. I didn't know you were coming."

"Tripp, it's okay. Really it is." She cracks her knuckles and stares at her hands. "Who is she?"

"Ummm... The thing is. I don't—"

"God, Tripp. If you didn't want me here, you can just be a man and say it." Bailey stands up and is halfway towards my room before I catch up to her.

"It is not like that. It's..." I take a long breath. "It's Willow."

"Willow who?" she snaps back.

"Willow. Like... Super Bowl halftime show Willow." My voice is small.

"No way. How do you go from dating no one to dating the queen of pop music? I saw your whole stunt with Champagne and the asking her out, but I thought it was just you being you."

"Believe me, I'm also surprised." I laugh.

"Well, the least you can do is make me a drink and give me the details."

"Are you sure?" This is uncharted territory, talking about another woman with Bailey.

"Tripp come on. We've been friends forever. There are lots of times we spent time together, without the sex. And if you just let me straddle you while you're trying to date this woman, you might need some help."

Fuck, she isn't wrong.

"Get the bourbon and tell me everything."

# **Chapter 19**
## Willow

Something came up. That was the only explanation he offered. My cheeks are hot with embarrassment, or maybe it's disappointment.

Earlier, when I stepped into the inky black lingerie—the one Tripp picked out—it made me feel good. Confident. Like dance-in-front-of-the-mirror confident. The lingerie went from a cheeky, uplifting secret to mocking me—making me feel like an idiot.

Tonight tastes like rejection and I wish I didn't care. How is it that excitement can immediately fall into disappointment? If you don't get your hopes up, there's nothing to drag you down.

Tripp cancelling makes me think of Dexter. I will say this, whenever Dexter and I made plans, they were solid. He wasn't one to deter from a plan, always craving consistency, and time for his own things.

I *almost* want to text Dexter. He was just making out with some supermodel a few nights ago. I know it's not Dexter I crave but the comfort of something familiar.

The lingerie, mostly lace and sheer fabric, itches and pricks my skin. I need to change.

After I put on my favorite leggings and crewneck, I'm in the studio writing sad words to melancholy melodies. I feel like this piano is fueled by my tears some days. It's insufferable even to think something like that to myself, but I'm being honest. I wish I could let things like this roll off my back and not bother me. I'm a sensitive soul; I always have been. People have told me this my whole life. Friends who pushed me out of their friend group, guys who dumped me, and critics who deemed my music too immature or cliché. They all fell back on the, "Willow, you shouldn't be so sensitive."

Do you know what it feels like when people don't want you? Even when those people aren't worth wanting, it still hurts.

Because tonight isn't painful enough, I think back to my first group of friends in middle school. Inseparable for years, we even made a band and would practice in my garage after school. No one really knew anything about music, besides me, so I'd teach them to play enough of the guitar or piano, enough to string a song or two together. I knew we weren't super talented, but it was fun to spend time doing something I loved with girls my age. The only place we played in front of others was the school talent show.

It wasn't until the tenth grade that they pushed me out. I was starting to get attention from labels, and they didn't like it. I think they thought the label would want to do something with our hodge-podge band, but that wasn't the case.

All of a sudden, I was the bad guy. Lies and rumors spread like wildfire. The parents even got involved and started a petition to ban me from singing at school talent shows and events. There was a meeting with the school principal where my parents and I sat across from this man who had no idea what to do with me. My dad was livid, and my mom was heartbroken. Not because of the petition exactly, but because people I called my friends could do something like that.

I was fifteen when I learned two valuable lessons.

1. People will choose their own insecurity over celebrating someone else's success.

2. Sometimes, you're just not worth it.

Tonight, I'm thinking hard about that second lesson. I didn't think that'd be the case with Tripp. With his public distractions and asking me out in front of a paparazzi camp, I thought this would be something different. The way he kissed me was unlike anything I'd ever felt before.

I know I'm being dramatic, so I try to put my feelings into words and music. Something I can manipulate, shift, and edit. Something I'm in control of. Something that needs me as much as I need it.

When the words and feelings finally stop coming, I look at the clock: midnight. I pick my phone up only to see no texts or calls from Tripp.

It hurts more than I wish it did.

# **Chapter 20**
## Tripp

BAILEY SPENT THE NIGHT. She took the master bedroom—I took the guest room—and it still felt like I was breaking a rule. She offered to go back to her hotel after we dissected and discussed anything and everything Willow related, but it was too late.

I'm not the most experienced when it comes to dating, or whatever the hell it is Willow and I are doing, but I know that cancelling plans, as another woman sleeps in your penthouse, isn't the key to happiness.

Even I know I shouldn't have stood Willow up. Why can I hear Zack in my head, telling me what a jackass I am? If he was right next to me, he'd still be right.

If there's one thing my idiotic behavior taught me, it's that Willow is moving up on my list of all the things that deserve my time. My focus.

It's time I learn how to make room for something other than football. I wish I came up with that, but it's a direct quote from Bailey.

Last night, I almost called Willow. I'd pick up my phone, open our recent messages, and hover my finger above the call button. I didn't have it in me to actually call her. Instead, thoughts of Willow ran through my mind until I fell asleep. Her wrapped around me. How she smells like vanilla. Those perfect pink lips. The way her eyes went wide with pleasure when I backed her up against the door. The little noises she made when I kissed her.

Mostly, I think about how I probably have fucked up this whole thing.

Our last preseason game is this week. Everyone on the team is ready for the season to get going. Right now, it's mostly speculation about a group of guys who've never played together before and it's time to just figure shit out.

On my way home from practice, I call Willow.

"Didn't expect to hear from you." Her voice is cold and level when she answers.

"I owe you an explanation."

"Tripp, we don't have to do this. If you're not into it, it's fine—"

"That is so far from the truth. What are you doing tonight?"

"Nothing." I can tell I've caught her off guard. "I need to get some writing done."

"Do you mind if I come over?"

"Don't you have your yoga class tonight?" She asks, skeptical.

I typically take a restorative yoga class on Thursday nights. I almost let myself smile when I think about how she remembered this small detail.

"I'm skipping it." Guilt pulls at the corner of my brain, but I wave it off.

"Sure. I'll be home around eight. You can come over if you want," she says.

"Perfect. Just enough time to switch cars. I'll be on my way shortly." In this moment, I plead with the traffic gods to just let me have this one.

"You don't have to switch cars if it's annoying..." Her words fade a bit.

"You're right. I don't have to, but I want to."

# Chapter 21
## Willow

"This is *my* fucking show, and I can do whatever I want…?"

"Willow. Not a question. A statement. Try it again." Claire says in a way that makes me want to follow all of her instructions.

"This is *my* fucking show, and I can do WHATEVER I WANT!" I yell the last part just to make sure it's not a question.

"There it is. Remember, we're in and out of this meeting. Give them enough but no negotiation or deep discussion today. They're going to need time. Also, we have a late lunch reservation at the place with the spicy salmon wontons and we will *not* be late," Claire says, looking back and forth between me and Emilie.

I tuck my phone into one of my favorite bags—a black leather Prada—before I walk into the meeting to discuss my next project with the label. Beads of sweat form on my lower back. Tripp calling right before we left was a good thing. Kind of like he knew I needed a distraction. Between Tripp and Claire's affirmations, my brain is busy in a good way.

His call gave me hope there's something between us. Right now, I'm choosing to hold onto that. I tend to lean into the negative but I'm working on it.

My label and I have a solid relationship, which is a good thing since the industry is so tumultuous. With so many talented artists breaking through on new channels, all thanks to social media, we're all looking for what's next.

My most recent album and stadium tour exceeded all expectations, and everyone was insanely pleased with the outcome. I was successful before the tour, but I've blown other markets wide open—people who didn't listen to me before are inhaling my previous albums. I'm guessing the label knows just how much based on the suits sitting around the conference room.

Cue even more sweating.

"There she is... our girl, Willow," Erik, my product manager, announces as I walk in. He's the type who needs control of the details or at least having a hand in them.

If announcing my arrival wasn't terrible enough, he starts to clap, and the entire room follows his lead. My cheeks turn hot, and it takes everything I have not to stare at my shoes.

"Oh, stop it. It's nice to see everyone." I reach for handshakes because if I'm shaking their hands, they certainly can't be clapping.

When the introduction fanfare is complete, thank god, I grab "my seat", determined by the steaming mug of peppermint tea.

Claire takes a chair next to me, reaching for the foamy cappuccino waiting for her and sucking down her first drink. Claire is a lot of things: a tenacious manager and a caffeine addict are just a few of them.

Emilie sits on the other side, an iced coffee in front of her. I pat her shoulder as we get settled. This is her first label meeting—she was so nervous she didn't want to come. I don't *need* her here, but part of hiring her was about growing her portfolio and giving her the gift of experience. To be honest, she's the type of person who could learn anything and kick everyone's ass in the process.

"First, let's recognize a job well done by Willow and the whole team." The sound of clapping fills the room again, making it hard to grab a breath. Claire squeezes my knee under the table, knowing how much I hate this.

"Yes, yes. We know she's the queen. Hate to rush this part, but we've got another meeting to get to." She gives me the smallest of Claire smirks, the kind only I can detect.

I try not to laugh because Claire's meeting really entails sushi and spicy salmon wontons.

"Sure, our girl's got things to do." The way my skin crawls every time they do that. *Our girl.* Gives me the ick. "Obviously, the last tour and album were a homerun. Wouldn't change a thing. Well, except for a few more international dates, right?" he says with a wink. "Kidding, kidding."

I know he's not. The label wanted to add more international dates, but I didn't have it in me. I'd already been touring for almost a year, on and off. I ached for home and my own space. Plus, the tension with Dexter was too high, and I knew another international leg would kill us. Without a doubt.

Didn't matter anyway.

Before I can respond to the subtle jab about more tour dates, Erik gets focused.

"You asked for a bit of a break from planning and solidifying what's next. So, I'll kick it to you. Why don't you tell us what's on your mind, what you've been working on, whatever you got." He claps a bit too loudly and then leans forward, clasping his hands, which are borderline too big for his body, on the table. Erik is muscular in a way that makes you wonder if it's a healthy choice.

I can feel Claire looking at me, trying to channel all her bad bitch energy. Generally, the label execs and bigwigs don't bother me. She knows I'm about to flip the script and we have no idea what kind of response we'll get it.

Why is it so damn difficult to ask for what I want? I've done my part, put in my time, paid my dues, but that doesn't still the shaking hands and anxiety. I reach my hands around the mug of hot tea, a perfect distraction.

"Thank you for everyone's time and the kind words about the tour. It was such a great experience. Core memories. But I'm ready to get into what's next." I take a breath to slow my heart rate.

"Don't tell me you want to act," Erik says, panic all over his face.

"What? No! It's nothing like that." I put the tea to my lips, dragging the silence a second too long. "The next album, I want it to be more acoustic vibes. More like someone's sitting next to me when they listen to the record. I also want to play all the music for it. I don't want to use a band." My mouth is like sandpaper.

"What happened with the band? We can find someone else—" Erik's voice cuts me off.

"Nothing happened. I love the band and we'll most likely work together in the future. Here's the thing, I need this album to be more... intimate." I feel like I'm a teenager, trying to convince my parents to let me go do something.

The room is filled with mixed reactions, as expected. Some of the suits sit back with their arms crossed, and some lean in forward with what I'm hoping is intrigue.

"I've done the massive tours. The press. The appearances. The million-dollar stage designs and costumes. For this next album, I want to play intimate, acoustic shows. Like venues that hold a thousand or less."

"That's *definitely* a direction," Erik scoffs, his voice dripping with sarcasm.

"It's a massive pivot. But the music I'm writing will be perfect for this. It will give me a chance to really connect with fans." My voice wants to drift off at the end, but I fight it.

"Is this about the ticket prices?" Erik asks.

The damn ticket prices. I could not *believe* what people were paying to come to my concert. By the time I caught wind of it, it was too late to change, or at least that's what the label insisted. The guilt ate at me, and I made a promise to myself I'd never let that happen again.

"That's part of it but I want to do something different. I want to showcase other areas of talent. I think an album like this will resonate with my fan base. And to be honest, I need this." My voice cracks a little at the end, but I think I'm the only one who notices.

"The thing about smaller venues like you're talking about is that they're not very lucrative," someone points out. I knew this would be the sticking point.

"You deserve to be paid for your hard work—" someone else interjects like it's not just about the money for them and sounds of agreement follow.

"I've been paid. I have more money than I'll get to spend in this lifetime. My last album sold more units across more formats than anyone projected, by a long shot. There's no reason to think this one won't do the same, or better."

Erik leans back and clasps his hands behind his neck. He stares at the ceiling, kind of rocking in his chair.

"Here's the deal. I don't even need to be paid for the tour. Keep my cut. Pay the team, the venue, and the label can have what's left."

I know what I'm proposing is unhinged, and while it's insane to have an artist work for free, the people across from me seem to relax a bit at the offer.

"How many songs do you have?" Erik questions with a side-eye look.

"She has enough but that's under lock and key until we all get on the same page. I know this wasn't what you were expecting, so we'll let you mull it over," Claire says while starting to gather her things, indicating we're ready to go. This is why she's my manager.

"We can't just buy into something without hearing any of it," Erik says.

"Come on, it's *our girl*, Willow. You know it's going to be fucking great. We don't need the greenlight today. Think about it. Let us know if you have questions or ideas. Let's get together soon. Emilie, you'll schedule that for us?" Claire stands.

Emilie nods and follows suit.

"I know this is surprising, but I'm really excited about what I've got. I can bring a sample next week, just in case." I stand up and smile. I try to make eye contact with everyone in the room because I know I'm asking for something that's hard for them to give. But I've given a lot too.

I follow Claire and Emilie, not breathing until we're far from the conference room.

"Honestly, that went better than I thought it would. Proud of you," Claire says as we exit the building.

Emilie bursts out laughing.

"I'm sorry. It's not funny. I was so nervous in there and you know how I get," Emilie says, trying to smooth her reaction. Her first reaction is always laughter.

"Thank you for not doing *that* in there," Claire says but smiles at the end.

My stomach flips thinking about going against the grain, what I've asked for.

"Claire, I've got to hand it to you. You've got some balls," Emilie says.

My head snaps to Claire, worrying that she'll be offended. But she smiles.

"Thank you, Emilie." Claire puts her hand on her chest in gratitude. "I do have balls. And you know what? They're bigger than Erik's."

"I don't think anyone doubts that," Emilie says.

# **Chapter 22**
## Tripp

After switching cars, asking my assistant to make it seem like I was headed somewhere else, and stopping to grab snacks, I pull into Willow's driveway almost an hour late. I try to quiet the voice in my head saying, *You should be training.* I shouldn't be training. I'm allowed to take a break.

My apology is more important.

I suck in a deep breath before knocking on Willow's door. My hands feel heavy and awkward. The seconds after stretch, making my stomach flip like it's a few minutes before kickoff. Can't remember when something besides the promise of a big game made me feel like this.

The door opens and Willow is wearing black leggings with a baggy quarter-zip sweatshirt. It's this light purple color, like lilacs. My mom's favorite flower.

"Hey, you made it," she says while leaning on one foot, a light jab at me being late. "And you brought...?"

"Snacks are always a must," I say, lifting the bag up.

"Well, if you brought snacks. Come on in." She holds the door open for me. Her mood is hard to read.

Immediately, I'm surprised by how open everything feels. Vaulted ceilings, open floor plan, lots of space. My apartment isn't small, by any means, but I love the way it feels in here.

"You're going to need to tell me the story behind this place." Before I finish my thought, I don't want to let her know that I may or may not know where her typical New York spots are to stay, and this one is never mentioned. I swear, I'm not a creep. I just know things.

"Sure, it's a good one." She takes the bag and walks into the kitchen, setting it on the island. "Can I get you something to drink?" Willow opens a white cabinet and grabs a glass. "I have peppermint iced tea... does that sound good?"

"Sounds great." She gives me a small smile as she pours me a glass. I hate how we're moving around each other like we're just friends.

I take a drink, and it's so refreshing. I make a mental note to start putting this in my fridge at home.

"I owe you an apology," I say, after almost drinking the entire glass, jumping right in.

"I'm listening," she says with her arms crossed across her chest.

"Last night, I bailed because Bailey showed up at my apartment. I didn't invite her, but this is the sort of thing she does when she's in town. She'll just show up."

"Bailey, like friends with benefits Bailey?" She scrunches her eyebrows and glares at me.

"Yes. I mean no. I mean, yes, it was Bailey, but there were no benefits." She stands still as stone, like a statue.

"She did kiss me and that's when I spilled all the beans about you. Now that I'm standing here, I'm not sure there was anything to spill." Willow's expression is icy. "But I told her everything." Willow doesn't say anything, and it feels like the doubt could swallow me whole. "Bailey thinks I'm a jackass, if that helps this situation at all."

"What else did she say?" She's direct and I know I'm walking the thinnest of lines.

"Well, she insisted I needed help. She's not wrong. Believe me. She was pissed that I let her kiss me and I didn't say anything before, but she really just showed up. I don't typically greet people with HEY I WENT OUT

ON A DATE WITH WILLOW SO PLEASE DON'T COME ON TO ME." I know I'm being over the top but it's my only move.

Willow looks at me with a slow blink and presses her lips in a thin line before shaking her head. It almost looks like she's trying to hold back a laugh.

"Nothing else happened?" Willow presses.

"Nothing. I spilled my guts while we drank bourbon. We played Scrabble. She beat me like she always does. It was late so she slept in my bed, but I took the guest bed. My neck has the tight muscles to prove it." I'm rambling at this point.

Willow stands without saying anything. Part of me wants to run to her. The other part is too nervous.

"I don't think you're a jackass. But you did hurt my feelings." Her voice gets terribly tiny at the end. It hurts to hear.

"I'm sorry. Really, I am."

"I thought we had this connection and then you blew off plans, after it took forever for you to find time to even make them. It felt like you were trying to get rid of me. No second date. I thought maybe I imagined our first night just being better than it was. Or something. I don't know. I can't chase people who don't want me. Not any more." She puts her hands on her forehead, like she's trying to block her eyes from mine.

Now I feel like an even bigger jackass. I take a couple steps so I'm standing in front of her. I put my fingers under her chin and lift her face up. I lean in for a kiss but pause with my lips in front of hers. I let her make the decision and close the distance. Her lips on mine, soft and intentional, make me feel even more sorry.

"I'm a dick. I didn't mean to make you feel like that. It is not in your head. I couldn't stop thinking about you. If last night taught me anything it's that you're the only one I want kissing me."

I give her another chaste kiss.

"In all transparency, I have no idea how to do this. I'm terrible at making time for things other than football and training. But you make me want to try." She smiles at me for the first time tonight. "Plus, I know you like your privacy. And fuck, I want to date you, only you. Even though I barely know how."

Willow grabs my shirt and pulls me in for a kiss.

"You showed up, in gray joggers, with snacks. I think you know how to do this. Give yourself a little credit. And you're right. I do like my privacy to an extent. I would love to keep this place under wraps," she gestures to her home. "My last boyfriend couldn't do the public thing. It hurt more than I thought it did. I don't want to do that again."

"Wait. What is the public thing?"

"He acted like being photographed was the most inconvenient thing and it just... it... wasn't for me." She picks at her fingernails.

This motherfucker.

"Believe me, I don't have a problem being seen out in public with you, if that's what you're asking. I don't know what went on with your last guy but that sounds like his own issue to work through." I dip my face down to catch her eyes. "The press is whatever. I can handle a little press." And I kiss her to put a period at the end of the sentence.

"What do you want to do?" she asks.

"Date you. If you'll have me? Knowing I've never really done this. I'll probably get a lot of it wrong. But this is your play to call." I point at her.

"Hate to be this person but... exclusive? Just you and I?"

"Exclusive. No random sleepovers with anyone else besides you. Even ones where I'm in the guest bed."

She giggles and looks at me, tilting her head.

"Dating. It sounds fun, and I'm due for some fun," Willow says. Her eyes are golden, and the corners scrunch up when she grins.

I wrap her up in a hug. I smell her hair: coconut and vanilla. I unclench my jaw and feel the relief. Part of me thought she was going to shut me down and say this was a bad idea.

"What kind of snacks do we have?" she asks, trying to change the subject.

I reach my hands into the bag and start pulling out the goods. "First, we've got caprese salad. I don't know what the fuck they put in this, and I've tried to recreate it, but it's so good. Next, these savory croissants. And last, but certainly not least, banana pudding and tiramisu. In all honesty, I picked up the tiramisu last night, so I don't know how well it held up in the fridge."

Willow nods each time I set something on the island.

"Random? Yes. But perfect. My mouth is watering." She fakes wiping drool from her mouth. And I can't do anything but stare at those lips. The same ones I've been thinking about all week.

"What?" she asks, her voice going up at the end.

And like the impulsive bastard I am. I move in front of her as she stands in front of the island and reach for her waist.

"What are you doing—" she asks while I pick her up and set her on the edge. "Oooh. Okay." She giggles. I consider that the green light.

I step even closer and put both of my hands on the sides of her face. She grins, her cheeks pressing into my palms. Before I can make the first real move, she wraps her legs around me, closing any remaining distance, and puts her mouth on mine.

That perfect fucking mouth. Which I can feel pulling up at the corners as she kisses me. My hands go from her face to her hair, weaving my fingers into it and lightly pulling. She moans in response—I pull a little harder.

Gone is the anxiety of the unknown. She kisses me back in a way that says she wants me too.

"I didn't even ask. Are we alone?" I put my forehead to hers.

She lightly pushes my chest.

"It's just you and me." She wraps her arms around my shoulders and pulls me closer to her.

She nips at my lower lip, and I can't get enough. My hands reach for the hem of her sweatshirt, not to pull it off, but to put my hands on her. I slowly rake my fingers up, feeling her bare skin, until I reach the soft fabric of her bra.

"Is this okay?" I stop and ask. Not trying to kill the mood but I don't want to get ahead of myself.

Willow nods in agreement, her cheeks flushed, and her lips red. She grabs the bottom of her shirt and lifts it up and over her head. I'm stopped cold.

She's wearing a charcoal gray bra with lace on the top of the cups.

"Fuck. Are you kidding me?"

"No, I'm not kidding you." She leans back on the island, putting weight in her arms. She pretends to look around the room as I get a good look. My eyes take her in, like I want to memorize every inch of her skin.

I kiss the soft spot between her neck and her collarbone. She tilts her head to the side giving me more access. My dick is hard and there's no way to hide it. I'm wearing joggers and I press into her. The whole island set-up is really working for me.

"Tripp," she rasps and makes this little noise as I grind into her. My mouth finds the tops of her breasts. My hands go to her back, feeling her shoulder blades. I run my knuckles down her spine and she shivers at the light touch.

She takes her hands on each side of my face, locking her eyes onto mine, and then pulls me in for a long, sweet kiss. Her arms reach up and around my neck and she rests her head in the crook of my neck.

Sensing the shift, I hug her back.

"Okay, definitely wasn't imagining this," she says, quietly, her mouth right by my ear.

"Huh?"

I jokingly glance down at my strained joggers. She laughs and it's the most beautiful sound I've ever heard.

# Chapter 23
## Willow

My heart races, echoing in my chest, as I reach for Tripp's shirt and pull him into me. Closer. I need him closer. His stubble is rough on my chin and I kind of love it.

The canceled plans and the whole Bailey situation are in the back of my mind. I have no reason not to trust him, but it feels like I'm blindfolded while trying to walk a straight line.

Is this worth it? Putting myself out there for him? Tripp makes this sound while kissing me that snaps me back to the present. I feel guilty for letting my mind wander.

I think I owe it to myself to give him a chance. Give us a chance. Hell, if it doesn't work, put that in the pile of failed relationships. There's a corner of my chest that pricks and tingles. Doesn't feel quite right. It's the voice that whispers, *Get out while you can*, before asking, *Why would Tripp stay when everyone else has left?*

How many times can I put myself back together?

Thinking these things while wrapped up in Tripp feels wrong.

"Want to take the snacks out to the pool?" I ask, pulling away from him long enough to get the words out. I need to quit spiraling.

Tripp picks me up from the island, spinning me around, before he sets me down with a kiss on my forehead. It's like two of the cutest gestures I've ever dreamt of in the same three-second blur.

Instantly, I feel better. The pinch in my chest is almost gone. I grab my shirt, reluctantly putting it back on.

We walk out to the pool, which is one of my favorite parts of the house. Well, the whole patio. This was one of the first home renovation projects we dreamt up, my parents and I. I've always loved the water—pools, hot tubs, the ocean, you name it.

"Wow. It's beautiful out here," Tripp says, spinning around, taking in the details.

"Thanks. We re-did this whole backyard patio area when we bought it."

"Who is we?"

"I bought it, but I had no idea what I was doing. My parents helped."

I can still feel the excitement of planning this whole space. I was so conscious about spending money because I truly hadn't grasped what was happening with my career.

"I bought it the month I turned eighteen. I had signed my first record deal. Claire, my manager, had always encouraged me to find a place kind of conspicuous, and to do it early on. She gave me all these tricks for keeping it a secret and it's worked, so far."

"That's amazing. What was out here before you redid it?"

"Nothing. We planned everything... the pool, hot tub, sitting area, hammock, bar, fireplace, all of it."

This is something I'm proud of. With Tripp, I don't feel the need to play it down.

"How fun was it? Dreaming this up and bringing it to life." We sit down in the loveseat, near the fireplace, and set the snacks on the table in front of us.

"At first, not so much. I was ridiculously stressed about spending too much money. My parents finally convinced me to relax. I had no idea how much money I had since my mom and dad did all of the right things and kept it in several accounts until I was eighteen. We didn't have much growing up, and I wanted to scrounge and save every penny I made."

I know I'm lucky. There are tons of tales of musicians, under eighteen, who didn't have cautious parents like mine.

"What was the first thing you bought? When you got your first check, or whatever the NFL gives you?" I ask because I have no clue how athletes and their salary work.

"Technically? A bouquet of lilacs. I walked to my favorite flower shop in town and then went to the bank to pay off my mom's mortgage."

"You had a favorite flower shop?" My heart is on the floor. In a puddle.

"Yes." His cheeks flush just enough to know this means something to him. "I went back home to tell my mom the house was completely paid off, and she needed to pick out a new place since I got drafted."

"And you just moved again, right?"

"I did. I decided to get a penthouse in the city. Didn't want to do a house. Not yet. My mom has a place five blocks from me."

"It's nice that you're close."

"It's always been the two of us."

Talking to Tripp is like wrapping yourself up in your favorite blanket—comfortable and warm. Obviously, the physical chemistry is there. I keep thinking about what it would be like to straddle him on this loveseat. Hold my body over top of his, creating friction where I need it.

This might be too easy considering I look at the clock and it's almost midnight. Tripp and I are still on the loveseat, long gone are the snacks. He sits with my feet in his lap, and we each have a blanket. It's still a relatively warm night for August; the blankets are just right.

"I had no idea it was so late," I say, looking at the time on my phone.

"What? How did that happen?" He looks flabbergasted as he runs a hand through his dark hair and grabs his phone out of his jogger pocket.

"Early morning tomorrow?"

"Yes, like five in the morning early. I've gotta get going."

We reluctantly pull ourselves from the cozy loveseat, collect our snack remnants, and head inside. Once everything is put away, we walk to the door.

"Tonight was—"

"Please don't say nice," Tripp sighs for dramatic effect.

"Fun. I was going to say fun." I laugh and lightly nudge his shoulder. "Thank you for coming over. For being honest."

He responds by wrapping his arms around my waist, lightly touching my lower back. Tripp doesn't need to pull me in because I'm meeting him halfway with a kiss.

It feels like this is brand new and also like we've been doing it forever. He quickly learns what it takes for me to make the little noises he seems so eager for. I search for the ways to make him want to press into me further.

He bites my lip and then slowly pulls away. "Good, because I'm not that nice," he says before kissing my forehead one last time and reaching for the door handle.

"Text me when you get home, please."

"You got it, Lo. Goodnight."

I watch Tripp leave through the window.

I can't help but smile to myself. How can things change so much in a few short hours? Hours that flew like minutes, nonetheless? The doubt comes in waves, but I fight back with the feeling of his lips on mine.

I can't explain it, but I have a feeling things are going to get very interesting.

# Chapter 24
## Willow

> still coming over?

yes a thousand times yes

can't wait to see you :)

I WATCHED THIS PRESEASON game like a hawk, clued in for every single play. Tripp Owens in joggers is something special but seeing him in a football uniform is *something else.*

He only played the first half. The team went comfortably up a few scores with their starters and then held onto the win with backups and third stringers. Pre-season is all about solidifying roster spots, according to Tripp.

Watching football isn't new for me. My family always had it on during the weekends when I was a kid. It's harder to keep up with when I go on tour and am on my own type of schedule. Now I have a completely different reason to tune in.

Everything between us is still light and exciting. I love the feeling of something fresh and new. I can't get enough of this man—It's like I crave Tripp's stories and details.

I haven't seen him since last week when he came over after practice, but we've FaceTimed every night. Doing the thing where you talk about nothing and everything for far too long.

Good thing because I haven't heard anything from Erik or the label. Claire told me not to stress about it but I am; the lack of response has me second guessing myself. Am I talented enough to pull something off intimate and small? Who am I without the lights, costumes, and effects?

I like that Tripp is busy with his own thing because it gives me time to work. I've finished a few more songs this week and am playing with some new melodies on my piano. All my homes have a small recording studio just in case I get a wave of inspiration and need to get a rough cut of something recorded.

I catch myself smiling when I think about Tripp, the kiss I'll greet him with. I decide to write and play the piano until he gets here.

THREE MISSED CALLS, A notification flashes on my phone. I look at the time and it's clear I've completely zoned out.

Tripp.

I call him back and run up the stairs to the main floor. He answers after the first ring.

"I am so sorry! Did you go back to your—" I open the door to see Tripp sitting on my front steps. When I expect to see a frustrated or annoyed version of him, I'm surprised when he's nothing but smiles and greets me with a hug.

"I don't know what happened. I was writing and on the piano and I can't believe I just left you out here."

Before I can keep going, Tripp kisses me.

"Lo, Breathe. It's okay. You were in the zone." He claps his hands and rubs them together.

"You're not mad?"

"No way," he says while grabbing a bag from the steps.

This is not how I thought this would go. If this was Dexter, he'd be scolding me on how disrespectful it is to waste someone's time. Instead, Tripp walks inside like he's been here a thousand times.

He puts the bag on the kitchen island, pulling out cookies and a pint of something.

"What's all that?"

"These are my favorite cookies, oatmeal scotchies, and before you make fun of me, I don't care. And this *was* a pint of ice-cream. A poor choice for the long drive and then the delayed entry." His voice is light and carefree.

"I'm sorry."

"Tell you what... if you want to make it up to me, you can show me your studio."

I reach for his hand to lead him down to the basement. His hand in mine immediately makes me want his hands everywhere.

"This is so cool," Tripp says as he looks around. He sits down at the piano and starts playing "Mary Had a Little Lamb". I sit down next to him, our legs touching.

"Very nice," I say as he wraps up the song.

"Play me something," he says. "Please."

"Ugh, I don't know," I chew on the inside of my cheek, embarrassed that he even asked. "I don't usually play live for people I know." His mouth drops.

"Global superstar Willow doesn't like to play for people she knows?"

"No, not really. I usually bring in recorded cuts to my label. I don't think I've ever played in front of them in a small setting." I tuck the same strand of hair behind my ear.

"Even the greats get nervous. Means you got something to lose." He squeezes my knee.

"That's sweet. Who said that?"

"My mom. I used to get so nervous before college games that I'd throw up. Just the ones where I was going to start." He laughs and puts his hands through his dark hair.

"Do you still do that? Throw up before games?"

"No. I saw a sports psychologist, and that's one of the first things we worked on."

The sports psychologist doesn't surprise me. If there's one thing I've learned, early on, is Tripp does anything and everything to take care of himself.

He takes his finger and taps a few of the keys.

"What's your favorite song?" I ask him.

He jokingly covers his eyes. "Don't make me pick."

"Just pick a favorite. I'll *probably* play it. You can sing." I lean into his side with a playful nudge, trying to mask my internal alarms screaming "don't do it".

Tripp breathes in slow and deep, completely exhaling before he says, "Let's do... City Lights Say."

A smile creeps over my face since he picked one of my favorites. I place my fingers over the keys and start to play. Even though it's one I recorded with the full band, I love this song on piano—it feels right. This is the type of feeling I'm after for my next album.

Right before the lyrics are supposed to come in, I sneak a look at Tripp. His eyes are closed and he's nodding along to the beat. I don't have to tell him to come in because he starts singing at the exact right time.

Hearing someone else sing my music is always an experience, but this 6'2" NFL player takes the cake. His voice isn't half-bad, and he knows all the words.

<br>

*They were out for blood*
*And all I had was grace*
*The city lights tell tales and lies*
*Just like you, the skyline was all about the chase*

Tripp dramatically finishes the chorus with some freestyle singing, and it has me in a fit of laughter, missing some keys at the end of the song. I clap for him as he stands to bow.

"Wow! You knew where to come in and everything."

"Well, that's because it's on my warmup playlist. I listen to it almost every day. I've also sang it at a team karaoke night."

I can't explain it, but it's like he's giving me the greatest compliment. Does it get better than hearing your song is on someone's playlist? The thought of him singing my songs, in public, in I'm sure true Tripp fashion, brings me joy.

"You are something else," I say as I stand up and wrap him in a hug. "Did you know this song is the reason it was The Skyline Tour?"

He gasps, "I knew it! Or I had my theories!" He puts his hands on my shoulders and lightly presses, so I can see his face.

Tripp in my studio, eyes wide and vibrant, voice enthusiastic and excited, is a memory I'll keep a mental bookmark on for a long time.

# Chapter 25
## Tripp

I sink into the hotel bed and stare at the ceiling. Tomorrow is our season opener. Typically, I'd be wired, packed full of energy, itching to play the game I know and love.

Instead, I'm thinking about how quiet this room is. How it's too put together. The white comforter tucked into the king bed, doesn't have a wrinkle on it. It screams "wash your hands" before getting too close. Empty bedside tables and a generic photo of a beach make me hurt for something familiar. It's too sterile, like a hospital room but with a bigger bed.

Truth is, being on a new team is fucking tough. There are so many things with established fans and organizations you don't realize you appreciate until it's gone. The buzz I'm used to feels a million miles away, on a roster I don't belong to anymore.

My heart hurts over my old team. It squeezes and pinches in my chest, all the while soaking in this quiet, too staged hotel room. I thought I had come to terms with the trade and what the rest of my career was going to look like. Guess not.

I reach my arms out. The California king bed, large enough to fit my entire body, feels like it could swallow me whole.

*I wish Willow was here.*

The thought is quick as sweat beads on my forehead. My heart feels like it stops and starts, erratically, with no rhyme or reason. Like it forgot how to beat. Why is the air so heavy? It's like my lungs can barely expand.

My mouth is dry. Pins and needles creep from my shoulders down my whole body, right to my fingertips. I flex and stretch my hand, trying to ease the prickling.

The room tilts just enough for the familiar feeling to hit me like the cornerbacks are going to tomorrow.

Oh no. Not fucking now.

I'm about to have a panic attack. It's been years but the feeling brings me back like it was yesterday. Just like riding a bike, I put my legs off the edge of the bed and put my head between my knees. I breathe in for five, hold for as long as I can, and breathe out for five. I visualize waves, rolling in, rolling out, with the pace of my breathing.

In.

Hold.

Out.

Eventually, the pin sensation leaves my hands. I don't know how long I do the breathing exercise for, but I feel better. Not great but better.

It's after 9 PM on the west coast, meaning it's past midnight back home.

I need a distraction. Otherwise, I'm going to be like this all night.

The phone rings. And rings. Until Willow answers.

"Hello?" she answers, her voice dripping with sleep.

"Fuck. I'm sorry. You were sleeping." I rub my hand over my face.

"It's okay. Is everything okay?"

I don't know what to tell her. This thing between us is so new. Does she really want to hear about this? Panic attacks? Over something as ridiculous as a bed that's too big.

"Tripp. What's wrong?" She says it in a way that makes me want to tell her everything.

"I have panic attacks. I just need to talk. Or listen to someone talk. I can't explain it but this fucking hotel room. It's empty and—"

"Tripp. Take a breath. You're okay," Willow interrupts my barely coherent rant. "I'm here."

And I do. I take deep breaths.

"Is this something that happens often?" she lightly presses.

"It used to." I stare at the floor. "I've done therapy on and off when it becomes an issue. But it's been a while."

"Are you nervous for tomorrow?"

"No. Not really. I feel like this game is one thing that I'm good at. I'm a key part of the team and they need me."

"Well, you're good at other things. Like singing," she jokes, and it brings me back to her piano. The lightness I felt when she played music and I sang along. "Do you want to talk about it?"

I sigh like a dramatic teenager.

"People don't play football forever. I've been thinking about what happens after this. And when I saw this stupid fucking bed it just made me feel like... I'm all by myself. I know it sounds ridiculous and it doesn't make sense but it's all I got."

"It doesn't sound ridiculous. You don't want to be alone."

"No, I don't," I say, my voice quiet.

Alone. My mind races. Did I go about this the wrong way? I've done nothing but pour myself into a game, a thing that is temporary. It's always been this way, but I've acted like it's forever. Me. My mom. Football.

The list is small.

"You're not alone. I'm here. I wish I was there with you."

"This doesn't scare you? Me, calling you in the middle of the night because I'm spiraling? You probably thought I had a better grasp on all of this."

Willow laughs. Actually laughs.

"What? Why are you laughing?" Insecurity runs through my blood.

"I shouldn't laugh but I like that you think everyone has it together besides you. No one knows what's going on. Tripp, hear me when I say this, this doesn't scare me. Not at all."

A wave of relief runs over me, and I can feel my shoulders moving away from my ears.

"Are you sure?" I'm a needy bastard right now.

"I'm sure. So sure. If you were perfect this would be so boring."

To my surprise, I laugh. Just for a second. But this is the distraction I need.

"Is there anything I can do to help right now?"

Two choices: I can tell her that I'm fine, when I'm not and wrap this call up. or I can tell her what I need.

I've been honest up until this point. Don't see the need to change it. "Can you tell me a story? Distract me."

"Sure can. How about the time I was a concert opener and the head-liner got too drunk? Do you know this one?"

"No. Tell me everything."

I can hear her situating herself, probably sitting up in bed. I try to get comfortable while she launches into a story.

I fall asleep listening to Willow. And thinking about how the Willow I'm getting to know is better than I could've imagined.

○○○

THE UPSTATE COSMOS ARE undefeated. We stole a win on the road with a go-ahead field goal. Our kicker was fucking losing his mind. He had missed two easy kicks—wide right—throughout the game, and I can't imagine what it's like to walk up and kick like that. Everyone holding their breath, praying one way or another.

But he drilled it. A goddamn 50-yard field goal, like it was cake. Celebrating with the team was pivotal. Felt like we were creating something, not because we're all in the same place doing our job but deeper than that.

I had a solid game: 90 yards, 12 receptions, 1 touchdown. When I scored, I felt this weight lift. It was like I could relax. I'm still fucking good enough to be on a roster.

Talking to Willow was just what I needed last night. I can't believe I woke her up and she did nothing but try to help. She showed up for me.

I can't wait to see her.

I open the door to my apartment and see a bouquet of flowers on my kitchen island. Did I accidentally send myself flowers?

They are yellow and white peonies with tons of greenery. The card sticks out the top and I open the tiny envelope.

*Tripp – I don't know your favorite flower, so I sent you mine.*
*Congrats on the win.*
*Willow*

# **Chapter 26**
## Willow

I FINALLY HEARD FROM the label. They're open to *discussing* the idea of a more intimate tour. Erik sounded lukewarm at best. We're meeting with them today, and I'm bringing a rough cut of a few songs I've been working on.

Lukewarm is better than cold but stress sits under the small victory. The more I think about it, the more I agree with Claire; I've put in the time and should be able to make calls like this. I never wanted to put out the same type of music over and over again.

Don't get me wrong, I'm thankful for what I've accomplished, the opportunities I've had, and every single fan who knows any words to any of my music. I want to do something new.

Emilie, Claire, and I are in my car when my phone buzzes.

Tripp

pumped for your meeting?

Me

I wouldn't say pumped but I am excited to get it over with lol

if they don't let you do whatever you want, they're idiots

ha! You and Claire have the same thought

Don't even worry about them saying no

They'll hear the new stuff and be on board

you have no idea if the new stuff is any good

you haven't heard it

No, but I know you.

no pressure but the fan in me is dying to hear the new stuff

just throwing that out there

score two touchdowns on Sunday and you can hear it

you've got a deal

see you tonight

I've always kept new music close to me until the last minute. It drives my label crazy but it's how I operate. The only time I play it early is for Claire, or my parents, when I'm stuck or if I need an honest reaction. I may have been doing this for over ten years, but the imposter syndrome is there just like the first album I put out. The little voice nagging, putting the doubt and second-guessing in your brain.

"Wonder who *that* could be," Emilie says, her eyebrows raised, looking at my phone.

I shoot her a look.

"I still think it's crazy I saw his apartment before you did," she says.

The flowers. We're still trying to keep this between us which meant I had to be careful with getting something sent to his apartment. Between Seth taking care of the security logistics and Emilie dropping them off, I was successful.

You know what I like about Tripp? He calls. When he wants to talk about something, he picks the phone up and calls. He's available and I didn't know that was something I needed until now. My bar might be too low.

Instead of looking at everything as an obstacle, he finds a way to do what he wants. I still can't believe he has his assistant leave in the car, that everyone knows Tripp drives, when he comes to my home. All in the name of keeping my secret.

He was adorable when he came home to the flowers I sent. For someone who loves sending them, I'm not sure he's received many. I was afraid he'd think it was stupid or not something "women should do for men". Instead, he was thankful and excited. Now, he's trying to figure out what his favorite flower is.

Lining up our schedules has been difficult. His day off is on Tuesday but Tripp doesn't believe in a day off, considering he always has something scheduled.

Tonight, he's coming to my place. I'm going to make dinner and he's in charge of dessert.

The thought of seeing Tripp tonight is what's getting me through this meeting that I'm absolutely dreading.

Peppermint tea is waiting for me when I come in. I have a single copy of a burned CD, like it's 2005, of a few rough songs. I'm paranoid about emailing any files and even though it's not final music, I'd always rather be safe than sorry.

"Let's get this show on the road," Erik says, his voice lined with agitation, matching the arms folded across his chest.

I can tell he's in a mood. *Great.* I hand him the CD, which they knew I'd bring, and they play it.

There are only three songs, and they still need work. Everyone listens while I feel like I could crawl out of my skin. My hands are folded on the table, and I'm staring at them, hating every second.

Once the final song wraps, Erik says nothing, leans back in his chair, and sucks in a long, drawn-out breath.

"This is—"

"Great. Even for an early stage," Claire interrupts. She knows this bothers Erik to no end, but she doesn't care.

"You don't even know what I was going to say," he responds. This isn't new. Claire and Erik bicker like siblings. When she really wants to get under his skin, she calls him "Ricky" and I will never forget the color his face turned the first time she said it.

"You didn't need to say anything. With your sighing and furrowed eyebrows while you were listening. I know what you're thinking. You're concerned about revenue."

She called it perfectly. I love her for that.

"It's a different approach. We know what works, I'm not sure the need to divert so far from that."

"Because she wants to. That should be enough. For you. For all of you." She points around the table like a disappointed mom.

"Claire, I've got this," I say as Claire sits back in her chair. "I've been with this label for nine years. You signed me to my current deal when I was twenty-one, and I've put out the same type of music. I'm at a different stage of life. I want different things. And if we're being honest, I don't have it in me to write the album you want me to. Even if I did, there's no way I'd tour that album."

"Do you need more time?" Erik asks.

"You're not hearing me. I can't do it." I hit every letter of the words, pleading for him to listen. Tears flood my eyes, but I barter with any god who will listen to not let them spill.

No one breathes. No one moves. Claire's eyes are saucers out of my peripheral vision. I feel like my skin could fall off. I hate going against the grain, asking for things outside of what's considered the norm, but this is necessary. I called my lawyer this morning. I wanted a refresher on the contract and what is outstanding.

"Our current contract ends in eleven months. I've put out the music required. I can wait to put this out." I've done everything I've agreed to.

"Is that true?" Erik turns to someone, who I suspect knows the contract details down to the nitty gritty.

He slowly nods. "Willow is right. She's satisfied the album and tour quota, plus some. She technically doesn't need to do anything else while under contract."

The room stills.

I look over at Emilie, and she is holding back a laugh, which makes me feel better.

"Fine. Let's explore this route and see what other markets we can unlock," Erik says, which is code for "you win but I'm going to pretend like this is an opportunity I thought of".

"Good idea, Erik," Claire croons sarcastically.

"Thank you for giving this a chance. I'll check in once I'm halfway through the tracks so we can get the details nailed down."

"Works for us. Happy writing," Erik says as he gets up, checking his phone. He's done here.

# Chapter 27
## Tripp

THE STOPPED TRAFFIC IS taunting me. As I sit in my unmoving car, my fingers tapping impatiently on the steering wheel, I think about the wasted time. It's the middle of the week, nowhere near the weekend, yet the roads are jam-packed. The minutes tick by, just like the stop-and-go traffic.

I hate that I'm missing a bonus hyperbaric chamber session but know that spending time with Lo is a different type of "worth it."

I'm exhausted. I stayed late at the training facility yesterday and my muscles are paying for it today. I mentally put TRX bands on the no-list for bonus workouts. It's been a while since I've been this sore.

I'm talking to my mom, one of my favorite ways to pass the time on a drive.

"Where did you end up, Tripp?" She knows something is up as I pull into Willow's driveway.

"What do you mean?" I try to bluff.

"You know what I mean. I just heard you whisper some hush-hush words to what sounded like a security gate."

The guilt creeps up my neck, giving me goosebumps. I hate keeping things from my mom.

"I'm at Willow's. We've been sort of—"

"Seeing each other? I know. I wanted you to tell me."

"How did you know?" My brain runs through how I could've let this slip.

"You left your bonus phone on the end table while you were making one of those disgusting green juices the other day. Saw her name pop up." Her smile is clear as glass over the phone. I'm amazed she waited this long to ask me. That was days ago. "She seems lovely."

"She is. It's been a little over a month." There's a rock in my stomach. More guilt. "Listen, Mom, I'm sorry—"

"Don't you dare apologize, Tripp James." Is there anything more severe than a mom using your middle name? "You're allowed to live and have your own secrets. Now, get off the phone. I love you." She hangs up before I even have time to register the conversation.

My phone screen goes dark in my lap. I smile, feeling lighter now that my mom knows.

I approach Willow's door, each step slow and sore. A smile tugs at the corners of my lips, eager to reveal itself. In my hands, I carry a small box containing tiramisu from our favorite restaurant, a sweet reminder of our first date. Willow had insisted I walk in when I arrived, so that's what I do.

With a gentle push, the door swings open, revealing the warmth of her home, her space. The vaulted ceilings and open floor plan could feel empty, or lacking, but not with Willow. Music plays louder than you'd expect, and when I see Willow dancing in the kitchen, the frustration from the terrible traffic and the guilt of keeping this secret from my mom is gone. My mood flips and it's like I'm a little lighter just by being in her presence—how does she do that?

I close my eyes, breathe in, and whatever she's cooking makes my mouth water. A smile stretches my lips as I let the door close.

She hears the door shut, stops dancing, and snaps her eyes to me. Willow's hair is up in a bun, messy, pieces of hair framing her face.

"Just in time. The stir fry is almost done," she says while turning the stove off and wiping her fingers on a towel that's thrown over her shoulder.

I walk up to her and can't help but kiss her. I wrap my arms around her lower back and pick her up a little bit, which makes her giggle, as she's kissing me back.

"Do it again," I say, my nose still touching hers.

"Do what again?"

"Make that sound," I practically plead and put my lips back on hers, a touch more forceful than before. I feel her lips smile into mine as she quietly laughs in response.

"I'm so glad you're here," Willow says, her arms wrapped around my neck.

Reluctantly, I set her down.

"Let's eat." She reaches for my hand and leads me to the kitchen table.

I do my best to keep my mind out of the gutter, but her ass sways in front of me as she leads me to the kitchen table.

AFTER TWO PLATES OF stir fry, with fresh vegetables and a ginger sesame sauce, I'm full and completely content.

"Thank you for cooking," I say, scooping the last bit of sauce and some rogue rice on my fork.

"No problem. This is one of my go-tos. I eat it probably once a week."

I stand up to take my plate to the sink and my muscles ache.

"What's wrong?" Willow asks as she watches me walk.

"It's nothing. Sore from a workout. A workout I will not be doing again for a very long time," I joke.

"You know what's good for sore muscles?" Willow asks, her lips pulled up on one side in a mischievous grin. "Hot tub." She tilts her head to the patio door.

"That sounds amazing, but I don't have a suit."

"You can wear those shorts or whatever you have underneath them," she says nonchalantly. "If you think about it, swim shorts are just shorts,"

There's nothing I wouldn't do to get in a hot tub with Willow right now.

"Let's do it."

Willow points me to a bathroom to get a towel and change. Essentially, strip.

I take everything off, besides my briefs. I fold and set my clothes on the counter and look at myself in the mirror. I'm surprised by my own reflection: lips pressed together, eyes wider than field goal posts, and my shoulders damn near my jaw.

*Fuck, I'm nervous.*

I turn on the water and take a deep breath. I hold onto it for a few seconds before loudly sighing it out. My hands cup together, holding cool water in between my fingers and palms. I splash water on my face, a few times, before wiping the water away; my cheeks are hot to the touch.

I open the door to the hallway and listen for Willow. Nothing. I peek out far enough to see her out on the patio.

I close the bathroom door and roll my shoulders up, down, and back.

"Tripp, you nervous bastard, you can do this," my voice cracks as I fixate on where the tile floor meets the rug I'm standing on. I sound pathetic. I do another shoulder roll and tip my chin up and look at myself in the mirror, pointing at my reflection, "This was her idea. If she didn't want you here, she wouldn't invite you in the hot tub wearing only your fucking underwear."

My hands go into my hair, gripping it, taking another deep breath and sighing it out.

"You can do this," I say to myself one last time as I wrap the towel around me.

I walk out to the patio with a towel wrapped around my waist, only my black briefs on underneath. My heart thuds in my chest, getting faster with each step I take toward Willow.

She's already in the hot tub, a black bikini top enveloping her breasts, and I'm trying not to stare. We catch each other's eyes, both wide, just for a second. Cups of iced tea are on the ledge, in plastic cups, of course.

After losing the towel and catching Willow smirk at me from my peripheral vision, I step into the water. The water immediately feels like heaven on my sore muscles. I slowly sink into a spot across from Willow, the only thing out of the water is my head.

"Ughhhhhh. This was a great idea," I say as I lean back and let the jets hit my muscles.

"Told you," Willow says, taking a drink of her iced tea, and then slipping into the water just a little further.

Our feet and legs touch as we both kind of spread out. We sit in silence for a few minutes with nothing but the sound of the water whooshing around us.

"How are you feeling?" Willow asks and I know it's not about my muscles.

"Pretty good. It usually takes a few days to bounce back from a panic attack, but this wasn't as bad." I know exactly why too. The way she was there for me, talking to me until I fell asleep. I don't know if she'll ever realize what that meant.

"That's good."

"I've been seeing a therapist, so we'll talk about it at my next appointment."

"I'm proud of you," Willow says, and it catches me off guard.

"For what?" I scoff.

"For taking care of yourself. For talking about it. For calling me and not just suffering. A lot of people don't do any of those things."

I look down at my hands floating on the surface of the water. I know she's right. I'm still bothered that this is something I must work through. I thought I'd already done this but that's the thing about mental health, it's never ending.

"Need another distraction?" she says, interrupting my internal pity party. Before I can say anything, she's making her way over to me. I don't know if I'd consider myself lucky, but I don't know how else I ended up in a hot tub with Willow—my fucking dream girl.

"I always want your distractions," I say, my voice low.

Willow takes her hands and puts them on my chest before reaching up around my neck. Her nose is almost touching mine, her eyes the color of dark honey, and she grins at me before pressing into a kiss. There is nothing else in the world besides her and this water.

"This is the best distraction," I say in between kisses. Her lips are soft and full.

When she puts her hands on my shoulders, making the space to pull her legs up and straddle me, I'm aware of how hard I am. Fuck. She sinks in further, deeper, feeling my dick through the fabric, and she groans.

I am a fucking goner.

# Chapter 28
## Willow

MY BODY HAS TRICKED my brain. At first, I wanted nothing more than to wrap Tripp up and sweetly sit together in this hot tub. But then he came out here in that towel, all his muscles on display. This might be the first time a man's chest had me in a puddle.

When I say I wasn't prepared to see him in his briefs, I mean it. My mouth like sandpaper had me reaching for my iced tea like I was parched.

I also wasn't prepared for the way he looked at me.

Now, I'm straddling this man. This professional athlete. His hands, strong and massive, rest on my hips.

I can feel his dick through his briefs, and it hits me in just the right spot. I can't help but moan into his mouth before throwing my head back.

He uses that opportunity to pull me closer to him and put his mouth on my neck. We're flush as he nips from the soft spot behind my ear before kissing a path all the way down to my collarbone.

"Fuck. You're so gorgeous," he says, making eye contact, his blue eyes piercing, before peppering my breasts with kisses. His lips, red from kissing, are the perfect contrast to my skin. He holds me close to him with one arm and then uses the other to lightly graze the skin right above my bikini top.

Tripp touching me like this, has me feeling like I can do anything. He makes me feel confident. Without a second thought, I untie the top around my neck and let it fall. I know what I want and I'm going to ask for it. Or try to at least.

The water hits right below my now bare breasts. Tripp leans his head back, brows raised, and mouth pressed together, as he takes me in.

"Perfect. You're perfect. I feel like I'm fucking dreaming." His words fall on top of each other before he puts his mouth to one of my nipples, sucking and lightly using his teeth, before rolling the other in his hands.

"That—" I gasp as he bites, "feels so good." My voice is ragged as I take in his reaction, and I open my chest up to him. Giving him the green light to keep going.

It's instinct, but I move my hips enough to feel his length hitting my clit.

"Such a good girl. Going for what she wants," Tripp says going from my nipples to my mouth. It's like he knew exactly what I needed to hear.

He kisses me hard, bites at my bottom lip, while I keep moving my hips, creating friction anyway I can.

Tripp takes the hand from my breast and slowly moves down my stomach. He stops right at the place where my bottoms start. His finger plays with the fabric.

"Is this okay?" he asks.

"Yes," I say, practically breathless.

Tripp teases me by pinching the fabric. My chest quickly rises and falls, waiting for him to continue. He reaches down into my bottoms but it's too slow. He touches me, but not where I want to be touched. He's just outside and I know he's doing it on purpose.

I tip my head to the side, arch my back, trying to get the right touch.

"Tell me what you want, Lo." Tripp's voice teases just like his fingers.

"You know what I want," I say as I lean into him, kissing his jaw before finding his lips. His beard is rough on my face and I can't get enough.

"Need you to ask, baby." This man just called me baby while having his finger so close to my clit I can taste the orgasm. It flips a switch. He puts his mouth on one of my nipples, pink and peaked with desire.

"Tripp. Put your fingers on my clit." I don't ask or say please. I'm commanding and it feels right.

"Fuck, that's so hot," Tripp says and then touches my bundle of nerves. "Always tell me what you want." He bites at one of my nipples and I'm already so close. The burn in my center gets closer to the edge.

"Good boy, Tripp." The words fly out of my mouth before my brain has a chance to register.

"Fuck, Lo." And this man goes wild. His fingers. His mouth. His groans. It's exactly what I need. He's everywhere.

I reach the top of the hill and then roll all the way down. I shudder and pulse against Tripp with my orgasm and he doesn't take his fingers away. He's there, all the way until the end. When the shocks are gone, I'm practically draped over him, my breasts touching his chest, my breath ragged, chest heaving.

I pull my face away and catch his eyes.

"I could watch you come undone forever," he says, before pressing a kiss to my mouth.

In this moment, I'm not insecure about Tripp seeing me or feeling my soft spots. There was no second-guessing him with his hands and mouth on me. I want all of it. It's like he knows exactly what I need.

I smile at him and put my hand down on his dick.

"I think you should sit up on the ledge," I say, my voice syrupy sweet.

He lets me slink back off his lap and takes my suggestion. Seeing him like this makes my low belly ache. He's wet, wearing black briefs, with his length aggressively pushing against them. His cheeks are flushed and lips red. His chest rises and falls as he looks from me, down to his erection, and back to me again.

I put my hands on his thighs and the muscles are such a turn-on. I love how strong he is.

"You don't have to," he says.

"I know I don't. But I want to," I say as I reach for the waistband. I pull them down far enough for his cock to spring out. Pink from the warm water and thicker than anything I've seen, in person at least, has a whimper escaping my mouth.

I kneel on the bench and am at the right level to take him in my mouth— as much of it as I can, at least. I lick my lips before looking up at him.

"Lo, you're killing me," Tripp says, putting his arms behind him, leaning his weight back.

First, I take my hand and slowly stroke from tip to base. My touch is light and excruciatingly slow. Tripp groans, and it spurs me on.

I tease with my fingers, changing the pressure, but never letting go. His breath is ragged and deep.

His cock is heavy in my hand and I pause with it right in front of my lips. I slowly blink and look up at him. We make eye contact, and it makes me feel like a queen.

"Keep looking at me like that and this is going to be embarrassingly short." He laughs in a tortured way.

Making him feel like this, with a look, and my hands, is empowering. I love feeling like I'm in control. I put a too-soft kiss on the tip while using my fingers to tease his base. He shudders when my lips first touch. I could live off those shudders.

When I take him in my mouth, as much as I can, the sound of his breath makes that once sated ache throb again. Hearing him like this is such a turn on.

I swirl my tongue on the head before licking down to my hands and kissing my way back before taking him all in my mouth again.

Tilting my chin up, so I can steal a look at Tripp, my mouth and hands team up.

"Are you kidding? Fuck, this is so good," he says when I look at him. He reaches for my head to take a bit more control. I love that he changes the pace to his liking. He's not too rough.

We work together and I know he's close. I can feel his muscles start to clench.

"I'm—ugh—fuck—I'm." The man can't get words out. "I'm going to come." I want him to finish in my mouth, so I keep going.

I moan around his cock and that's all it takes to get him over the edge.

He shakes, his hand still on the back of my head. I look up at him and take in this moment. The way he leans into me makes me feel like a goddess.

Tripp reaches for me, under my arms, and lifts me up enough to plant a soft kiss on my mouth.

"Wow. What a distraction," Tripp says, taking a drink of his iced tea.

I reach up to tie my bikini and a gentle hand stops me.

"Woah. Don't rush that. I could go for a few minutes of soaking." He looks down at the water.

I let my top fall back down. The way he looks at me is startling. A good kind of startling but I know he could get me to do almost anything he wanted with that look.

He pulls up his briefs, gets back in the water, and then pulls me to him. I'm in between his legs, leaning back on his chest.

No words are said but none are needed. We soak each other in until the jets turn off.

"I wish we could stay like this forever," Tripp says, his voice tired and happy.

It's like he read my mind. I'm so relaxed.

"Wish you could stay." I say it knowing well he can't. I know what his practice schedule is like tomorrow and how early his day starts. It's not lost on me the time he loses making the drive to and from my place.

"We need a sleepover."

"That's the most adorable thing I've ever heard," I say with a grin that reaches my eyes.

"I can promise you, it wouldn't be *that* adorable," Tripp says while nipping at my ear lobe.

"You say when, MVP. My schedule is basically wide open for the next few weeks." Tripp has another away game this week.

"You got it," he whispers in my ear before resuming our position.

We stay for just a few more minutes, surrounded by the dark and whisper of the trees.

And I am completely wrapped up in Tripp.

# Chapter 29
## Tripp

THERE'S NOTHING LIKE YOUR first home game of the season. We've been preparing and having a fucking blast. The team is on fire.

Today was one of those practices where every pass felt a little more dialed in, each catch secured, and every route damn near perfect.

I need to be feeling it. Willow drives a mean bargain. We won our last game, but I did not score two touchdowns, leaving her new music unheard. She said, "Let me know when you get two."

That's the goal for this week.

Zack and I are walking back to the locker room after getting some treatment—most of the guys have left.

"Is your girl coming to the game?"

*My girl.* I love the way that sounds.

"Umm, we haven't really talked about it. As in, we haven't really talked about public outings yet."

"Wait a second. You forgot about bringing your mega-hot, superstar girlfriend to the first game in a brand-new stadium? It's going to be epic!" Zack's enthusiasm is contagious.

"It's not that I forgot about her. I don't want to pressure her."

"Maybe tomorrow is the time? Didn't you get a suite for the season? That seems low pressure. Well, in the sense that she won't be out with just standard fans."

The general manager of the Cosmos included a suite when I got traded. Didn't have the heart to tell him I didn't have a ton of friends and family to fill it with. This is the first time in my career I've had one. I've opened it up to a few of the guys so their girlfriends and parents can watch the game from there.

I do have extra tickets.

"I can see your wheels turning. Plus, your mom will be there. Isn't that a fun first meeting?"

He's way too excited about this but I do love where he's going. Willow and I haven't seen each other since our night in the hot tub. I had some PR events get added to my calendar this week and she's been in writing mode.

I'm itching to see her and not through a phone screen.

Going public means I can also have her at my place. I told her I'd keep driving out to her as much as I can, but it would be nice to stay in the city. I think that also opens up the possibility for her to stay over. And fuck do I want that.

"Okay, I'm going to do it."

"Don't forget to chat with security," Zack says while collecting his things and heading for the door.

Once I'm in my car, I call my assistant because I need a favor.

I'M FINISHING UP COOKING dinner when my phone rings. Willow.

"What's up, pretty girl?"

"Seth just brought me an *urgent* flower arrangement."

"Is that so?" Like I don't know he got them to her. Instead of just asking her over text, or on the phone, I thought of sending her flowers with a note and the tickets. Well, they're not real tickets. Our stadium is mobile-ticket entry only, but I wanted "real ones". Luckily, my assistant has a ton of connections and had someone photoshop some very realistic looking tickets for the gesture.

"I'd love to come to the game!" Her voice is enthusiastic and eager. It makes me do a fist pump in the safety of my own home, that no one can see. Thank God.

"You would?"

"Yes! I wouldn't miss watching you play in person!"

"This means being public." I take a deep breath. Why am I nervous? "It's your call and I don't want you to feel like you have to do anything—"

"Tripp. I want to. A resounding yes. Let's do it."

"You've made my night." My cheeks cramp from smiling.

"Seth is already making the calls and arrangements for Sunday."

"Perfect. Also, you'll be in a suite. My mom will be there, plus some other players' wives and family. Is it cool if I give them a heads up? I want everyone to be on their best behavior."

"I can't wait to meet your mom!" she practically screams into the phone. "And yes, you can tell whoever. It'll be easier if the press doesn't know until I'm there but if it gets out, there's nothing we can do."

"How do you feel about packing a bag? Staying at my place? The Cosmos General Manager booked out an entire restaurant for players and families to celebrate the first home game. Figured we could make an appearance and then you could stay over."

"You don't even have to ask. I'm there."

*I'm there.* My heart races. This feels significant, me and her being seen together, but there's no hesitation on her end, or at least what I'm hearing.

"You're amazing," I tell her.

"Thank you for inviting me. I'm really looking forward to it. But *especially* looking forward to our sleepover."

"Fuck. Me too."

And I don't think she knows how much.

# Chapter 30
## Willow

I WAKE UP BEFORE my alarm and hop out of bed. It's game day! I've been to NFL games before but never to watch a friend or someone I know. Here I am, about to see my Super Bowl champ-caliber guy do the thing he loves most.

When I fly around my room getting ready, excitement bubbles under my skin. I'm about to tell the entire world that I took Tripp up on his offer. Usually, this part of a relationship is stressful and feels like walking on eggshells, but Tripp makes this part fun. I have no idea what to expect but the sinking feeling in my belly is barely there.

I'd be lying if I wasn't scared to tell everyone I'm dating someone. I know it's going to get to Dexter. And if something goes wrong, it will be hashed out, over and over again.

Wouldn't be the first time.

Tripp has already shown me so much good that I refuse to miss out because of the possibility of it falling apart. Or, at least that's what I tell myself as I look at the outfit hanging in my closet, specifically for today's game.

For my outfit, I've got a top in Cosmos blue, a black leather skirt, and knee-high black boots. It's late September in the city which means perfect boot weather, no tights needed. Plus, I'm having a stellar body image day and I'm thankful.

Tripp gave me some extra tickets if I had anyone else to invite. When I asked Emilie to come, I thought she was going to pass out. Not only is she a music fiend, but she watches football every weekend. Watches *and* yells at the TV.

"Willow, are you ready?" Emilie yells impatiently from downstairs.

I take one last look at myself in the mirror. My dark hair is lightly curled away from my face, pink lips a perfect contrast to the team colors. I look good which means I feel even better. Isn't it satisfying when everything goes as planned—outfit *and* makeup? I grab my overnight bag and go downstairs.

"A bag? GIRL. YES. I say that coming from friend Emilie and not your assistant." Emilie literally claps before opening the door and we laugh as we walk to the car.

All I can think about is watching Tripp do the thing he loves most.

Seth pulls up to the specific entrance outside the stadium while he confirms something on the phone with stadium security. He's coming to the game but insists on staying outside the suite the entire time. I told him that was unnecessary, but he insisted that that's the only way he agreed to this with Tripp. The man takes his job very seriously.

Seth gets out of the car, opens my door, and I step out. I'm relieved to not see a single camera. It's just a few people, using the same entrance, and security.

Emilie and I walk into the stadium, hand in hand. She has this thing about holding hands and it makes me feel like we've known each other our whole lives. Good thing because suddenly, I'm nervous. My head feels like it's full of feathers and I'm a tad unsteady on my heels. She stops walking for a second, pretending to fix my hair, and squeezes my hand.

"You good?" She mouths, concern etched on her face.

I take a breath, and when I'm sure I'm not going to fall over, I nod yes. My free hand goes to my stomach, one of my most insecure places—I'm thankful for the oversized top. When I'm overwhelmed, my brain lets me hear the body image doubts a tiny bit louder.

We give our names, they check a list, and move us on through security. There are a few spots to walk through a metal detector. It's funny being someone people know because they use your name like you've been friends forever.

"Willow, right through here." One of the staff indicates where to walk through. I take off my jacket, jewelry, and follow Seth and Emilie. All good.

Seth leads the way with a stadium staff member and turns giving me a look that says *there are cameras ahead.* This isn't a surprise. We knew they'd be here and it's one-hundred-percent fine. I do know that once I make this walk, it'll only be minutes before people will know I'm here. The press will not wait; they'll post the photos as soon as they're able.

There's no turning back. And you know what? I don't want to.

Emilie squeezes my hand.

"Let's do this," I respond as the nerves make my voice quicker than intended.

I step into the suite and am met with wide eyes and nervous shuffling. I know they've been prepped that I'd be here but it's still weird for people. The best thing, I think, is to immediately start introducing myself.

Before I can do anything, someone comes up and wraps me in a sweet hug.

"Willow! I'm Wendy. Tripp's mom. It's so nice to meet you. He's told me so much about you. I mean, I knew some of it already, but, well, you know how it goes." She pulls away and the excited light in her eyes makes me emotional.

I go in for another hug.

"Wendy, it's so nice to meet you! It feels like I know you already." I lean back and we're holding forearms, in a half hug.

"Oh, don't make an old gal blush. When Tripp told me you were coming to the game, I just couldn't believe it. It's going to be such a good day."

This woman has won me over in a single interaction. There's not a moment of awkwardness or hesitation. She jumped all the way in, and I love her energy.

After I introduce Emilie to Wendy, I make my way around the suite. I shake hands with everyone, offer to sign anything they may have hidden in their bags, and try to show them I'm excited to see the game. It's my attempt to show them I'm not that different from them.

I order myself a craft beer from the bar and grab a plate of snacks. Wendy has spots saved for Emilie and me, right next to her, near the front of the suite.

Kick-off is in about twenty minutes. The energy grows with each minute that passes like it's something I could reach out and grab.

I finally let myself sneak a look at the field to find number seventeen, Tripp Owens. Wendy must know what I'm doing because she points him out to me.

He's warming up in a light blue top and charcoal gray shorts. Even among an NFL roster, Tripp stands out. I feel like I could pick his silhouette out of a lineup at this point. He's running routes, pushing the dark hair from his eyes, and catching passes from his quarterback.

This man. This is so hot.

I've never dated an athlete before, and I feel like I've been missing out. Or maybe Tripp is an anomaly.

"How do you like the new place? Tripp mentioned you recently moved." I turn my attention to Wendy, so she doesn't see me drooling.

"I like it. It's much busier than I'm used to, but I love being close to Tripp. I go to every game I can. Plus, there's a club for everything here. I joined a puzzle and knitting club in the same week!" she answers with a smile that reaches her eyes.

A knitting club? Adorable.

"There's always something going on. I've also always wanted to learn to knit," I say, taking a drink of my IPA.

"Oh, say less. I can teach you! It's easy. You'll be knitting scarves in no time," she hands me her phone to put my number in. Her offer isn't an empty one.

The Jumbotron shows the guys warming up and they zoom in on the Super Bowl MVP. He's laughing and tossing balls back forth from the sideline. When he starts hyping up teammates, giving them chest bumps and yelling, I find myself grinning and feeling that fluttery feeling throughout my whole body. I hope the Cosmos can pull off a win and extend their unexpected winning streak.

According to Tripp, and the research I did online, this matchup is even. The Cosmos are favored by 2.5, which means the gambling gods expect them to win by three. Many people aren't sure what to make of the Cosmos quite yet; there's no previous seasons to compare to. Seems like most new teams have a bit of trouble finding their groove but these guys seem to have something going for them.

The game is about to kick off, and the players are lined up on their respective sidelines. Tripp told me there's sometimes awkward pauses which are really media timeouts for the telecast.

Tripp lines up, his back to the suite. He's wearing his jersey, number seventeen proud on his back, the light blue contrasting his tan arms and dark hair. He sways back and forth, his hands behind his back. I watch him turn around, find the suite, and stop when he sees me. I can't make out his facial expression, but he waves. To me, to his mom, to the suite, it doesn't matter.

He's managed to push all my doubts to the side with a single gesture.

I'm in for this man.

In it.

And it feels good.

# **Chapter 31**
## Tripp

THE COSMOS ADD ANOTHER win to the column. We might have traded touchdowns throughout the entire game, but we had a special teams turnover that favored the Cosmos. There's nothing better than an electric special teams play.

The locker room is deafening. You'd think we just made the playoffs but it's just a bunch of guys pumped after a solid game—it feels fucking great. Not only did we win, but I had 156 yards, 13 receptions, and *two* touchdowns. This means I can cash in on Willow's bet. I can't wait to listen to her new music before anyone else.

During warmups, I knew she was there, but I was too nervous to even look at the suite. I only let myself a single glance when we were waiting for the anthem.

There she was. Wearing a Cosmos blue top, sitting in the front, right next to my mom. I couldn't look for long because it fucking filled my eyes with tears. Happy ones. But no one wants to be crying before an NFL game.

Plus, the second I found her, so did everyone else. There were multiple times she, Emilie, and my mom were shown on the Jumbotron. Cat's out of the bag. It's been roughly two months and I can't believe word hasn't gotten out before this.

I'm itching to get out of the locker-room. I turn my phone on and it's a barrage of text messages from friends, family, and old teammates. Almost all of them have something in common: Willow. Some just ask me how I've held out, but some include clips of her celebrating when I scored during today's game.

*Fuck me.* Is this for real? She's jumping up and down, hugging my mom, random friends and family from the team, like she's having the time of her life. Emilie is right with her, always screaming. They're so into it and I can't get enough.

"Huddle up, it's time to give away the team ball," Coach says, trying to get us all to pay attention.

"Hell of a game today. Our defense was flying around in the way we know it takes to win football games. Special teams, you pulled off some trick plays that I never would've allowed if I knew what was happening." Coach laughs and looks at the coordinators. "But we have got to give it up for our guy, Tripp Owens. Over 150 yards, two touchdowns, and he may have been showing off for his girlfriend but if that's how you play when she's here, she's welcome any time." He winks at me. "Game ball goes to Tripp."

A ball of emotion is in my throat. *Our guy, Tripp Owens.* I figured news about Willow would spread quickly throughout the team, but I didn't think about coach. Why do I feel like my dad is calling me out for having a girlfriend?

When the guys start clapping and hollering, I go from borderline crying to pumped. The moment is quick, but it feels like I'm living it in slow motion. It may not be as significant as others, but this means something to me. Some guys hit my back and shake my shoulders while others give me shit for not telling them about Willow.

Today, I'm not boring. I know this much. I'll always remember this game, taking home the game ball, and my girl in Cosmos blue.

Once the hype dies down, everyone starts leaving to meet friends and family before we go to team dinner. I let the locker room empty, hoping it will be less chaotic when I go out there. The thought of Willow out there with the other family members, and my mom, has me itching to get out of here.

When it's finally time, I walk into the friends and family area. Before I can look for anyone, my mom runs up and wraps me in a hug. I know it's her by the touch.

"Tripp! Two touchdowns. You were SO GOOD TODAY. I mean, you're good *most* days, but you really had it going." She squeezes me tight. I can feel and hear her pride.

"Thanks, Mom. I try," I joke because I don't really know what else to say. She praises me no matter how much of a dud I play.

She gives me a kiss on the cheek and steps away. That's when I see her.

Willow. Leather skirt. Boots. Cosmos Blue. A signature pink lip. And a smile that makes time fucking stop.

I walk towards her and she meets me—wrapping her arms around my neck.

"You were incredible! I just, ugh, I can't get my heart to stop racing. I can't imagine what it's like playing!" Her words come a mile a minute and the enthusiasm doesn't go unnoticed.

"Means a lot that you came. I had about a hundred text messages sending me clips of you at the game," I say into her ear; it's just for me and her.

"Well, in that case..." she says before brushing her lips on mine. Kissing me in front of all these people. Winning a game is a good time but kissing your girl after is much better.

"Tripp, I'm going home. You guys have fun at team dinner. Call me tomorrow," my mom says knowingly.

"Love you, Mom." I wrap her in a final hug.

"Willow, such a pleasure. Hope we can do lunch or something soon. I'll bring you some knitting needles!" my mom says while reaching for Willow's hand.

"Sounds good, Wendy. Text me what day works best for you."

Text her? What is happening? She must sense my question.

"Your mom and I sort of hit it off." She shrugs like it's common knowledge.

"Wow, okay. Hope you'll still have time for me."

"I'll see if I can fit you in," she says while planting a sweet kiss on my mouth.

"All right, lovebirds. I'm out of here. Tripp, great game. Hope to see another one soon," Emilie says, trying to make her exit.

"I'll put you on the suite list for the rest of the season. You're always welcome. If you ever need a plus one, let me know and I can make it happen," I say and shake her hand.

Emilie shoots Willow a look. One that says, I know what you're about to do and have some fun. Someone else from Willow's security detail will follow us to the team dinner and then to my apartment before calling it a night.

"Are you ready?" I ask.

"More than ready, Mr. MVP," she tells me, and I try not to blush.

I reach for her hand and we walk to my car. She and I both know this is where some of the media will be waiting to get a picture of us together. We talked about it before the game and I can't wait for people to see her with me. I'd see her in secret if I needed to, but I love that we're going public.

The media is respectful and quiet. They mostly take our pictures without saying anything and Willow smiles and waves when we pass.

My girl's so good at this.

# Chapter 32
## Willow

I'm sitting in a booth next to Tripp and across from some of his teammates. Everyone has been welcoming. It feels like I'm Willow, a semi-normal human, meeting her boyfriend's friends.

We keep finding ways to touch. Leaning into one another. Knees touching under the table. Holding hands. An arm wrapped around shoulders.

While I try not to be that disgustingly smitten woman who keeps stealing looks of Tripp when she thinks no one is looking, I can't really help it.

The best part? I don't think Tripp is much different. There's been quite a few times when I find he's already looking at me. I love the feel of his soft, gray eyes on me.

Someone slides into the booth, and they have this look. Their eyes are wide, posture is too straight, and I haven't seen them blink or breathe. I know this look.

"Hi! I'm Willow," I say, extra cheer in my voice, and reach out to shake this man's hand.

The way he slowly lifts his hand to mine makes me want to laugh. Not at him. It's surreal to think I elicit these kinds of reactions from people. Some days my brain can't make sense of it.

"I'm FJ. That's what people call me. My name," he sucks in a breath, "isn't two letters. I have a name—"

"Are you kidding me right now? We practiced this..." Zack says while bumping his shoulder into FJ's. Tripp puts his head in his hands, I think he's also trying not to laugh.

"Fritz. My name is Fritz," he says, and Zack gives him a high-five. It's adorable.

"Great to meet you. What position do you play?"

He responds with a laugh. A belly laugh. Zack whips his head to him, with a massive grin on his face.

"I love when that happens," he says through his laugh. "I'm an equipment manager, not a player. But did y'all see that? She thought I was *on the team*," he says playfully and it makes me like him. Immediately.

"We're never going to hear the end of this. You know that right?" Tripp softly says in my ear, his lips kissing my temple, like he's done it a million times before. The act of affection, in front of his guys, melts me.

"FJ or Fritz, it's great to meet you."

"This is probably annoying, but my wife will never forgive me. I have a four-year-old daughter, Ruby, who is obsessed with you. Like, I'm convinced your music is the only reason she started talking. She did it so she could sing along. Is there any way we could take a picture or something?" He holds onto his phone like it's gold.

"Ruby?! I love that name! And you're not annoying. If you want, we could do a quick FaceTime this week? I'm pretty open and would love to chat with her."

As I'm saying this, FJ's jaw is about to hit the table. His chin is almost touching his chest and his eyelashes are almost touching his forehead. His teammates laugh at his reaction, but you can tell it's all in good fun.

"Yes. 100% yes to that. I should mention my wife is also obsessed, but I thought the daughter would be a good lead in."

The guys laugh even harder. My cheeks are starting to warm but it's only because this is wholesome. I give him my phone so he can put his number in. I promise to text him to find a time that works this week. He fidgets and kicks his feet under the table, saying how he wants it to be a surprise.

The night is dying down, and I'm ready to get out of here. Most of the guys have left. Besides Zack.

"You know that you're about to make FJ the coolest dad and husband of the year, right?" he says, leaning his forearms on the table. "That was pretty cool. Gotta say. How'd you end up with this knuckle ball?" He laughs and points to Tripp.

"That's our cue," Tripp smiles, putting an end to the evening. We stand and Zack does the same.

"It was great to meet you, Willow. Thanks for hanging out and for giving this guy something to do other than football."

I'm a twelve-year-old boy, because I'm trying not to giggle over "something to do".

Zack leans in to hug me and I let him. He has dirty blonde hair, eyes that are like the blue of a sunny sky. He's taller than Tripp. He's like a golden retriever. You see him for just a second and you just want to wrap him up. Also, you know he'll be getting into trouble ten minutes later.

I jot down a few thank you notes, smiling as I put my 'W' stickers to seal the envelopes, to hand to our server and bartender on the way out. I can feel Tripp looking at me.

"You ready?" Tripp asks, like he read my mind.

"Absolutely." He helps me put my jacket on and then reaches for my hand.

We say quick goodbyes to everyone still there on the way out and I make a promise to be at the next home game. A promise I fully intend to keep.

Tripp opens the door, and the flashes and screams are aggressive. While the inside has been a safe space for the team and significant others, all bets are off about twenty feet from the door.

"Holy shit," Tripp says, trying to keep a smile on his face, knowing that every moment is being recorded. Cataloged. Kept.

It's a barrage of questions and screaming. *Are you dating? How long has this been going on? Is that an engagement ring? Over here! Look! Comment?!*

I suck in a deep breath, trying not to let my facial expression give them a single ounce of rattling me. I've got this because Tripp's got me.

"It's okay. Don't let go though," I say, looking down at the hand he's holding. He winks at me and then reaches in for a chaste kiss, in front of everyone, like we've done it a thousand times. I swear I can hear the clicks of the cameras speed up.

I know my security team is nearby and I'm not necessarily nervous but it's a jarring shift from the cozy restaurant to this. Tripp squeezes my hand and leads the way.

Once we're in the car, buckled in, and pulling away from the paparazzi, I let out a sigh.

"Well, there's no going back now," Tripp jokes with one hand on the steering wheel and uses the other to squeeze my leg. His hand on my midthigh has me wanting him to speed all the way home.

"Wouldn't dream of it," I say.

THE PRIVATE ELEVATOR DOORS close, and Tripp is in front of me, hands in my hair, pulling me to him. His kisses are feverish, quick, like he's trying to grab hold of as much of me as possible. I drop my overnight bag and use my arms to put my hands at the nape of his neck. I moan against his lips, the burn in my low belly growing.

He picks me up, my back against the elevator wall. Tripp's mouth finds the spot on my neck that makes me forget my own name.

And, too fast, the doors open.

Tripp gives me a final kiss before grabbing my bag, my hand, and leading me to his place.

This apartment is stunning. We're one step in and lights turn on. The ceilings are tall, and the windows are massive. It feels open and exactly what you'd expect for a penthouse in the city.

"Let's do a quick tour," he says emphasizing *quick*. "This is the kitchen. There are always snacks and food in my fridge. Help yourself to whatever you'd like." We walk into the living room, and it screams cozy even though it's in such a modern space. Plush furniture, the kind you can sink into, all in dark tones, create a welcoming vibe. There are ottomans and tons of blankets. Different textures, colors, all pulling the darkness of the room together.

It's the windows that cause me to stop.

"This is not your view," I say, getting as close as what's acceptable to the windows.

"This is my view." He crosses his arms and takes it in with me.

It's a sparkling New York City skyline. Feels like his apartment is wrapped in miles of it.

"This is beautiful."

"I know something more beautiful." He reaches for me, pulling me in for a kiss. "Thank you for coming to the game." He wraps me in a hug.

"Stop it," I blush at the cheesiness of the line. "Thanks for the invite. Also, you're stuck with me for next week's home game at least," I joke.

"Happily stuck. Hopefully for much longer than that." He laughs. It's a tiny comment but it sticks in my brain. The part where it's like I can't think about this right now and I need to file it away for later.

"You were amazing today. I mean, you look fast on TV, but in person, it's different."

I swear his cheeks blush.

"Thank you. Today was good. Sometimes, it's like that."

Tripp leads me down a hallway, his hand on my lower back, showing me the guest bedroom and bathroom before we're in the master suite.

"This is my room."

I walk in and sit on the edge of his bed. I lean back a little, putting the weight in my arms behind me, before lying all the way back. I let my arms touch the softness of his duvet.

It's only a second and Tripp is leaning over me. He straddles me and holds himself up on his forearms. His hair dips into his eyes. Instinctually, I brush it away. I already want to bring my hips to meet him.

"Are you sure about this?" he asks, his voice husky like the end of a breath.

"Don't make me beg," I say.

In a swift second, he grabs my wrists and pins them above my head with one arm.

"Now I'm going to." His mouth is on mine, urgent and hungry. I pick my head up as fast as I can, pushing the kiss further, exploring his tongue with mine. I reach as far as he'll let me, and he pulls away each time I reach this imaginary line.

Painfully slow, he puts his mouth to my jaw, and then he's biting my ear lobe. When he takes his tongue and draws it down my neck, I can't help but let out a whimper. My hips are dying to move but Tripp holds me in place, his strength on the best kind of display.

His free hand lightly touches the top of my breasts. My nipples tingle and harden in anticipation of his hands. His mouth. His bite. I want all of it.

"Tripp," I gasp and put my head to the side.

"Tell me what you want," he says, moving his hips just enough for me to feel his dick through his pants. "If you're good, I'll let you have it." When his lips pull into a sly smirk, I can't help but respond with a sigh.

"Less clothes."

"Promise to be good?" He grabs the hem of my shirt, pulling it up away from my skin.

"I promise." Before the word is out of my mouth, he's got both hands on the side of my stomach, raking up my skin, while pushing my shirt over my breasts.

My hands reach for his shirt, and he's back to pinning my arms above my head. He buries his head in between my breasts before using his free hand and putting a nipple in between his fingers. He rolls and squeezes, my hips follow.

"My god, Tripp." The need for him intensifies with each held back touch. I throw my head side to side.

"Not yet, baby. Does this have any sort of sentimental value?" He touches the black lacy bra.

"No." It comes out more like a breath than a response.

"Good." With a brisk movement he goes from pinning my hands to grabbing for my bra and ripping it down the middle.

I let out a moan because I could explode. My back arches off the bed, my tits exposed.

"Ask nicely and I'll consider it." Tripp's voice melts but in a way that I know he's still in control. I love it.

"Your mouth on me." My voice sounds like it doesn't belong to me, raspy and needy.

"Where?" Tripp's response is slow—deliberate.

"Anywhere."

"Only if you put your hands behind your back." I can't follow his instructions fast enough. When he takes the other nipple in his mouth, I so badly want to reach my arms out and touch him. Touch myself. Pull him closer. Now, I know why he was specific about the hand placement.

"Don't even think about using your hands." He's firm and goes back to biting my nipple, just hard enough.

I shiver as he plants a delicate line of kisses down my body, starting at my sternum. I'm so thankful I didn't put tights on today. I bite my lip and smile at the thought. My body shudders in response, a delicious torture.

"What's that for?" he prods.

"Just thinking about how I'm glad I left the tights at home."

"Why is that?" he asks while pulling his hand painfully slow down the front of my leather skirt. My heart races and I shiver in anticipation. He takes his hand from my knee to the inside of my thigh, drawing lazy circles.

"Fuck, that's so hot. You looking at me over my leather skirt. Your face, right, there." Words are hard. I can't remember a time I was ever this turned on during foreplay.

"How is this?" When he takes a finger and slides it under my panties, so close to my center, I gasp. I know I'm dripping at this point.

"Even. Hotter."

"Is all this for me? You're so wet, Lo." Two fingers enter me, and I pick my shoulders off the bed, while keeping my arms behind my back.

"Yes. All for you."

"What should we do about this?" He is slowly killing me. He knows it, too.

"Use your mouth." I'm pleading at this point.

"How should I use my mouth?" he counters with a devilish tone.

He's going to make me say it. Say exactly what I want.

"I want you to put your mouth on my pussy. My clit." The words jammed together coming out too fast.

Tripp bites his lip before using his fingers to pull my soaked panties to the side. He moves his mouth closer but stops right before making contact. Tripp lightly blows, and I let out a whine.

When he uses his tongue, licking me agonizingly slow, I pick my head up and see his head hidden under my skirt. My skin feels like it could catch fire.

"Tripp!" I call out, digging my own arms which are still behind my back. I'm following the rules like a good girl.

He bites my inner thigh and then blows on my clit again, inching me closer and closer. My nerves are shot, and I feel like I could come at any second.

"I know you're close," he says. "You're so wet. You're not coming until I say."

Before I can respond, he fills me with his fingers and flicks me with his tongue.

"Do you remember what I told you?" He pulls away before using his tongue where his fingers were. "I told you I wasn't that nice." And he licks so close to where I need it, where I crave him. He's teasing me and it's fucking delicious.

Then he's back on his knees, but reaching for his shirt, taking it off. Muscles ripple but he's calm and collected. Meanwhile, my chest heaves with heavy breaths.

"Can I touch?" I ask because I know he wants me to. He nods yes and my hands fly from behind my back and hit his chest. I scratch my nails down his front. When I reach the top of his pants, he stops my hands and lightly pushes me back on the bed.

His head is back under my skirt.

"Do you want to come, Lo?" he asks me like it's a common talking point.

"Yes."

"Yes, what?" he says, the air hitting my clit. His mouth is so close. My climax is within reach.

"Yes, please," I practically yell.

And then he kisses my bundle of nerves the way I need. He fills me up with his fingers and pinches the inside of my thigh. It's the perfect balance of bliss and welcomed stings of pain.

He pulls back, giving me long strokes up and down my lips, joining his fingers before coming back to my center. When he moans, it's over. The vibration from his mouth has me at the peak. Waves of bliss and need wash over me. I contract around Tripp's fingers.

"Right! There!" I scream in his bedroom. He moans as I come on his fingers. His face.

Before I'm fully out of it, he's unbuckling his pants. I'm panting on his bed.

"Do you want me to use a condom? I was tested at the beginning of the season," he asks, taking his pants off.

"No, I have an IUD. I got tested... before our first date." I can't help but overshare.

His grin is devilish as he shakes his head. He's kissing me in a way that makes me feel like I'm exactly what he needs. Like if he doesn't have me, every last piece, he'll drown.

The only break he takes from my mouth is to pull my skirt and panties off. I sit up and reach for his dick. Just getting a touch in before he is towering over me.

He slides his dick inside me. I'm still ridiculously sensitive.

"Fuck, you feel so good," he says, his mouth close to my ear. "This pussy is all mine."

Tripp catches my lips with his, and I groan into him. His pace is slow, deliberate. He uses his arms to hold himself up. They dig into the mattress.

"Tell me you're all mine." His voice low and demanding.

"I'm all yours, Tripp." I say, as he thrusts all the way in.

When he slowly pulls out of me, it's brutal. He keeps the tip of his cock inside before pressing in. He does this three or four times before I wrap my arms around his neck and pull my hips to speed up the pace.

"Someone is eager," he says with pleasant restraint.

I respond with a bite to his lower lip, harder than I originally planned, which he matches by covering my body with his. The weight of him on me inching me that much closer. I moan into the crook of his neck, pull my fingers down his back. I might be leaving a mark, but I don't care.

My hands pull at the nape of his neck before they're tangled in his hair. I pull. Hard. Tripp immediately slams into me, giving me exactly what I want.

I can't catch my breath. His breath mingles with mine, with each thrust—filling me.

I lift my hips, just enough, and I'm close.

"Fuck, Lo." He speeds up, taking advantage of the new angle. I use an arm to lift him up and somehow, it's even better.

My skin is ice and fire, all at once. He can't be touching me enough—it's impossible to be close enough. I've never wanted more of him. He looks at me, his steely eyes like storm clouds.

I stretch around him. He kisses my neck before biting my shoulder. And that's all it takes. I grind against him a final time before I throb around his dick—then he's coming with me.

He groans, low and slow. My eyes roll back. Each toe curls. He keeps thrusting as he rides out his own wave. Tripp lies on top of me, solid weight pressing me into the mattress. I feel his breathing, heavy and quick, against my chest. It's the most wonderful feeling. Like being someone's matching puzzle piece. We fit.

It's like Tripp knows what I need before I do. He presses the sweetest kiss on my mouth. His tongue lightly touching mine. He falls to the side of me.

He uses his hand to delicately move a rogue strand of hair, getting it off my face. When he tucks it behind my ear, and locks his eyes on mine, I know this is something. Really something.

My heart squeezes. I swallow the lump of emotion. This is new territory for me.

And there's nothing I want more than to explore it.

# **Chapter 33**
## Tripp

I'M ALWAYS UP EARLY. There's always something to do, somewhere to go, something on the schedule. But right now, I can't think of a single thing I'm supposed to do because a naked Willow is in my bed. Wrapped in my sheets.

I prop myself up, watching her sleep. I'm aware this is either romantic and acceptable or extreme-creep behavior. She's stunning. Her dark hair is fanned around her, contrasting against the white pillowcase. Her eyelashes flutter. Maybe she's dreaming?

Fuck. It feels like *I'm* dreaming.

Her chest rises and falls—she stirs a little. I could pretend to be asleep, but I don't. Willow wakes up and sees me watching her and she gives me a sleepy grin.

"Morning," she says, while stretching her arms above her head.

"Morning." I lie down on my side, facing her. Once she's done stretching, she mirrors me.

"What time is it?" she asks with her eyes closed.

"It's 5:45."

"Gah! Why are you up so early?" She squints her eyes shut and dramatically throws her arm over her face.

"I'm always up early. Also, thought we could grab some breakfast before I have to go to the facility. Today is a corrections and adjustment day."

"Do we have to go right now?"

"No, we have some time. Should leave here around seven. But thought we could take a shower." I nuzzle her nose with mine.

"Mmmm, a shower sounds great."

I take my arm and throw it around her waist, drawing circles on the top of her hip. I then cup her ass.

Her eyes, golden and bright, pop open. We're on the same page.

I stand at the edge of the bed, reach for her hands, and pull her out of the bed.

I lead her to the bathroom and ditch my briefs before I turn the water on. Willow stands in front of me but covers parts of herself with her hands.

"Why the hands?" I ask.

"It's bright in here." Her voice is strained and sleepy. "I'm wildly aware that you are a professional athlete and I," she looks down her body and back up to me, "am not."

Fuck no. I don't want her feeling like this. Not for a minute.

"Lo. Believe me, I love that I can see you. And not to give away all my cards, but you're sort of my dream girl." I look down at my dick and then back up to her.

Her eyes go wide when she sees my erection.

"You're gorgeous. Seeing you like this…" I gesture to her and take in a deep breath. "It makes me want to put my mouth, my hands, all of me, all over you."

Her worried face cracks into a sly smile. I take a step back into the shower. She meets me with a kiss, soft but urgent. It's like she wants me to prove something to her.

*Happy to.*

Without breaking the kiss, we step in until we're under the water. I'm closest to the shower head. Steam rolls around us.

Her hands massage my scalp, playing with my hair, and that's new. Never had someone do that. My hair isn't that long but Willow's hands lightly coiling it around her fingers and scratching my scalp is incredible. Something I didn't know I was missing out on. Or fucking loved.

I groan into her mouth and pull my lips from her perfect pink pout to her jawline. Down her neck. Spending time at the delicate base. Her hands help direct me on where I should put my mouth next.

She glides a hand from my hair, slowly down my chest, stopping right above my cock. I laugh when she stops.

"What?" Lo teases, scratching my skin with her fingernails. Soft. Delicate. Tortuous. Her golden eyes snap to mine and it's like a punch. This moment. Willow here. Touching me like this. How I can't get enough of her.

"Love when you tease me," I say into her ear, her dark, wet locks touching my lips.

"Is that so?" she asks while she still runs her fingers on the lowest part of my stomach. My muscles flex on and off, reacting to her touch.

"Yes, baby." I think I'd love anything this woman did to me.

Willow turns us, switching our positions. She's now under the shower head, but just for a second. She takes her hands and lightly presses me back, into the bench. Her fingers dig into the top of my shoulders and she pushes down, making me sit.

I lean my weight back on my arms, for a second, taking her in, from her head to her toes. Her skin is pink from the hot water. She's fucking beautiful. And strong. Her legs are muscular; muscles flex in her arms when she massages the top of my shoulders from the front.

I'm in a perfect position to put my mouth on one of her breasts. I bite her nipple. When she arches her back she presses further into me. I swirl my tongue and use one hand to grab her ass. That ass. I love that there's something to grab.

Her hands move from my shoulders to the tip of my cock. She's delicate with her touch, exploring the head. I knead her ass with my fingers before giving it a light slap.

She yelps but smiles in a way that tells me she likes it.

"Tripp!"

"I can't get enough of that ass," I say, my face between her breasts, looking up at her.

When she laughs and tips her head up, I look up to one of the most beautiful things I've ever seen. Willow. Naked in my shower. Smiling.

She comes back to my dick and moves to the shaft. Both hands work in tandem, up and down. I get impatient and move my hips to deepen the touch.

"Someone is needy," Willow says in my ear before biting my ear lobe.

"For you? Always." My voice is like gravel.

Willow gets on her knees in front of me. She has one hand around the shaft of my throbbing cock and her mouth is close to the tip. She looks at me and I swear I almost come right then and there.

"You can't look at me like that," I say, looking down at this fucking siren in my shower.

"Like what?" she says before she puts my dick in her mouth.

"Fuuuck," I groan and lean back, my arms behind me. My chest heaves every time she pulls me in and out of her mouth. I can't look at her. If I do, I'll come early. Like a chump.

It's her hands. Her mouth. Her lips. Everything stacks on one another and I'm close.

"Lo, stand up," I say, my voice like a growl.

She pulls my cock out of her mouth, with a pop sound. When she stands, I grab one of her legs and pull it over my thigh. Willow knows where I'm going, and she straddles me.

Bit by bit, she slides on top of my length. I use my fingers to touch her clit. Each touch elicits those moans I love so much. Willow wraps her arms around my neck, giving her a bit of leverage for her to ride me while I sit.

I use one hand to guide her by holding her lower back. The other touches her bundle of nerves.

"Keep touching me like that. Just like that." Her pace picks up. Hearing her like this makes me want to come undone, but it's not time yet.

She leans a little further into me. I let her dictate the rhythm.

"My," she sucks in a breath, "my ass!" she demands. My hand goes from her low back to slapping her ass. The sharp sound spurs her on. My fingers move faster, I rock my hips forward. Back. Forward.

And there she goes.

Willow throws her head back, thrusting her tits into my face. I put one in my mouth. She shakes and trembles while I come inside her.

"Fuck, Lo."

We ride out the aftershocks together. She flips her hair forward before putting her forehead to mine. Her breath is quick. We match.

I put my hands into her hair and pull her to me for a kiss.

"I guess that was worth waking up for," she laughs, and I can feel her smile in the way she kisses me.

⚬ ⚬ ⚬

I take Willow to one of my favorite breakfast spots. It's a hidden gem, and I can text the staff if I'm planning to come in. They do their best to give me one of their back booths or tables. That way, people can't see me from the front window.

Honestly, it's rare that people pick me out of a lineup. I think I've changed the game a bit, going public with Willow, and definitely by bringing her here.

We eat our breakfast uninterrupted. Pancakes for her and an omelet for me. She holds her cup of coffee like it's a life source.

"No one's going to take that from you," I joke.

"They better not." She closes her eyes and takes a long sip. "Someone kept me up late last night." She smirks at me, steam in front of her eyes, like smoke on a sandy beach. "This is not me complaining but merely pointing out I will need copious amounts of coffee."

We're about to leave when she pulls out a thank you note from her bag. She takes a minute to write something and leaves it on the table for the server.

She reaches for my hand and we're one step out the door before paparazzi run towards us. Gone is the peacefulness of the morning.

The thing that pisses me off is how they are screaming at Willow. I've had my run-ins with these people, and it may be annoying, but I'd rarely call it disrespectful.

People shout things at her, like they did last night, but it's the way they crowd us. We each have security that was posted up and instructed to stay to themselves unless they were needed. When they come to our sides, I know this has the potential to get out of hand.

*Willow, what makes you think you can keep Tripp entertained?*

What the fuck? Did someone seriously say that? I look at her, and she's focused on nothing but the ground.

*What happened with Dexter? How long do you think this one will last?*

This is fucked up. The audacity these people have to scream at someone like this.

"Tripp. Don't." She squeezes my hand to get my attention. Her voice is barely loud enough for me to hear.

*Willow, ever think the problem is you?*

*Tripp, she isn't worth it!*

I stop. My security bumps into my back. No one expected me to stop. I know I should let this go but I fucking can't. Anger floods my veins.

I turn to the man who just screamed in my face about her not being worth it. He doesn't even stop taking photos.

There's a line I need to walk. Otherwise, I'll find myself in deep shit. Legal shit. Annoying shit.

With the lightest possible touch, I put a single finger on his camera. He pulls his eye from the finder, and I gently move this far enough that I can see his face.

"What did you say?" I keep my voice level and make eye contact with this sorry excuse of a person in front of me.

"Come on, you know how it is." He shrugs his shoulders. Nonchalant. Fucking asshole.

"I don't know how it is. You can take your stupid fucking pictures and sell them to whoever cares, but I'd appreciate if you didn't scream about shit you know nothing about." I say it through a sickly fake smile.

"Tripp, let's go," Willow says. She's tugging on the hand she's still holding.

"Did you hear me?" I ask the man who shrinks in front of me.

He doesn't say anything, but he nods in understanding. He backs himself out of the crowd of people. I know the entire interaction was documented and I don't care.

Willow and I get back to my car.

"Sorry, I know that's a lot to handle and—"

"Why are you apologizing? Are you okay?"

"It's not the worst thing I've heard, to be honest..." Her voice fades away and she stares at her hands resting on her knees.

"That's not okay." I place one of my hands on top of hers. She doesn't look at me.

"You don't have to do that. Try to get them to stop. It's not worth it."

"If I can get one of these losers to realize this is not how you treat fucking humans, I'm going to do it. Every time. I don't have to, but I want to."

"Tripp."

"Don't tell me it's not worth it. It is," I say, softer than before.

"I appreciate you. Really I do." She takes a deep breath. "I don't need you to call out the press though. You will never win. There are too many of them. Things like what just happened, they make me uncomfortable. I worry someone's going to lose it. I don't trust anyone to keep their cool."

Immediately, I feel bad. I want her to feel safe when she's with me. Not sure I accomplished that this morning.

"I've been doing this a long time. They've said everything there is to say. I'd prefer to not feed into it." Her voice cracks. She looks up with her eyes a tiny bit glassy. "I don't mean to get emotional. It just surprised me. The yelling about Dexter. I typically have thicker skin than this."

"That was. A lot. Don't apologize for having a reaction." I want her to hear me.

I take the hand from her leg, and reach for her with my other, each on her cheeks. I pull her in for a kiss. Sweet and tame compared to this morning.

"Thanks for taking me out to breakfast." I can tell she's trying to bounce back.

I kiss her hand.

"I hope there are many more breakfasts in our future, Lo."

# Chapter 34
## Willow

It's only a few hours later before my publicist calls, giving me a heads-up about the headlines. None of them are from reputable sources, but it doesn't mean people won't see them.

***And She's on to the Next: Willow Picks Up Her Next Boytoy***

***Will a Player Get Played? Willow Dating NFL Player Tripp Owens***

***Willow's Career Might Be Stalled but Not Her Love Life***

***Tripp Owens Uses Force with Paparazzi***

It's the last one that stings. Tripp did not use force. Everyone could tell how much he was holding back. No one was violent. That's the thing about the press, no one cares what really happened, they only care about clicks.

I text Tripp to give him a heads-up, including the link to the last headline.

What a shift.

Yesterday was one of the best days I've had in a long time. The game. Meeting Tripp's mom. Hanging with the team. My night with Tripp.

Nothing like a nice reality check with a bunch of strangers who live to take you down a notch, whenever they can. It's part of the deal. I know that. I love my life and the ability to create. Sadly, the press comes with it.

What if it gets to be too much for Tripp? I could tell by the way he took it all in, that's not a normal interaction for him. The thought runs and tumbles in my brain. Nagging me.

He said I was worth it today. How long will that last?

When my brain won't stop, there's always something that helps. Music. I take myself to the studio and get to work.

I'VE BEEN IN THE zone the last few hours. New music. New verses. It feels good to be productive. My phone vibrates.

Tripp

uses force lol

that's a piss poor headline

didn't even use a football pun

missed opportunity

Me

glad you think it's funny

how else am I going to be? doesn't bother me

Really? Not even a little?

Not even a little

I'm done with meetings

plan for tonight?

hoping to collect on a bet

??

did you already forget the touchdowns?!

you owe me music baby!

ahhh that bet

Tomorrow is my day off. That means I can stay over

not sick of me yet?

quit it

plus, the hot tub is calling my name

see you soon. I'm working in the studio

i'll tell Seth to let you in

My cheeks pinch from smiling.

Tripp cautiously opens the door to the studio, like he's trying to not disturb me. When he sees me sitting with a guitar, but taking a break, he walks to me and kisses my cheek.

"How's the writing today?"

"Surprisingly good," I say, taking the guitar off and setting it next to me.

"Don't stop on my account."

"No, I need a break."

"Well, then I've got perfect timing," he says while sitting next to me.

I lean into him and he wraps an arm around my shoulders.

"I'm very excited about the music sneak peek though. Not going to even try to lie."

"Ahh. That makes one of us." I cover my eyes with one of my hands. "I never play music early for people. Like, it makes me cringe. Getting that first reaction on something. From someone who counts."

"Someone who counts, huh?" He leans into me and squeezes my shoulder.

Why did I say that? I swear, sometimes my brain just runs from one thought to the other. Heat creeps up my neck and part of me wishes I'd melt into the floor.

Tripp uses two fingers to tip my face to his and puts his lips on mine.

"I like being someone who counts," he says in between kisses, a massive grin pulling at his lips.

I keep falling deeper and deeper. Every time he says something like this, it's like the magnetic pull gets stronger. Not even the words he says, but how he says it. He means it.

"Alright, let's get this over with. I have two complete songs and a snippet of another that are ready for playback. I change the output on the soundboard so it will play through the whole studio and not my headphones.

Tripp rubs his hands together and sits up tall.

Music fills the studio. The first two are piano only and the partial song is on guitar. I pace while my voice comes in and out. I can play it for him but the farther I am from him the better. My heart races and my hands shake a bit.

We're in the middle of the second song when I steal the quickest of glances. Tripp has his eyes closed, a smile on his face, and he's sort of swaying with the beat. This reaction eases my anxiety, just a bit.

I love the bridge for this one. It's one that fell out of my brain, onto the piano keys, and hit me in the right spot while I was writing. I mouth the words as they play.

*You and I dance, under the night sky,*
*nothing but a gleam*
*Entwined, a fleeting moment, on the fringe*
*of this cosmic dream*
*Each star, its own, bright beauty*
*In the spaces between*
*We dance and you kiss me like it counts,*
*A promise unseen*

The music stops. Tripp stands up and, to my horror, claps.

"Stop it." I put my hand on my forehead, pretending to hide from him.

"I will not. This is a fan's dream! I am living the dream." He walks toward me. "Willow, this is so good. The piano is delicate and powerful and ugh, you sound so good when you sing with the piano."

"It's still rough, lots of work to be done, and things to smooth out."

"Your rough version is better than many people's polished. Seriously."

"That is one of the kindest things someone has said to me. Thank you." And it is. People tell me the music is good, the lyrics make sense, they feel something. Tripp has given me such lovely feedback in just a few minutes after a couple songs.

"I know you don't like playing things early but thank you. I won't forget it. Especially when the new stuff is all over the radio, taking over the world. I'll know I was one of the people to hear it first."

"Tripp Owens. What am I going to do with you?" I say with flushed cheeks as he reaches for my hands.

"Well, first, I say we soak our troubles away in the hot tub. And then, I have a few other ideas." He smirks, mischievous and gorgeous, all at once.

# Chapter 35
## Tripp

IF I THOUGHT THINGS got wild after I very-publicly asked Willow out, I don't know the word for whatever the fuck is going on now.

People hang out by my apartment, trying to get a glimpse of us out together, doing literally anything. Per Willow's security team, we've hired a few more people for the time being.

Every day, ten new headlines pop up, still using pictures from Willow at the first game and our breakfast date. Most of them make me eye-roll, laugh, and then text my mom to make sure she knows it isn't true.

That part sucks.

But there's a part of the press or media frenzy who have chosen to focus on the positives. Plus, Willow's massive fan base has latched on to these and they seem to get more traction than the bullshit ones.

***Willow and Tripp – From Super Bowl to Super Cute Couple***
***Tripp Owens with the Catch of His Life: Willow***
These are the types of headlines that make me want to drop everything and spend all my time with Willow. Even though it's impossible.

Since we're no longer a secret, Willow has been at my place almost every night this week. She even rented some studio space in the city. The commute back and forth to her place isn't short. The fact that she'd rather work on her new album at a studio closer to my place makes my heart hurt, in a good way.

Honestly, my trainers haven't seen much of me these last few weeks. I'm doing everything team related but I'd typically have more one-on-one during my "off time". It's the cost I must pay to spend more time with the beautiful woman posted up at my apartment.

Tonight, we have a charity Gala hosted by the Cosmos owner. It's for a new charity dedicated to the well-being, health, and safety of animals. All I know is that there will be dogs there. Also, Willow is going with me.

Emilie called me to line up all the glam team details for today. It was easier once she explained what the hell a glam team was. I look at my watch and bet they're still in my apartment.

I open my apartment door to see, what I'm guessing, is the glam team on their way out. They smile and tell me to have fun tonight. The only one I recognize is Claire, her manager. And I don't think she's there for hair and makeup.

Once everyone is gone, besides Claire, and before I can look for Willow, she walks into the living room. My feet are planted to this floor. I can't move. She looks fucking incredible.

Her dress is black, but a mix of fabrics. The top is structured, tight to her body, while the bottom is fluffy layers of chiffon. When you're an only child and your dad is a dead beat, you spend a lot of time with your mom, learning words like chiffon.

"There he is," Willow says as she walks to me.

"You look—Wow." I reach for her hand and twirl her once she accepts. Her laugh fills the penthouse and it's the most beautiful sound. "This dress is stunning."

"Thank you. It's an up-and-coming designer. Emilie made the connection, they sent the dress, and I knew I had to wear it tonight. I love it." She picks up layers of chiffon letting them rise and fall.

"You should be all set for tonight. I know you're sitting with Zack, maybe a couple other singles. I didn't want some random plus one being all nosy at your first major event together," Claire says as she lays out the game plan.

"You're the best. Thanks for knocking out some stuff while I was getting ready," Willow says to Claire, grabbing her hand.

"For sure. Don't let Emilie get wild tonight," Claire says. I know Emilie is going to be sitting at a table near us. Each player had some extra tickets to give out because a packed gala means more money for the charity. Emilie was an easy invite. We asked Claire if she wanted to come and she scoffed at us and actually never answered. Long story short, she won't be making it.

Claire is still working on the label when it comes to Willow's new tour. Seems like she handles a lot of the behind-the-scenes things, especially when Willow is in the recording stage.

I can't stop staring at Lo. She literally makes it hard for me to breathe. Her lips are painted a dark pink, almost magenta. I love her signature pink lip. I feel like most women wear a red lipstick for things like this, and I love that Willow has her own spin.

"MVP, you better go and get ready," she says while smoothing her hands down the front of her dress.

Claire chimes in. "Don't forget to wash your face. You've got some drool," she jokes as she gestures to my mouth. She claps me on the back before she leaves.

○○○

THE CAR STOPS AND I can already hear the incessant click of the cameras. I open the door and step out first. My hands brush the front of my black suit, and I double check the buttons. The crowd is getting unruly quick. They know Willow is in the car. Waiting.

I stand in front of the opening for a few seconds, giving everyone a slight smirk. When the sound is at what I think is an appropriate hype level, I reach my hand in and help Willow out. Her foot hits the carpet. The clicks are constant, and the screams are deafening—goosebumps pebble my arms under my designer suit.

Instead of letting her hand go, I give her a quick spin. She's caught off guard, and it leads to an earnest smile. We hold hands after, and I know I'm feeding into exactly what the paparazzi want. Sure, I may yell at the ones who cross a line but I'm also here to give a shot to press who follow the rules.

We walk to the carpet, hand in hand.

*Willow! Willow! Over here! Tripp!*

It's overwhelming but I actually don't mind it. This is the first time I've attended something like this with a date. I swallow back the emotion—I will not cry on this red carpet. I try to soak in the cheers, Willow's hand firmly in mine, and the coy look she gives me. Our eyes lock for a moment, long enough for me to know I want to swim in that golden gaze.

While we're posing and slowly making our way down the red carpet, I hear a laugh I could pick out of a lineup. Zack. I look back just in time to see him reach for Emilie's hand. She's confused but grabs it and he pulls her in for a pose. The press loves it. Emilie quickly bounces back, replacing her furrowed brows with a face fit for the red carpet, like she's done it a hundred times.

"What in the world?!" Willow says while seeing what I see. "I swear, that woman can do anything." She shakes her head and laughs.

"Zack and I share the same kind of spontaneity," I say as I dip her so fast she grabs my arms like I'm going to drop her. I would never. When she realizes what I'm doing, she wears a pink smirk that I can't help but kiss.

It feels like every camera turns our way and leans in. I prolong our kiss, because I fucking want to, and I know everyone is eating this up. This famous thing? Not so bad when you're kissing your gorgeous girlfriend who kisses back like she means it.

I know this isn't typical red-carpet behavior. The Cosmos PR team briefed us about the event and used words like high-brow, sophisticated, and refined. Whoops.

WE HAVE MORE FUN than I ever remember having at something like this. Emilie ended up joining our table since Zack said he was bringing a plus one but that didn't work out. Who knows what flavor of the week he was planning on.

Everyone acted like Willow and Emilie were part of the crew. The drinks were flowing, the snacks never stopped, and now I'm listening to Willow moan over a piece of caramel popcorn cheesecake.

*That fucking moan.*

Not me adjusting my crotch while the owner of the team holds a golden retriever puppy, trying to get someone to take this dog home. Sneaky bastard.

After the festivities, it's more drinks and music. Some people approach our table and ask to take pictures with Willow. She's a queen and says yes to every single one of them.

We're standing at a high-top, just the two of us. Zack and Emilie ditched us an hour ago to dance. I'm pleasantly buzzed. Not drunk but everything is soft enough around the edges. I can tell Willow is feeling the same way.

Her hand finds the nape of my neck where she draws slow circles as she leans into me. I hold her hand and plant kisses on the inside of her wrist. She wraps her arms around my neck, and we dance during a slow song.

"How about one more drink and then we go home?" she croons into my ear.

"Home. I fucking love when you say that." I wrap my arms around her lower back and then lift her up, spinning in a circle. She throws her head back with a laugh that's a little louder than it would've been two glasses of Champagne ago.

I set her down, plant a kiss on the sensitive spot between her jaw and ear. She acts like it tickles but I know it's *one* of her favorite spots for my mouth.

I walk to the bar and find myself next to a sweaty Zack, chugging a glass of water.

"Maybe your plus one was afraid she would drown if she came tonight." I look him up and down, pull him in by the shoulder, and shake him when we both laugh.

"The dance floor is where it's at! You'd know if you weren't wrapped up in what I'm guessing is going to end up being the love of your life." Zack puts the gin and tonic to his lips. His words hit me. I let them land. What if he's right? *Fuck*. I hope he is right.

"I can't get over how chill she is with the guys. Like, I want to hang out. Not at a fancy gala where there are sad puppies being paraded around but how about a bar? We could totally do that." Zack runs his hands through his hair which looks much darker because of the sweat.

I look over at the high top and see Willow with someone. A guy. Someone I don't know. He leans his arms on the high-top table while they talk.

I order her a Champagne and a neat bourbon for myself. I keep looking over my shoulder to see what she's doing with him. Maybe they know each other? She knows a ton of people. That must be it.

"What's with the scowl?" Zack asks and looks over to Willow.

"Nothing. It's nothing. Do you know who that is?" I ask, my words running into each other.

Zack squints. "No clue."

"Wonder how he got an invite." I scoff, looking for the bartender. I want my drinks. The uneasiness feels like it could choke me.

"What are you even talking about?" Zack laughs. He thinks I'm joking. I don't think I am. Fitting this guy would find his way over as soon as I left.

Willow laughs and puts her hand on his arm. My stomach twists.

The bartender sets the drinks down in front of me. I put a twenty in the tip jar and swipe the glasses. I spill some bourbon on my sleeve.

"Woah, woah. Tripp. Whatever you're going to do—don't," Zack tries to convince me, practically jogging to keep up with me.

I set my bourbon down harder than intended. Or maybe not. Both of their eyes snap to me.

"Here you are, Lo." I hand her the glass of Champagne. Zack awkwardly stands next to me.

"Tripp Owens! You were the man in the Super Bowl last year," the guy says. Willow sips on her drink.

"That's me," I say while taking a sip of the bourbon, welcoming the burn.

"Just a massive Willow fan. Wanted to come and introduce myself. Didn't want to miss my chance." He winks at me. Or at her. Or who the fuck knows. I know I'm being a jealous prick, but I can't help it.

"Bet you didn't." I take another drink, looking at him through the glass. Zack puts his hand on my shoulder and squeezes.

"Actually, Oliver is from home, a small town in Virginia, about fifteen minutes from mine. Isn't that wild?" Willow says, trying to bring me back. She gently puts her hand on my arm before gesturing to Oliver.

"What a coincidence," I say less than entertained and not breaking eye contact with this guy.

"It's a small world, and all of that..." Zack tries to jump in, smooth the bumps, but what's done is done.

"Hey, I don't know what I did. Didn't mean to offend you. Or..." Oliver stumbles over his words. He looks at Willow. "It was great to meet you. Honestly. Can't wait for your next album." He reaches out a hand to shake and she takes it.

Oliver leaves without a second look back to us at the high-top.

Willow turns to me, razor sharp. Like knives could come out of her eyes.

"Are you kidding me?" she asks with a voice rigid as steel.

# Chapter 36
## Willow

*What. The. Fuck.*

Tripp basically sprints over here and is a sarcastic asshole to this guy who was doing nothing wrong. I put my hands on my hips and stare at Tripp, willing him to speak. Instead, it's Zack who talks first.

"That's my cue." He claps his hands and rubs them together. "If I don't see you again, tonight was fun," Zack says, in a way that he's trying to convince himself, pulling me into a hug. I keep my gaze on Tripp. "I'll see you at practice," Zack says to Tripp and waves at me before putting his hands in his pocket and going back to the dance floor.

"Why are you acting like that?" I ask, rephrasing the question.

"Like what?" he responds, like he has no idea what I'm talking about. Is there anything more infuriating?

"Like this." I point to him, up and down. "How you're being right now."

"The second I leave, he runs up to the table? Sure. He's a *big fan.*" Sarcasm drips from his voice. "He had you over here cracking up. What was so funny?"

The only thing I can do is laugh. I put my forehead to my hands.

"Tripp. Do you know how nice it is to meet someone from home? He was reminiscing about rural Virginia. High school things. That's it. If you thought he was over here declaring his love for me, you're wrong."

He looks at me but doesn't say anything. I'm trying to understand what the hell just happened but he's not giving me much.

"Tripp." I lean in closer to him. "What has gotten into you?"

"I don't fucking know. I was at the bar and just saw you laughing with him, being touchy-feely. I just. Didn't like it. I know how it sounds."

Ah, there it is.

"It sounds like you're being a jealous ass." I don't give him a pass.

The look on his face tells me I've nailed it. It would feel like a win if this all wasn't so bizarre and borderline pathetic.

"I am being a jealous ass. You make me want to be jealous and keep you to myself. I just—"

"Let me stop you right there." I close the remaining distance and put a finger to his chest. I look up to him; he doesn't move back. "We're adults. I can't do the jealousy thing. I need you to trust me. Otherwise." I look down. "Otherwise, this won't work."

He lets out a long breath before stretching his neck, side to side, looking for a reset.

"I do trust you," he says, quiet enough so I'm the only one who can hear.

"The version of you from two minutes ago did not." I want to be as clear as possible.

"I do. I told you. I'm not good at this." His hands go through his hair and then hang from the nape of his neck. It looks like he blinks away tears.

This man. He's jealous. Insecure.

I do the only thing I can think of to bring the man I know back to me. I put a sweet kiss on his mouth.

"You were good at this for 98% of the evening. If something bothers you, you need to tell me. But, most of all, you need to trust me. Plus, out of all the people I'll meet and will want something from me, that guy was pretty tame." I kiss him once more.

"I'm sorry. I should've slowed down. Thought things through." I know it's hard for him to admit this.

I reach for one of his hands and hold it at my chest.

"Yes, you should've." I kiss him again. I don't want to drag this out but it's not something I'm going to easily forget.

Tripp and I move in silence as we get out of our gala attire and into pajamas. I pull on a pair of pink satin shorts and a matching top. I walk by Tripp and he rubs his hand on my back, touching the softness of the fabric.

He wraps me up, from behind, my back on his front. He sways a tiny bit, back and forth, as I hold onto his arms. Tripp puts his chin on my shoulder before he kisses my neck.

I know he's embarrassed for the way he acted. The silence itches and is almost uncomfortable, but I won't be the first one to speak   .

"Lo, I'm sorry for acting like a jealous prick," he says, his voice level and smooth.

"I know you are." I rub his forearms and tilt my head so it's touching the side of his face.

"What do we do now?" he asks, tinged with sadness.

"We go to bed," I say while turning to face him. His arms wrap around my lower back. "And we try to do better next time."

# **Chapter 37**
## Tripp

"How do you feel about the new team? It seems to be going well." My sports psychologist, who sometimes doubles as a therapist, sits across from me.

Her office is minimal. Modern. With light and airy paint colors, soft light, and about five different seating options designed to offer maximum comfort. I've been seeing her since I made the move to New York. She pushes me in the right direction and is always willing to explore other areas outside of football once we've covered all the key topics.

"Winning makes it easier. The game is still fun." I know that's what she's about to ask me next.

"Fulfilling because of the winning or because of something other than that?"

"I feel like I have a place here. I'm not playing because a bunch of guys got hurt but because they want me to. I'm good enough. It also brought me Willow." My cheeks feel hot bringing her up.

"Willow. This sounds like your first adult relationship. How's the balance? How do you feel about that?" she asks. That's all she does, ask questions. I know it's her job but sometimes I wonder how someone can fit so many questions in a fifty-minute session.

"It is. I'm trying to do as much as I can. I do any and all of the bonus training things when we're not together. Some days, I feel like I'm doing something wrong or not committing to an opportunity. But when I'm with Willow, those thoughts are quiet." I rub my hands together, almost too hard. "I think it's going well. I had something happen recently but…"

"You can share it if you'd like."

That's the thing, I'm notorious for letting my mouth run while digging myself a deeper therapy hole.

"We were at this charity event and out of nowhere, I was so jealous. Like, a type of feeling creeping into me that I've not felt in a long time. She was just talking to some guy and I couldn't keep it together."

"What do you mean?"

"I acted like a dick, or a toddler, the whole time it was happening. It felt like I was watching from the outside and I was so fucking embarrassed by how I was acting but I still didn't stop. I made the guy feel uncomfortable. Willow was upset."

"Interesting. Why do you think you couldn't stop?" She shifts in her chair.

"My brain hurts. I don't know why I couldn't. I feel like *you* might know…" Occasionally, I try to flip the script. It rarely works.

She laughs before crossing her legs and leaning back in her chair.

"Could it be that you're developing feelings? Substantial feelings?"

Of course she would answer with another goddamn question.

"Well, yeah. I am. But I'm not following."

"Tripp, when things feel important to us, we want to do anything we can to protect them. Sometimes, it doesn't make sense. Sometimes, our actions run faster than our brains. Which is already something you struggle with, yes?"

"Yes. I'm an impulsive jackass and sometimes it really bites me. I know I need to keep working on it."

"The only reason I'm pointing this out is because of the way your anxiety and panic attacks have almost completely dissipated since you've started spending time with Willow. This is significant. I don't want you to overlook the importance of that." Her voice is stern and caring at the same time.

She's right. My anxiety has been almost non-existent, and I find I'm naturally in a better mood. It's also helpful being home for back-to-back weeks.

"I wish I could tell you it was going to get easier, but I'm afraid it won't. Things worth keeping are hard work." She gazes at her notebook, flipping back a page. "Did you get to work on your homework from our last session?"

Ah, I was supposed to outline three possible paths for what I do when there is no more football. I only did one of the three.

"Part of it. Sort of. An option would be to find a way to use my college degree, do something with non-profits. I was looking at a few of the non-profits headed up by someone in the Cosmos organization and they have a few that are centered around kids. Giving them access to sports. Safe places to be after school. I think I would be happy doing that."

"One is better than none. I think that's a great start. For next time, let's find the other two ideas and expand on this first one. What are you hoping your day to day looks like? Do you want to stay in this area or move closer to your hometown, or maybe somewhere else completely? Is it just you? Is it you and your mom? Is there someone else with you?"

Yes. Willow.

I nod in agreement. I know our time is ending.

"Now, let's end with your affirmation."

"I am resilient. I am strong. I am here," I say, and I mean it. Those words run through my brain when I'm struggling. No matter how silly I thought it was when she first asked me to repeat after her.

I WALK INTO MY apartment and it feels like I'm in the wrong one. Music blasts through the house and it smells fucking delicious. Someone is cooking.

I walk into the kitchen to see Willow dancing at the stove. I don't think she heard me come in.

"Boo!" I yell when she's nowhere near the hot pan.

"AH!" she screams and steps back a bit before busting out laughing. "Don't do that!"

"How was shopping?" I ask her, knowing she had a date with my mom today.

"It was fun! I also went to knitting club. I'm not very good at it but it's awfully soothing." She laughs and points to a ball of yarn on the coffee table in the living room.

Mom has made her stance on Willow clear. She loves her. Like, can't get enough of her. I know they've gotten lunch a few times plus this shopping adventure. It's the sweetest fucking thing.

"What's going on in here?" I step closer to the stove to see a pan of shrimp and scallops. My mouth waters at the garlicky smell.

"You mentioned you were craving seafood, and I felt like cooking. I hope it's okay I took over your kitchen."

"You're always welcome to cook in here. Especially anything that smells this good." I waft the steam from the pan and breathe in. On the counter is a salad and a bowl of something that looks like rice.

"It's orzo. A little butter and parmesan cheese. Matches perfectly with the shrimp and scallops," she says like she's reading my mind.

I stand behind her, lean my head down into the crook of her neck, and wrap her up as she continues to cook. I soak in the sound of the pan, the music, and the bustling of Willow cooking me dinner.

WE'RE ABOUT TO KICK off. I know this game will be a grind and we're not favored to win. Technically, we're predicted to get our asses handed to us. Nothing like a little extra fuel for the guys.

It's the end of September and the air is cooler with the promise of fall. The Jumbotron starts showing celebrities and other athletes in attendance. I jump around a bit, keeping my muscles loose. And then the crowd is cheering. Loud.

I look up to see Willow. Wearing my jersey. It's not just a Cosmos blue top, it's my number on the front. She's in the suite, and I can see my mom clapping as Willow waves and then covers her eyes like she's embarrassed.

I can't help but smile.

Some of the other guys give me fist bumps, hit my helmet, and it's like the energy has kicked up a notch.

Zack claps me on the back. "Tripp, we gotta go off on these guys today. Your girl's wearing your jersey. Doesn't get better than that."

"Let's fucking go."

THE GAME WASN'T EVEN close. The opposing team's quarterback threw four interceptions in the first half and got benched, while my quarterback was on fire. Coach even let us call a trick play which set our quarterback up for a 52 yard touchdown pass, caught by yours truly.

We're undefeated. Fuck, it feels good. I'm wrapping up with a press conference before getting back to Willow.

"Tripp, looks like you caught a glimpse of Willow before kick-off. They showed it on the broadcast. Anything you want to share?"

I always underestimate how much people care about this. Not surprising that they tried to get a shot of me when they were showing her. Smart.

"Just that she looks damn good in Cosmos blue."

Reporters laugh and I know I've given them enough.

I walk out to Willow and my mom. Willow is easy to spot in my jersey, gray tights, black skirt, and thigh-high boots.

"Where did you get this?" I ask, pointing to her outfit.

"Your mom and I went shopping this week. I wanted it to be a surprise."

I pull her into my chest and kiss the top of her forehead.

"Definitely surprised."

"Tripp! Look. You're going viral." My mom shows a video on her phone. It's me when I see Willow, what the reporter was alluding to. The video is on a social media app and already has millions of likes and hundreds of thousands of comments.

Willow's phone dings. She takes it out of her pocket and furrows her eyebrows, before rolling her eyes.

"Everything good?" I ask.

She changes her face and forces a smile.

"Yes, all good. Nothing important."

# Chapter 38
## Willow



THAT'S THE TEXT I get while I'm with Tripp and his mom. It makes my skin crawl, like it doesn't fit my bones.

It's been months and I've heard nothing from Dexter. Not even as much as a drunk dial. Even if I didn't say it out loud, at first, his immediate absence hurt.

I'll never understand people who can just get rid of someone like they didn't share years of their lives together. A few months after, I had come to terms with him leaving. Now, I'm fine without him. Naturally, he's always had a knack for timing.

I don't respond to Dexter. In fact, I try to push him to the back of my mind as far as it will go, so I can be with Tripp—the one who deserves my attention. The one who makes me feel like I count, every time we're together.

"How does it feel to be undefeated, Mr. Owens?" I put a fake microphone in front of him and Wendy giggles.

"Pretty damn good," he jokes, grabbing my wrist, like I have a real mic and he needs it to be closer.

Instead of going out with the team, the three of us go out to dinner. Emilie set it up at one of my favorite restaurants, a place that specializes in small plates, that has a great track record of getting me in and out without much hassle. I know the press is inevitable, but I'll do what I can for Tripp and Wendy.

We arrive with no issue, probably since my security team has been changing up their vehicles. It's not a sustainable practice to do long-term but is doable for now.

It feels like we order the entire menu. Plus, our server brings out a few bonus chef plates. This is something that usually happens when I come in here and it's one of my favorite parts. I don't know how they do it, but they are always incredible. I don't think I've gotten a repeat yet either.

"I'm going to head home before I slip into a food coma at this table," Wendy says. She always has a driver on game days to get her home safe.

"Are we still on for lunch Thursday?" Wendy asks as she's hugging me goodbye.

"Absolutely. Wouldn't miss it." I can feel Tripp's eyes on me.

Tripp and Wendy say their goodbyes and Tripp slides into the booth seat next to me.

"Are you sure about going home tonight?" he says, running fingers on my tights, right under the hem of my skirt.

"I should. I have a label meeting in a few days and need to get some tracks squared away." His fingers keep drawing lazy lines.

Plus, I need to sort out this Dexter thing. I don't tell him that. Part of me feels guilty for keeping this from him. But I don't even know what *this* is. Who knows what Dexter wants?

Do I care? When the answer isn't immediately "no", a rush of guilt hits me.

"Fine. Responsibilities win this time. Are you ready?" Tripp asks, pulling my mind from Dexter.

I give him the one second gesture and take out a thank you note. He knows the drill. I leave the envelope on the table.

Tripp grabs me by the hand, and we go out the back way. Luckily, we don't meet a single paparazzi. Minus our drivers both waiting for us, it feels like we're a normal couple.

"Thanks for coming. And for wearing my jersey," Tripp whispers in my ear, nipping at my earlobe.

"Be good," I giggle.

"Only if you promise to wear that to bed." His voice is breathy and gravely low.

"As long as you're gentle. I'm particularly fond of this piece of clothing."

"Not sure if that's a promise I can keep," he jokes before kissing me goodbye.

I THOUGHT ABOUT WHAT Dexter could possibly want the whole way home, which bothers me. I don't want him to take up space. I pull out my phone to see his most recent text messages.

Dexter

Will. Come on. Call me.

Emilie is gone this weekend since she had some friends in town. Tripp gave her tickets for the game, outside of the suite, and she's staying in the city tonight. I'm out on the patio, lighting the outdoor fireplace, when my phone rings.

Dexter.

I roll my eyes even though there's no one around to notice it. I grab a blanket and put it in my lap before I answer.

"Hello," I say, like I don't know it's him calling.

"Will. I've been trying to get a hold of you." For a fleeting second, his voice feels like a warm blanket, like the one I just grabbed.

"I saw."

"Too busy at the game?"

He couldn't even get thirty seconds in before bringing up Tripp. The feeling of nostalgia is quickly washed away.

"I *was* busy," I scoff and look at my nails. "I just got home. I'm also not sure if I want to talk to you. Why don't you tell me what you need so we can get this over with?" The blanket is no longer soft on my skin, but itchy. Irritating.

"I have to have a reason to want to talk to you?"

Is he kidding?

"Well, that's what your first text said. We needed to talk. And yes, kind of. We've not been in contact for months. I don't think it's a coincidence you're trying to get a hold of me *now*."

"Fine. That's fair…" His voice drops off. I stay quiet. I wasn't the one who called him. "I just have been thinking a lot the last few weeks."

"I'm sure that has nothing to do with Tripp."

"When did you guys start dating?" he asks. Heat floods my face, and my lips press together, hard.

"Why does that matter?" My voice is flat, and I think I know where he's going, but I'm going to make him say it.

"Well, he did that whole thing the night of the Super Bowl. It made me wonder, is all."

There it is.

"Dexter. *You* left me. *You* were the one who decided I wasn't worth keeping. And if you're asking if anything was going on when we were together, I'm disappointed. Thought you knew me better than that."

"I don't know! I think I fucked this up. I shouldn't have left. I want to do this right. You and me, how it was always supposed to be."

Wow. I shake my head in amazement. The audacity of this man.

"It's a little late for that, Dexter. Don't you think?"

"It's late but not too late. Come on, part of you must've wondered about this."

I laugh. That's the only reaction I have for him that isn't telling him to fuck off.

"Have you lost your mind? You call me out of nowhere and insinuate getting back together? Knowing I'm seeing someone else."

"Let me swing by the apartment. We can talk it out face to face."

"No. Do not come to the apartment." I do not tell him I'm somewhere else. I'll let him think I'm still there. "You're not quite grasping how inappropriate this is. I thought you were better than that."

"I'm not. When it comes to you, I'm not."

"Dexter. Stop. It's been months. You've got something built up in your head that isn't close to reality."

"What, are you going to tell me you're actually serious with a football player?" His voice is sharp, and I know he means it as a dig. He's always been good at putting his hooks where it hurts.

"Good to know you still pack a punch. And yes, I'm telling you that."

"I don't buy it," he says with a sigh.

"You don't have to. This isn't about you."

"He just doesn't seem like a good fit for you and your—"

"Let me stop you there. *You* weren't a good fit. You made me run into and out of restaurants. We took umbrellas when we went for walks in public just so people couldn't take our picture. We never went out." The words are practically falling out of my mouth. "Tripp loves being with me in public and private."

"It wasn't that—"

"Then why don't you tell me what it was," I interrupt.

"Do you know what it's like? Your success, it just, it made me realize how much I didn't have or didn't accomplish. It shouldn't bother me but it did, but I promise, I know how to be better, and—"

"You petulant child." I take a deep breath, putting my head in my hands.

"What? At least I'm being honest!" He pleads but even now, he doesn't get it.

"Do you want me to give you a gold medal for basically telling me, post breakup, not hearing from you for months, and during a three-year relationship, you essentially were too jealous? You couldn't be happy for me?"

"Let's talk about it now. Get it out in the open," He suggests.

"No. I'm not doing this right now. There is nothing to dissect. I'm with Tripp. I'm happy. And I'm begging you to leave it alone. He's different."

"How is he different?" he asks. I know there's one thing I can tell him that will make it click. Even though I don't want to give him anything else, any more of time or effort, but I want him to hear me.

"I played him rough cuts for my new album. He's the only one who's heard parts of it."

At first, the line is silent. I move the phone from my ear to see we're still connected. He lets out a sigh.

"Of course, you did." I know he's upset by the way his voice goes up at the end. I can hear him pacing back and forth, wherever he is.

"I hope you find someone who can make you happy. I'm not that person."

"You don't know that, Will—"

"Bye, Dexter."

Finally, I know the truth. Dexter was looking for someone he was bigger than, someone who would shine for him.

It was never me.

YOUR PLAY TO CALL

It was never me.

# Chapter 39
## Tripp

WE'VE LOST OUR THIRD game in a row. Easy come, easy go. The Upstate Cosmos are now 5-3 and dropped to third in our division. There's still lots of time before the playoff picture, but no one wants to lose like that.

It's worse when the games are close, like the last two losses. Sometimes, your opponent has everything clicking and going their way. We had some questionable calls against us, but that's part of the game.

The thing I can't stop thinking about is my dropped pass from today. I bobbled what would've been a touchdown in the end-zone. Not only a touchdown, but a winning touchdown. Fuck. That one stung.

Luckily, this game was against the other New York team. While it's technically an away game, we're taking our team charter bus, instead of a plane, back to our facility.

Willow watched the game at my mom's place. When Wendy doesn't travel, she hosts.

My heart squeezes thinking of Willow. When I'm not with her, I miss her. Even though she's meeting me at my place shortly, it's never soon enough.

We may be on a losing streak but things with Willow are fucking incredible. She has clothes at my place, stuff in my bathroom, and a carafe of peppermint tea in the fridge.

Schedules are tough but we do what we can to see each other. Even if it's for just a few minutes before one of us is falling asleep while the other is talking. Sometimes, I just like occupying the same space as her.

We're asking her parents to come to the city for Thanksgiving. No matter how shitty of a day I'm having, I can think to one of my favorite holidays, and what it will be like this year, to put me in a better mood. The thought of Willow and I hosting a holiday together... my god. My mom is thrilled to meet her parents and also probably to have a holiday where it's not just the two of us.

I walk into my apartment and see fresh flowers on the counter.

"Mr. MVP," Willow says while walking towards me in the doorway. She wraps me in a tight hug.

I've always been a competitor. It sucks to lose, but this is the first time I've had someone to come home to. Instead of throwing myself into solo film review or a rogue gym session, I have someone instead of something. I never considered having someone, not like this. The thought is startling but in a good way.

"Sorry about the game," she says into my chest.

"It's okay. Part of the gig."

"You'll get 'em next time." She claps me on the shoulder like she's one of the guys.

"Right," I say before kissing her forehead.

"Are you sure you still want to go out for dinner?"

"Absolutely. I'm starving and would love a distraction." I take my arms and run them down her back until I reach her ass.

"I've been known to be a good distraction," she says, kissing me.

SETH DROVE US TO dinner which gave me time to decompress and sit with Willow in the back seat. Before Willow, I'd be in such a sour mood, and wouldn't be able to do anything after a loss like that. I'm not thrilled about it, but there's other things to focus on. I'm focusing on being grateful.

"Ugh. This isn't ideal," Seth says from the front when he's stopped at what I'm guessing is the side entrance. "It seems like word has spread."

Restaurant staff are trying to get the press to step back from the building.

"What do you want to do, baby?" I ask Lo.

"I mean, the media isn't inside. Let's not let it ruin our plans."

"You got it."

Seth puts the car in park and walks over to my door. He opens it for me, I come out, and then reach for Willow's hand. She steps out wearing a forest green top paired with a black pleated skirt, and a black leather jacket. I've never paid much attention to fashion trends or clothes, but she always seems so effortlessly cool.

When she's out, I quickly kiss her temple and whisper, "Babe, you look so cool," I joke—my go-to compliment when I love her outfit.

There are lots of cameras and what I would call standard yelling. No one is screaming anything super inappropriate. To be honest, there's a lot of people asking about the loss today, which I'll take over screaming about Willow.

When we get inside, the manager is already apologizing up and down. They have no idea how it leaked that we were coming.

"Hey, it's no problem. I appreciate your staff out there trying to corral the herd." I laugh trying to get this poor man to relax.

"It really isn't a problem," Willow chimes in. "Let me know if my security team gets to be annoying. Seth is awfully stubborn."

"Follow me and let's get you to your table."

The restaurant insisted on a bottle of wine for the table. I don't typically drink during the season, peak muscle recovery and all that, but red wine sounds like a necessity at this point.

"We'll take your recommendation for a Cabernet Sauvignon," I say, knowing this is also one of Lo's favorite wine. "Two glasses."

"Oooh, what's the special occasion Mr. Owens," she jokes.

"Dinner with you is always a special occasion." I reach over and hold her hands on top of the table.

I used to see people do this and I'd make so much fun of them. Like, is it necessary, the touching in public? Now, I get it. The want to touch someone, constantly. Be as close as possible.

"Tell me about your meeting with the label. What's the latest?"

"Latest is they want me to finish at least three more songs by Wednesday. That way, we can start recording in the fancy studio. They're also trying to get me to sign a new contract." She rubs the top of my knuckles with her thumbs.

"Trying?"

"As long as they do what they promised, I'm happy to sign an extension for a few more years, but there's a few things I need to be sure of. Like the tour dates, cities, venues. Ticket prices. Basically, the things they pushed on me before letting me take this album in a different direction."

"That's smart. Are you excited to start planning a tour?" I feel like if I was an artist, this would be one of my favorite parts.

"I am. Mostly because it's going to be so different." She beams as she talks about her new album. It's contagious.

○○○

WE'RE INTO OUR SECOND bottle of wine and waiting for dessert. The wine is giving us a pleasantly heavy buzz. Willow's cheeks are flushed from the wine and my own hurt from smiling. Tonight was just what I needed.

There were even a few of her fans that came up before any food was at our table. If there's something I love, it's watching this woman interact with people who adore her as an artist.  She's always so kind and willing to sign anything, take photos. They're all respectful and it's fucking amazing to see.

I pour more wine in our glasses.

"I have a question for you," she giggles with her pink cheeks. "Do you hate when people scream 'Don't Tripp' when you have the ball?'"

"No, I don't hate it. I've heard it ever since I was in high school. Opposing teams used to make shirts and wear them to my high school games. I mean, it's a great pun."

She is cracking up which makes me do the same.

And then Willow's face shifts. She sits straight up, scrunching her forehead and squinting her eyes before they're as big as the plates waiting for our dessert.

"What's wrong?" I ask her.

She sighs in annoyance. And before I can try to see what she's looking at; someone stops at our table.

"Dexter, what are you doing here?" she asks through gritted teeth.

# Chapter 40
## Willow

Dexter.

Is standing at our table.

I thought my brain was playing tricks, or I had too much wine, because there's no way he could be here, right?

Tripp looks from me to him and back to me.

"Hate to barge in like this, but can we talk?" Dexter asks, more confident than he should be allowed.

My jaw drops.

"Absolutely not. What are you even doing here?" I shake my head from side to side and cross my arms. I don't even want to turn to face him.

"Will. Come on."

"Don't. Call. Me. That."

"I don't think we've been introduced. I'm Tripp. Guessing you're Dexter?" Tripp stands up from the booth and puts his hand out for a handshake—one this man doesn't deserve.

Dexter doesn't even pay attention to Tripp. He just stares at me. My skin crawls.

"How did you even know I was here?" I say through gritted teeth. Tripp is beside himself that Dexter wouldn't shake his hand.

"I, ugh, saw it. Online. Thought I'd take a chance and see if it was true." He rubs his hands on his pants.

"You've got to be fucking kidding me," I say, and Tripp's face says it all.

"It's time for you to go," Tripp says, stepping closer to Dexter. His voice is still quiet. I know he's trying to not cause a scene.

"I can't believe you. What do you want from me? Haven't you taken enough?"

"You won't answer my phone calls. I don't think you're staying at the apartment. What else am I supposed to do?"

"Not this. You're certainly not supposed to do this." I wish he'd leave. The balls on this man to come in here and do this, not shake Tripp's hand, and continue to ask me questions. I don't owe him anything.

"I told you, I thought we'd end up together. Ever since we talked a few weeks back, I just want to clear some things up." Dexter's voice sounds whiny and annoying to my ears.

Tripp doesn't know that I'd talked to Dexter. I didn't think it was even worth bringing up. I can see a flash of confusion on Tripp's face.

This is unreal. Tripp puts his hand on Dexter's shoulder, trying to turn him.

"Don't touch me," Dexter says, putting his finger in Tripp's face.

"Then get the fuck out of here. You weren't invited and she wants you to leave," Tripp says.

"Dexter. I can't believe you think this is okay. It's not. You followed a sleazy internet tip to ambush me. I'll tell you again, just like I told you during our very brief phone call, leave me alone. Don't call me. Don't text me. Don't come by my apartment or anywhere else you'll think I'll be."

He runs his hands through his hair. It seems like he thought this would go a different way.

"I can't believe this is it. It's just... I..." he tries to keep going. His eyes are glassy. I know he's about to cry.

For a moment, the anger subsides and all I feel is pity. Dexter isn't dangerous and he's not a stalker. He seems lost.

The manager approaches the table, knowing something isn't quite right.

"Is everything okay here?" he asks.

"Yup. Dexter was just leaving." Tripp claps a heavy hand on Dexter's shoulder.

"Willow. I still love you," he says in the tiniest voice.

"No, you don't. You think you love me, but you don't." A flash of understanding shows on his face. What I'm saying is resonating. "And Dexter, even if you did? You don't do this to people you love."

Dexter nods and slowly turns. When he's about to walk out of the building, Seth is there to greet him. I'm sure they'll have a nice chat.

"So, that's Dexter," Tripp says as he sits back down.

I wipe a tear from each of my eyes. My brain tries to process what just happened while every inch of my skin is flushed. I shiver with rage and embarrassment. I can't believe he showed up here like that. For someone who did everything he could not to be seen in public with me, he sure knows how to flip the script and make a scene.

"I feel like I know the answer but are you okay?" he asks.

"I just don't get it. He's harmless but this wasn't okay. Who does something like this?"

"Someone who is only worried about themselves."

"And I didn't tell you that he called me because there was nothing to say. I told him I was happy with you and that he should leave me alone—"

"Willow. Take a breath. I'm not mad at you because some dickbag ex has no boundaries."

I take his advice, breathing slowly in and out, and look across the table at Tripp.

"Okay. Thank you for being... you."

"Let's get out of here. We'll take the dessert to go and chill out at home."

I like the way he says home.

We gather our things, pretend people aren't staring at us as we do so and go to the exit, which is just as chaotic as when we arrived. Seth waits for us at the door.

"We're right there." He points to the car that's maybe a fifteen second walk away. Members of Tripp's security are strategically placed along the path.

Getting past the press isn't bad. They seem to be your standard, trying to get a thousand pictures, but not really going the extra mile to yell anything or cause a reaction. After we get through the mass of cameras and bodies, I relax. I just want to get back to the apartment and hide under a mound of blankets.

But there's another group of people coming our way.

"Tripp! Tripp Owens! Nice game today." Their words slur and they're wearing the opposing team jerseys.

"Today is awesome," Seth says. There's a little security glimmer in his eye because this man lives for the job. He's had more than enough run-ins today.

"Hey! ASSHOLE. Great catch today! Gonna start calling you butterfingers," one of them yells to us still kind of making their way towards us. They're right by our car.

*Great.*

"I aim to please," Tripp says and waves at them.

Seth puts his hand out for us to stop. The guys are still in front of the car.

"You got your digs in, very funny, now we need you to move along," Seth says, trying to get them to go anywhere else.

"Free country. Free street." These guys are hammered.

Tripp's security starts coming our way and the press follows. They may not have anything to do with this reaction, but they will capitalize on this situation.

The mass of people we just got through are behind me, starting to crowd on the sides. I'm not scared but it's more annoying than anything. Exhaustion falls on me like a too-heavy blanket. I just want to be home.

One of Tripp's guys comes and puts his hand on my back, letting me know he's nearby. Tripp is still holding my hand but putting his neck out, trying to see what's going on with Seth and the rowdy group of fans.

"I'm going to go help out."

"I don't think that's a good idea," I say.

"They're a bunch of drunk football fans. Maybe if I give them some attention they'll get their fill and get the fuck out of here."

"I don't know, Tripp."

"Stay here, Lo. I'll be right back."

Tripp picks my hand up and kisses it, before making eye contact with his security detail, who nods in understanding. He walks up to the guys; Seth puts his arm out stopping Tripp before he gets too close.

I can't hear what they're saying but that means no one is screaming which is a great sign at this point. Until one of them yells, "Tripp Owens is a little bitch!" And the rest of the group cackles. The press is trying to inch closer and closer.

Seth has gotten one of the Suburban doors open and the group has shifted enough for us to get in. Tripp turns to come back to get me.

And that's when one of the guys sucker punches Tripp, hitting him in the back of the head.

# **Chapter 41**
## Tripp

*WHAT THE FUCK WAS that*? I stumble a step forward, mostly because I was surprised. And then it clicks: one of these idiots hit me. Since they were drunk, and probably not very coordinated to begin with, they barely made contact.

I look up to see Willow with her hand over her mouth, eyes wide.

In a short second, things get worse. The security guards lose focus for a minute and take a few steps towards me.

And that's all it takes.

The crowd of press surrounding Willow rushes forward, trying to get pictures of my security detail, pinning the man who threw the punch on the sidewalk. When security took those few steps, they gave the press too much space, and they dash forward. They push her to the concrete. She catches herself with her hands.

"Lo!" I yell as I push through every person who stands in my way. I don't give a fuck who is taking what picture, I'm shoving people out of my way, and Seth is right behind me.

I reach Willow as she's pushing herself up, looking at her hands. I lean down to her level.

"Are you okay?!" I take her hands gently to see the damage. They look to be scraped, nothing more than that.

"No! I'm not okay. None of this is okay." Her eyes fill with tears as she is still on the ground.

I reach under her elbows and help her stand. Seth and I get her to the Suburban. Once she's inside, I slide next to her, and shut the door. Seth gets in the front seat, locks the doors, and looks back at us.

"Willow. Let me see your hands." She shows him. "Are you hurt? Do you want to get checked out? We can have someone come to the apartment."

Willow lightly touches her upper arms, flexes her elbows, and touches her knees.

"I'm not hurt."

"I'll take you back to the apartment. Tripp's team will take care of these guys."

"No," Willow says, her voice small. "I want to go home. To my place." She doesn't look at me.

"The press might recognize the car if we don't switch it," Seth explains.

"I don't care. I just want to go home," she says, defeated, slumping back in the seat.

"Do you want me to come with you?" I ask.

She takes a deep breath, still examining her hands.

"No. I want to be by myself. Today was too much." Tears fall down her cheeks.

"Okay, Okay. I get it."

Seth starts driving. It doesn't matter where we're going but staying here isn't an option.

"Why didn't you listen to me?" Her voice is firm but also pleading. "Engaging with those guys was not a good idea. We could've just gotten in the car and been on our way to your apartment."

"I just thought—" I try to explain.

"I don't think you thought much at all." She looks at me before staring at the floor of the car. "I know this might be new to you, this level of being known and seen. It isn't new for me."

I'm speechless. There are no words in my brain.

"You say you do things on a whim, but you can't do that with me. Not like that." Her voice is cold and shaky. "I already told you how much I hate things like what just happened. Actually, tonight is one of my greatest fears come to life." Each tear that rolls punches me in the stomach.

"I'm sorry." It's the only thing I can think of to say. She's right. I look over to see silent tears fall down her cheeks.

"I don't want you to be sorry. I want you to think before you do things. You can act however you want when it's just you. Go ahead and get in fist fights with random strangers on the street. Please don't be reckless with me." She's looking out the window now. Like she can't even stomach looking at me.

I don't respond because I don't know what to say. We ride in silence. When Seth gets me close enough to my apartment and I'm convinced no one is close enough to be a threat, I say, "Seth. This is close enough."

He finds a good stopping point and I open the door, getting out of the car. I look at Willow one final time.

"Will you text me when you get home?" I ask her.

She nods yes. I lean in and give her a featherlight kiss on her cheek. She doesn't turn away, which I think is a good sign.

"Seth, I'll have my team get me back to my place. That way you can get Willow home," I say, as I reach for the door.

"Sounds good, Mr. Owens."

I get out of the car. I try to look at Willow before I close the door, but she won't look at me.

There's a pit in my stomach as they drive off.

I'M BACK AT MY apartment for only thirty minutes before there's a knock at my door.

"Tripp. Let me in," my mom says from the other side of the door.

I open the door and she hugs me the second she's inside.

"Tell me everything."

So, I do. I tell her about Dexter. About everything with the press. How Willow wanted to go home, and I wasn't invited.

"Is that everything?" she asks, eyebrows raised.

"Yes, I think so."

And then she pushes me in the chest before launching into a rant.

"Tripp James. You should be ashamed of yourself. You thought giving some drunk idiots what they wanted was better than staying with her? What were you thinking?"

"I don't know! I thought if I gave them some attention it would end the interaction. My brain was all fucking jumbled from Dexter showing up." I put my head in my hands and try to think.

"You think she was safer *without* you? She'll never be safer than with you. You also wouldn't have gotten punched."

"I barely got punched," I point out.

My mom puts her hands in her lap and leans back into the couch. "You know what I'm talking about. Don't get smart with me," she says in her perfect mom voice, one I've heard countless times before.

"You'll never be able to get rid of the press. They will always be around with their annoying and terrible timing. What you can do is stand by Willow and make her a priority."

The words hurt because she's right. What was I trying to prove? The flash of Willow on the ground comes back and I feel fucking horrible. It was a fluke thing, but I could've done something. I could've caught her.

"You can also listen to what she says. She's giving you the playbook and you're going rogue." I know she uses football terminology because she's trying to soften the blow. It still hurts.

"I'm scared I fucked this up, Mom."

"One, language. Two, she needs time. Give her tonight, like she asked. You need to think about this and be ready to explain yourself tomorrow."

"And then there's this whole Dexter thing. He said they talked, and she never brought it up."

It stings that she didn't bring it up even though I said it wasn't a big deal. It wasn't, but then all of this happened, and I'm in my apartment stuck with my thoughts.

There's no way it was nothing. It was enough for him to show up like he did tonight. Before my thoughts run away without me, my mom interrupts.

"Who knows. You'll have to ask Willow. Also, he sounds like a giant tool."

I let out a small laugh because hearing my mom call someone a tool is not like her at all but she's not wrong.

"Where did you hear that term?" I can't help but give her a little smile.

"I listen to podcasts." She shrugs her shoulders. "You seem better with Willow—less anxious."

She's right. Willow has made a difference. And tonight, I did nothing but make her life more difficult.

"I think there's time to fix this. Not tonight, but tomorrow. And the day after. And the day after that. It's not about being perfect every day but working through things when you fall short."

Falling short. That's me.

# Chapter 42
## Willow

AFTER I TEXT TRIPP to let him know I'm home, I turn my phone off. I open the door to see Emilie sitting in the kitchen, a box in front of her.

"What are you doing here?"

"Well, I saw Dexter showed up to your dinner. Tripp also texted me, telling me you might need a friend."

"You have friends in town..."

"We had a full weekend, even without me staying there tonight. Believe me, you're sort of doing me a favor. Had my fill." She winks at me.

I have no words. From Emilie cutting her weekend short to Tripp telling her I might need someone. I walk to her, and she hugs me. She rubs my back, and we stay like this for a minute.

"I brought cookies. The ones you like with the stupid thick buttercream. Do you want to get cozy on the patio?"

"Sounds perfect."

AFTER HASHING EVERYTHING OUT, from Dexter showing up, to the paparazzi nightmare, we've each eaten almost the entire box of cookies.

"Were you scared?" Emilie asks, her voice gentle.

"For a few seconds. I thought I was going to get swallowed by the crowd. Like everyone would forget I was there, and I'd get trampled or something. It was nowhere near that dramatic, but that's what it felt like. For a blip, at least." I can be honest with Emilie, and she won't judge.

"I would've been scared. People are wild cards." Emilie sums up my fear in a few short words.

"Fitting end to the Dexter date crash, to be honest."

"Dexter. Woof. That is so cringe," she says, fake-covering her eyes in embarrassment.

"Cringe is one way to put it. I was so angry. My blood felt like it was boiling. It's one thing to infringe on my personal space but Tripp and I were having such a good night. He ruined it."

"But...?" Emilie baits me.

"I also feel kind of bad for Dexter. He seems to be having a hard time. It's not like I want to fix it or be friends or anything. It's just another complicated emotion layered on top of everything else."

Emilie mulls that over and nods in understanding.

"Men like Dexter are why we can't have nice things." She bites off a piece of cookie. "Are we mad at Tripp?"

"I'm mad. Disappointed. Sad. I don't understand why he can't pause for a second. This isn't the first time he's gotten into it when we've been out."

"But if we're keeping score, he didn't punch Dexter in the face, even though he probably wanted to."

"We shouldn't keep score, but you're right. He didn't."

"Lo, feel all the feelings. There's no right way to feel, whatever you're feeling is valid," she says with such conviction. "The thing you have to remember is they won't last forever."

"You are too wise for your age. Honestly," I say while I wrap a blanket around my shoulders.

"Long time therapy-goer, like my whole life." She puts her hand up like she's proud to be in the club. "Here's the thing, Tripp has never had to deal with the press like you. He's probably had other times, just like tonight, when his tactic worked."

"Yeah. Maybe."

"That man might be as thoughtful as they come. His intentions were probably good. That doesn't mean they were right."

"Damn you, Emilie. That's so good." I sigh. "I'm glad I gave myself the space without Tripp tonight. With Dexter, I always put myself second, did whatever I thought was best for him. That never worked out because turns out, we were both putting me second."

"Space isn't bad either. Seems like everyone needed some time to reflect. I'm sure you guys will talk tomorrow. Switching gears, what are you going to do about Dexter?"

"I hope I don't have to do anything. I don't think he'll try to contact me again."

"I can't believe he told you he still loved you. Bold."

"I honestly don't think he does. It's the whole him seeing me with someone else. I hadn't heard from him until pictures and news about Tripp and me started making their rounds. He wants to put his hooks in me, think there's something there, but I know there isn't. When we first broke up, this would've worked, which scares me."

"Scares you?"

"I just would've bought it. It feels like I've not been with someone who has been good for me. Until now. Tripp is thoughtful, hardworking, and he looks at me in this way which makes me feel like I'm worth it. He gives and doesn't only take. The man has put everything into perspective for me. Maybe that's another reason I'm being so hard on him about tonight." The realization lifts a piece of the weight from my chest.

"I really like Tripp. He's not at all what I expected. In a good way," she says.

"I don't know what I expected but it's better."

"If Tripp has some single friends on the team who are like him, I'd be interested," she says, laughing at the end.

THE NEXT MORNING, I decide to do yoga by the pool before my morning swim. The pool is heated, and the air is chilly: a stellar combination. Plus, I love the feeling of an October morning.

When I'm dried off, I go inside to have breakfast with Emilie. She's making pancakes and dirty chai lattes. The spicy smell of the tea pairs perfectly with the buttery smell of the batter.

"It's early and so much has already happened," Emilie says, handing her phone to me.

It's a Google search for "Dexter Stone" and it has the most recent headlines:

***The Girl Is Mine! Tripp and Dexter Face Off for Willow***

***Dexter Stone crashes Willow's Date- He's Not Over Her!***

***Bye, Bye Dexter!*** is my favorite because it's accompanied with a photo of Seth leading him out of the restaurant.

"Again, this man has been in the press more since our breakup than our years together." I roll my eyes and hand back the phone.

She points. "Those were delivered this morning."

There's a bouquet of yellow peonies on the counter. Flowers that weren't there when I went out to the patio an hour ago. Flowers so bright it's hard not to smile when you see them.

"Who are those from?" I ask.

She gives me a side-eye look. "You know who they're from. There's a card."

I reach into the flowers and pull out what is a folded piece of paper. A note from Tripp.

*Lo – I'm sorry about yesterday. I know we need to talk about it, but I want to give you time. Let me know when you're ready.*

*If you're interested, I do have a possible adventure for us. Next week is a bye week which means I'll have a free weekend. Think about it and let me know.*

*xx- Tripp*

Me

the flowers are gorgeous. Thank you.

also got your note. I'd like to take the day to decompress. Turn my phone off, work on some music, and try to miss out on the barrage of headlines surely floating around already.

Let's chat tomorrow. I can come to your apartment after practice, if that's okay.

Tripp

That's more than okay. See you tomorrow.

# Chapter 43
## Tripp

Practice is going to be a fucking bummer. I know we're going to get our asses beat into the ground, and maybe we need it, considering we're on a losing streak.

We have an away game this week. I dread every single one. Statistically, this is where I'm most likely to have a panic attack. Even the thought of it brings a wave of anxiety.

The guys keep giving me shit about everything on Sunday. Of course, there were pictures of Dexter ambushing our dinner, plus the whole fan fiasco. It's team shit, and we do the same thing to the other guys when things like this happen to them.

I had to come in early to meet with the team doctors, which caught wind of the "punch". I had to be cleared to practice which was truly laughable. Even though the guy barely touched me, the pictures and videos looked worse.

After I was medically cleared, I was lucky enough to be handed off to coach, our offensive coordinator, and members from the PR team.

The meeting was short as was the message: *Don't interact with drunk fans. If something does happen, get a hold of someone who can do damage control for the team. Would you like to do a quick round of media training?*

Plus, there was the message they conveyed without coming outright and saying it: *Are you going to be a liability moving forward?*

My head coach couldn't eye roll hard enough throughout the meeting.

"Okay, Tripp is a bad boy for talking to those idiots, his brain is safe and cleared to practice, and he will not do this again. If he wants to do the media training, he knows where to find you. Can we get him to practice? The thing we pay him for?" he asks while standing up.

The meeting is over, and I've never been more thankful for this man.

We walk out of the room together.

Coach gives me a small smile and claps my back, "Looks like you had a rough Sunday. For what it's worth, I probably would've done the same thing,"

His confession makes me feel a little better.

"But I also was nowhere near your caliber when it came to talent. You're a key piece of the team. I'm betting on you not to screw this up."

"Yes, coach." There really isn't anything else to say—it's almost like talking to a disappointed parent.

"I also know this is the first time something like this has happened. You're not known for causing problems. That's why I ended the meeting. There are probably ten other guys on the team who could use a talking to. I'll see you out there." Coach keeps walking out to the field where my team is practicing.

I'm in the locker-room, and I need a minute. I knew what I did was stupid but never really thought about it affecting my job. Or my health. Hell, that guy could've gotten a real punch in and I could be on the injury report.

I sit down in front of my locker. My name and number are on the top. I love this sport. I love that I'm thirty, almost thirty-one, and still playing at a high level. It's such a key part of me. Who I am. What I've accomplished.

There will be a time where there is no locker, no mom in a suite watching me play, no team meetings, no practice, no team dinners. I swallow the lump in my throat and press my lips together.

I breathe deeply through the anxiety surge. My chest expands in short bursts as I try to get the breathing under control. My fingers tingle as I put my head between my knees and try to catch my breath. I stay like this until the breathing calms the waves.

Today, I'm still playing football.

I PRACTICALLY JOG INTO my apartment, knowing Willow is waiting for me.

I wrap her in a hug, not saying anything. I could give her space, but I don't want to. When she doesn't pull away, a piece of my anxiety falls away.

"How's your head? I saw something about you being medically cleared to play." She looks at me and touches a soft hand to the side of my head.

"I'm one hundred percent fine. I can barely feel where he tried to punch me. Mostly missed." My chest warms at the thought of her being worried about me.

We sit on the couch.

"Can I go first?" I rub my fingers together. She nods in agreement. "This all is new to me. Not just you and me, but the team, and people knowing who I am. I'm not used to situations like Sunday. That isn't an excuse because I know I have to fucking do better. I'm sorry. I want to be better. And above all, I want you to feel safe with me. I didn't make you feel safe and that's what I'm most sorry about."

Willow reaches over for my hand. She squeezes it.

"Thank you. And I do feel safe with you. I've never been able to let my guard down like I can when we're together. Sunday was a lot. And not just because of you." She takes in a slow, deep breath. "I'm sorry for not telling you Dexter called. For keeping it a secret when it didn't need to be. I truly thought it was not even worth mentioning. Thought it would be more stressful bringing it up. I didn't want to be too much."

"It was a surprise, but I hope you know I'll always keep your secrets. And, let me tell you when something is too much."

"I trust you. I know you can. Dexter is ... a mess."

"Gathered that when he stood at the end of our table at dinner." I joke, trying to lighten the mood.

She rubs her thumbs over my knuckles. "He called to tell me he thought we should get back together. That he thought we'd end up together. I told him he was wrong. That I was happy with you. And you're unlike anyone I've ever been with."

My fucking heart. It's racing, warming my chest, and it feels like it could explode.

"With other guys, I always had to bargain pieces of myself. You don't ask me to do that. It's a cliché, but I feel like myself when I'm with you.

"Tell me all the cliché's."

"I think Dexter panicked when he started seeing photos of us together. We were never a good fit. I settled for him when we started dating and for every year after. One day, he'll realize that too."

"Look, I get it. He's jealous. Maybe having a bit of a what the fuck did I do? The thing I want you to know is you can tell me anything. I'll do my best to listen without judgment and just be here for you. I'm not jealous of Dexter."

"You're a good man, Tripp Owens."

"I don't know about that, but I definitely want to be better for you."

"I need you to hear me, really listen to this next part," she puts a hand on her chest. "I can handle you being impulsive for many things, but not when it comes to my safety, or yours, especially in public."

"I know," I interrupt, and she quickly tilts her head. I don't think she liked that, so I cover my mouth to show her I'm ready to listen.

"You say that, but your actions need to match. Trust is important. I want to be able to trust you, with all I have, and vice versa." She stops.

I wait a few long seconds, making sure she's said everything she wanted to. "I know I let you down. I want to be a person you can trust, with no second guessing."

She leans in and kisses me. It's sweet and slow.

"And I do trust you. That night I called you, when I was having a panic attack, it was all about thinking about what comes after football. This isn't something I talk about, unless you're my therapist, but you're the first person I've told." I nervously crack my knuckles. "Football is all I've had for most of my life. I'd be a liar if I said I'm not concerned about that time coming to an end, but my brain has shifted. I think about having more time to do things with you. Taking trips. Going to dinner, hopefully without Dexter. Random coffee dates. Seeing movies during the week. You make the thought of life after this bearable."

She crawls into my lap and melts into me. I pull her against me and hold on.

"Tell me about this potential adventure," she almost whispers into my ear.

"How about a little road trip? To my hometown. They do this fall carnival every year, and it's next weekend. Lined up perfectly with the bye week. Take a break from the city and the press and mentions of Dexter and drunk fans."

"A fall carnival? That sounds so fun. What do you mean take a break from the press?"

"Can you keep one of my secrets?"

She nods excitedly.

"Besides the people in my hometown, there are only a handful who know where it is. The real one. I transferred to a different school when I was a junior in high school, to try and get more visibility for football scouts. But that isn't my hometown... it's just what everyone thinks it is."

Anticipation fills me when I think about taking her to my real hometown.

"How has this never come out?"

"Mostly because I don't think many people care. Also, my town knows how to keep a secret."

"That is... amazing. I'm in. A break sounds perfect. Plus, a whole weekend with you." She plants a trail of kisses from the top of my neck to my collarbone.

# Chapter 44
## Willow

"You're doing it!" Wendy cheers as I do what is barely considered sewing. It's a pattern with my first initial and a small heart.

She claps her hands in excitement, smiling wide, and I would do anything she asked me to if I knew she'd give me this reaction every time. We were out to lunch today when she had to leave to make it to her sewing club—which is different than her knitting club—she asked if I wanted to go and there was no way I could say no.

Here's the thing, I know nothing about sewing. I didn't dabble with any of this when I was younger. Wendy is the best cheerleader. She even clapped when I finished my first "W" pattern, even though it looked nothing like the actual letter.

Using my hands, the delicate manner of the needle, it's refreshing. I tend to put the pattern and needle five inches in front of my face, paired with a mean scowl. I'm just trying to focus. I want to get it right.

Wendy's sewing club is only a handful of women. They were not expecting me to join them, but they welcomed me with open arms. I'm pretty sure Wendy promised a photo at the end if they were all on their best behavior.

I finish my fourth W, and it finally looks like a letter. My hands are starting to cramp, so I set down my embroidery loop to take a break.

I pour a glass of lemonade and sit back in my chair as the women around me continue their conversations—a pleasant distraction.

To be honest, I almost bailed on today's lunch. I didn't want to get into what happened with Dexter and Tripp. Or the press. Or anything. I'm exhausted thinking about it. My PR team has been working overtime on trying to keep ahead of the false headlines but it's no use.

I needed a break.

Wendy is a lovely human because as soon as she saw me, she wrapped me in a hug and whispered in my ear, "We're not going to talk about the dumb thing my son did or the dumber thing your ex-boyfriend did, unless you want to." My shoulders sagged in relief.

She knows Tripp isn't dumb, but his actions were.

I keep stacking these things together. The Champagne. Him asking me out. The new car. Confronting the press. The thing with the fans. By themselves, it might seem like spontaneity, but together, it's a definite pattern, which makes me nervous.

I'm falling for Tripp. Like, all the way down. He knows me. I love how he asks questions he really wants the answers to or is focusing on my details.

Typically, when I'm dating, I end up in this cycle of self-loathing. I have a streak of horrible body image days where I curse the gods for making my legs as big as they are. I wish my muscles away.

This is the adult and controlled version of what this behavior started as. But, thanks to years of therapy and building a positive relationship with food and exercise, it's much more contained.

I kind of forgot about this vicious cycle. It didn't really cross my mind to pick myself apart because Tripp acted like he's the lucky one. He makes me feel confident. Deserving. Like being with me is worthwhile. I know I shouldn't need someone else's validation on how my body looks, but he makes me feel like I'm the most beautiful person on the planet.

It's not like he's impulsive because he's wishy-washy about his feelings. Sometimes it could be the opposite. He cares so much that his judgement is clouded.

Quite the combination with someone as impetuous as Tripp.

Plus, he's had an iffy few days with his anxiety. It really takes a lot out of him to travel for away games. I think of him alone in the hotel room, having a panic attack, and my heart breaks. I hope he'll always call me if he needs me.

I'll never forget the night he called me. The way his voice sounded on the other line. How I was actually able to help him. How he needed me.

I pick the sewing back up and do a few more patches with my initial on them.

"Wow, those look so much better," Wendy says, looking at my most recent patches. Now I know how dismal my first few were.

"You're a good teacher. What do you do with patches like this?" I ask.

"Oh, you can sew them into any fabric really. Put them on a corner of a pillow, a blanket, a top."

Just like that, I have an idea.

Me

FJ – hey, I need your help with something…

Fritz (FJ) Cosmos

I'm listening

# Chapter 45
## Tripp

BEING TIRED BEFORE THE game kicks off is a bad sign. I couldn't sleep last night. Thankfully, I was anxious but didn't have any full-blown panic attacks. The only positive.

We're in California and I don't think I could ever live here. The traffic makes no sense. I don't know how anything the city offers could make up for the fucking traffic. I hate sitting in a car going nowhere.

Between the time zone and my overactive brain, I didn't get much quality sleep.

Today is going to suck.

"Earth to Tripp," Zack says, waving an arm at me in the locker room.

"Sorry, just beat."

"Well, get un-beat. We need you today!" Zack says, trying to get me hyped up.

"You need me every day," I shoot back.

"Exactly. Get it together." He claps his hand and reaches for his jersey and pulls it on over his pads.

I do the same thing just as Fritz comes up to me.

"Tripp, there's a hole in this one." He points to my jersey.

I look. There are no holes. Fritz seems a little jumpy. Definitely nervous.

"What are you talking about? This jersey is fine." I stand with my arms out, inspecting the front.

Fritz has a small pair of scissors and reaches for the bottom of the fabric and cuts it with one swift snip.

"What the fuck, Fritz? Have you lost it?" I ask and look down at the jersey that will certainly not get me through a game. The thing about a hole or a cut is that it will fray with a few tackles.

I'm too tired for this shit. If this is some prank, I'm not into it.

"Today isn't the day for this," I say to him as he hands me an envelope and a new jersey. It must have been on the chair behind him.

"You'll thank me later," he claps me on the back and immediately turns to leave the locker-room. I watch him leave in disbelief.

The card has a small T on the front. It looks like Willow's handwriting.

*Tripp --*
*Consider this jersey a special edition. Maybe put it on inside out.*
*Your eyes only.*
*Wish I was there with you today. This will have to do.*
*Xoxo – Willow*

What the fuck? I put the note in my locker and take off my current jersey. The one Fritz cut. I look around to see most of the guys are heading out to the field and anyone else isn't paying attention to me. I turn the new jersey inside out.

Oh my god. On the side of the jersey, is a small patch, a 'W' with a little heart connected to it. It's sewn into the side, so it will be touching my left ribcage when it's on. Like it's close to my heart.

Willow somehow got her hands on a jersey and pulled this off.

I rub my fingers over the hand-stitched 'W' and my heart feels like it could break out of my chest. I wipe a tear from my eyes because this is one of the nicest things anyone has ever done for me. Ever.

For the first time today, I'm excited to go out and play. The exhaustion that pressed on my bones feels lighter than it did a few minutes ago.

The quarterback reads the coverage, and I act like I've given up on the play. The defensive back bites which gives me the second I need to sprint, get open, and for my quarterback to drop a perfect pass, right in the end zone. It might be one of the easiest balls I catch all year.

A cameraman gets close to me and I use this as my shot.

I put my hand on my side, where the patch is, before touching my heart and making a "W" with my hands for the camera. I know I'll get shit for this later. People will say I'm whipped, unfocused, or embarrassing. And they'll be wrong.

I'm falling in love.

# **Chapter 46**
## Willow

CUE THE ANXIETY. I'M at a key planning meeting for the new album and tour. This is when the new music feels close and the reality of other people hearing it sets in.  Since this tour is going to be significantly different, I'm excited to get into the details.

"Will, you've been holding out!" Erik says, using the nickname Dexter used.

"I told you I'd bring in more music once I hit the twelve-track mark."

"No, not the music. Tripp! You're little miss Cosmo!"

"Jesus Christ," Claire mumbles under her breath.

"I'm sorry?" *Little Miss Cosmo?* I could throw up.

"Saw the clips of you in the suite!" I can't hold back my eye roll. "I'm kidding, I'm kidding. Unless you can get me a ticket for the next home game." He winks at me.

"Less talk about Willow's dating life and more about work." Claire literally snaps her fingers.

I badly want this meeting to go my way. Getting a couple tickets for the label wouldn't be a problem.

"I can get some tickets. But yes, let's get to it."

Someone passes out folders and a list of dates shows on the screen at the front of the room.

"What we're thinking is a tour that starts in August of next year. Sixty dates. They are color coordinated to indicate the venue size."

I read the key: Blue - ~5000. Pink - ~2500. Red - ~1000

I'm not surprised that I'm mostly seeing blue dates. There's also purple, but no key.

"What are the purple dates?"

"Well, those are stadium shows. I know you wanted to keep this small but when we looked at potential revenue, we need some of these to carry the tour."

"This isn't a stadium tour type of album."

"We thought you'd say that, and we think doing extended dates of the tour you just wrapped up would be a surprise. Fans would love it. Plus, it'd bring some hype to the new music," someone from Erik's team says.

There are so many things wrong with what they just said.

"We'll come back to that. Where are the ticket prices?" I ask while making eye contact with Claire. She is already looking for me, knowing this is on the verge of crashing and burning.

They put the ticket prices on the screen. While they're cheaper than the previous tour, it's not by much. One thing is for sure, it's not enough.

"First, why such a late start? I'm set to finish this album in a few weeks. We could announce it and start touring by March of next year. We don't need to wait until August."

"If we look at the ticket schedule for the last tour, it's not that far off."

"This tour is going to be on a much smaller scale. We should need almost no prep time. It's mostly confirming dates with the venues. I want to move it up."

I want to move it up because there's truly no need to wait. There's also a tiny thought of Tripp and his offseason in the back of my mind.

"Why March?" Erik asks like he knows the answer but doesn't want to say.

"Why not? Second, you can take those purple dates and cross them out. I don't want to do them. That tour is over. Done. It's been done for months."

"You won't consider doing any of those--?"

"No. I told you I wanted to do 1,000 capacity or less and since you did such a great job color coordinating, you'll realize there is barely any of those here." I flip back and forth between pages, feeling like I've been slapped in the face considering how little they took what I wanted into account.  This time, it's easier going for what I want, considering they did such a horrible job.

"Plus, those ticket prices are absurd. They need to be lower."

"Willow, you're not going to make any money. Especially if we attempt to find smaller venues."

"If finding the venues is the issue, leave that to Emilie." I look to my assistant as she awkwardly waves a hand. "I promise she'll have no issues finding cities and stops." I cross my arms across my chest.

"Let's cut to the chase. I'm disappointed in you, Ricky," Claire says while pointed at Erik. "Willow was clear as glass when she told you what she wanted. You're trying to give her 10% of what she asked and it's going to be a no. Quit with the bullshit."

"I told you. This tour isn't about money. I need you to respect this or I will hold this album for a different label. I'm not in a rush," I jump in on where Claire is taking the conversation.

"Why even tour?" Erik asks.

"To celebrate my new music. To play songs I love in front of fans who love me."

"We all sometimes need a change but you're wanting to completely change a proven formula. Is there any other reason you want to rush the tour? Do the ridiculously small cities?" He looks at me like I'm a child, not smart enough to make my own decisions.

"Because I want to," I say, each word deliberately slow. "We're done here. Everything here is a no, minus the dates in red. If you want Emilie to start finding other spots, let us know."

"Why don't we pick this up tomorrow? We can have lunch," Erik suggests.

"No. I'm busy. Going out of town. And there's not much else to discuss." I don't even take the folder Erik's team gave me. I know Emilie has hers and it's mostly trash anyways. I grab my peppermint tea and get to the door before turning back.

"Oh, and Erik? I'll make sure those tickets for the Cosmos home game get to you. I said I would, and I know the importance of follow-through."

Claire whistles in surprise. Emilie laughs and covers her mouth. I pretend like I'm not going to sweat about this comment all the way home.

MY BAGS ARE PACKED, and I'm waiting for Tripp to pick me up. No matter how horrendous the label meeting was, nothing is going to put a damper on my good mood.

Tripp's driving the two of us and my security details will follow in their own car. He's adamant security won't be necessary, but Seth is relentless. My security promised to stay out of the way unless it's needed.

There's a knock on the door, and I practically skip to let Tripp in. When he sees me, he picks me up and spins me around while giving me a kiss. Some moments with Tripp feel like I'm living inside a movie, one I'd pay to see again and again.

"Let's get this road trip started. I have the snacks covered. Also made a little treat bag for our security friends, including crossword puzzles, because they're going to be remarkably bored this weekend."

Weekend. A whole weekend. Me and Tripp. He grabs my bags, and we walk to the car.

"Where are we going?" Tripp has been secretive on where his hometown is.

"A little spot in Maine," he answers elusively but still with more information than he'd offered up until this point.

Maine. Wouldn't have guessed.

"How long is the drive?" I poke him for more details.

"Probably seven hours." He opens my door.

We're buckled in the Tesla, and Tripp hits something on the screen to get the navigation started.

"Are you ready?" he asks me, wearing a smile that makes his eyes shine.

"Born ready." I smirk back.

He meets his mouth to mine, surprising me with a quick kiss. He puts one hand on the nape of my neck, pulling me to him.

"I've never shown this to anyone. It's like telling your best friend a secret you've kept for years."

My chest warms at the sentiment. This man is ridiculously excited. Whenever I think about Tripp's lack of relationships, I'm surprised. Tripp is truly a romantic.

I wouldn't have it any other way.

# **Chapter 47**
## Tripp

*GOLDEN COVE, MAINE: WHERE Each Day Has the Chance to Glimmer.* The welcome sign is just as it was the last time. The wave of nostalgia hits me like a splash of cool water on a warm summer day—I haven't been back in years.

"Golden Cove? That doesn't even sound like a real place," Willow croons as she tries to take a picture of the welcome sign with her phone.

"Home sweet home." I earnestly put a hand on my chest.

"How many people live here?"

"Right around 5,000, last I checked."

We drive through town, and it takes me all the way back. It's the diner, where my mom and I had breakfast every Sunday, the only religion I'd ever known. It's the ice cream shop, where I got my first job and would work on the weekends.

This feels like it hasn't changed a bit. Just how I like it. There's always comfort in familiar places like this.

We pull into The Cove. It's the only bed and breakfast on the beach and my go-to place to stay.

"The game plan. We check in, drop our bags, and get to the carnival."

Willow gives me a thumbs up.

We walk in, the bell dings, and Sally pops up from behind the front desk.

"Tripp Owens! You made it. It's been too long." She walks out behind the desk, squeezes my cheeks, and then hugs me tight. The main area is still riddled with trinkets and shells.

"Couldn't miss the carnival when it fell on a bye week."

"Who did you bring?" she asks, a nosey glimmer in her eye.

"This is Willow. Trying to impress her with all Golden Cove has to offer." I wink at Sally, and she chuckles. Willow puts her hand out but Sally hugs her like they've known each other their whole life. "How has the beach been?"

"Unseasonably warm. Shouldn't be too windy tonight. Also, I chatted with a stern gentleman, Seth, they're all checked in down the road."

"Wait, you got Seth to stay somewhere else?" Willow questions.

"I did but it's barely a block away. If that."

Sally hands me the key to the room.

"Everything is like you remember. Let me know if you need anything. We still do breakfast in the morning."

"You know I wouldn't miss a breakfast," I scoff at her, picking up our bags, and leading the way to our room.

The Cove has been around since the 90s, but it does not have a 90s feel. It may be a bit eclectic in the main area, but the rooms can rival any of the 5-star hotels, in my opinion. As soon as you step in, you're caught off guard by the massive windows that go almost from wall to wall. The natural light is crisp and illuminates the room.

"Woah. This isn't what I expected," Willow says while sitting in a dark green velvet chair in the corner.

She sits for only a minute before switching to the king size bed. Canopy and all. It feels like it should be too much, or it shouldn't fit, but it does. For me, at least.

"This is amazing," she says, her voice dripping with admiration. "Look, an entire basket of blankets!" she squeals.

"You will never run out of pillows or blankets here. Promise you that."

"Can we just lie down for a minute? Stretch out before we go to the carnival?" Willow asks, getting comfortable.

I go to what would be my side of the bed back home. I lie on my back and Willow lies on her side, her arm draped across my chest. We stay in comfortable silence. There are no words. I play with her hair, turning the soft brunette strands between my fingers.

It's surreal being here with Willow. I've stayed in this room almost every time I've been back, but this bed has always been only for me. I like it even better with someone to share it with.

Who would've thought?

Is there anything better than October? It's always right when the football season is getting good. The air has a chill that soothes my bones. The best season. The best month.

Willow reaches for my hand as we walk into the fall carnival. I rub her palm with my thumb, like my body finds new ways to touch her. The security team, in normal day to day clothes, is also walking in. You'd never guess they were with us. I tried telling Seth that we wouldn't need them, but the compromise was they'd arrive and poke around, away from the two of us.

The sun hangs low in the sky bringing the chill at the edge of the day. The wind brings the smell of cider, pumpkin, and fried sugar. Sally was right, it's warmer than I thought it'd be.

"My mouth is watering," Willow says, sucking in a deep breath, and then leaning her head on my shoulder.

"First stop, the caramel apples. A must." I point to the stand.

"I will not argue with that."

Willow keeps looking around and seems a little antsy.

"What are you looking for?"

"Seth. Also, cameras."

"Seth is right over there." I point to the group of men about thirty feet away. If you looked closely, you'd think they were out of place. "And I told you, you won't meet any press here. Someone might ask to take a photo, but this place is the best at keeping secrets." I nudge her shoulder with mine.

"I trust you. It just seems... weird."

"Oh, it definitely is. Guess there are still some good people in the world. Present company included."

"A Ferris wheel?! My favorite!" Enthusiasm rolls off of her. Her eyes shine with excitement.

All color leaves my face. Willow notices right away.

"No way. Tell me big, bad Tripp Owens, Super Bowl MVP, isn't afraid of heights?" I can't help the flush showing in my cheeks.

"Heights are not my thing but I'm not afraid to admit it. If the Ferris wheel makes you smile like that, we're definitely doing it."

"You're a good man, Tripp Owens."

Something is clear in this moment: there's nothing I wouldn't do to see her smile like that. I'm at the mercy of Willow and her love of Ferris wheels and who knows what else.

How lucky am I?

# Chapter 48
## Willow

Tripp gets into the gondola and it takes all I have not to laugh. The man is gripping the bar like it's a lifeline, similar to how he held my hand while we waited our turn. He gets himself inside, and slides all the way in, settling the farthest he can from the gondola door. Luckily, this isn't your normal two-person Ferris wheel. Instead, the carriages are spacious with longer benches and could hold probably four adults.

I climb in and sit across from him, our knees intertwined. He closes his eyes as my movement causes the Gondola to shift and move.

"How are we doing? You are aware we watched a group of eight-year-olds get into one of these before us, right?"

"Ha! Your teasing will not bother me. I'll be fine once we get moving and I can't consider getting out." He laughs and my heart warms. The idea of someone doing something they'd rather not, all to make me happy, is new. It always felt like I was the one doing this, and it never was reciprocated.

Just like Tripp explained, no one had interrupted any of our time yet. Not that I'm bothered when people do that, it's the chaotic crowding after. Tonight, we're just a couple, enjoying an evening out. I haven't seen Seth or any of Tripp's security except for a few fleeting seconds in the background of our night.

This makes tonight feel real. It's hard to explain, but the absence of all the extra stuff, it's more authentic. We're simply Tripp and Willow, without the back of our mind distractions, wonders, logistics.

The carriage starts to move, and I see his hands grip the edge of the bench seat, making his knuckles white.

"Give me your hands," I say. He only gives me one, but I hold it in between mine, strong and secure.

"Want to tell me a secret?" He smiles nervously, intently focusing on me. Tripp, always wanting to know my secrets, makes my heart full. Even when he's nervous and making himself uncomfortable, he's still trying to figure me out.

"I'm thinking of leaving my label." I give him something good.

"Really? That seems big."

"It is. I just... it doesn't feel like it used to. Even though I've proven myself for years, they don't listen to me."

"Honestly, that seems like a solid reason to leave. I'm sure it wouldn't be hard finding a new label." His eyes are on me, gray and blue like waves on the sea—a look I could swim in.

"I don't know, I've never done it. I'm one to stick things out, waiting for the change, but I don't know if I can keep doing that." The words lift a heavy weight from my chest.

"You don't have to stick it out," he says in a way that makes me think he understands me.

"Are you happy you got picked in the expansion draft?" I ask. I wonder if I can get him to focus on something else besides the moving Ferris wheel.

"That's tough. At first, no. It felt like such a slap in the face. To show up for an organization, especially the way I did that year, and then they're just on to the next. But I'm happier with the Cosmos. I like this city. And then there's you." His thumbs rub the palms of my hand.

"Me, with my ex-boyfriends who crash dinner and the annoying press—"

"None of that is you. I'd take that every day if it meant I got to keep you. Without question," he interrupts.

I feel like I knew this or had hoped he felt this way but hearing it from him is different. It's moments when he says things like this where it's like he's stitching himself to me. He brings a comfort I feel deep within, all the way to my bones.

He leans over the small table in the carriage and I meet him halfway, my lips on his. Tripp anxiously holds my hands but his lips on mine tell me the truth of how much he means what he said.

I hold my breath since I don't trust my mouth. I know, at any moment, I could blurt out how much I love this man. I've thought about it, but my bones are telling me it's true.

In this moment, I know there's a song here. A song that will say the things I want to declare, promise, and swear. My brain is full of half lines and my ears are full of a melody I've been saving for something, or someone, monumental. It feels like I've been writing Tripp's song almost my entire life.

No matter how I feel, I don't have it in me to say it first. I know it's childish but it's self-preservation. What if he doesn't say it back? What if he's not ready?

We reach the apex of the Ferris wheel and are hit with a view that steals the air from your lungs. It's a line of the coast, waves from the Atlantic breaking at the shore, and the sun retreating. Tripp even leans a little closer to the edge to get a better look. The sun has started to set and it's showing off, littering the sky with blurred pinks, purples, and yellows. We couldn't have picked a better time to reach the top.

The Ferris wheel slowly comes to a stop. The gondola sways a tiny bit and I immediately look across to Tripp. He grips the edge of the bench with one hand, his knuckles straining, and his other holds my hand tighter. The muscles in his jaw flex and twitch as he stares out towards the sunset.

I stand up and the gondola sways, back and forth, as I sit next to Tripp. He snaps his face towards mine, clearly bothered with the movement.

"Must you do that?" he says through a nervous laugh.

"Do what?" I lean my weight back and then forward, causing us to rock. Tripp closes his eyes and takes a deep breath.

After a few seconds, which probably dragged on much longer for him, I use a hand to turn his face to mine. My fingers are chilled from the October dusk and Tripp's skin feels warm underneath. He opens his eyes just as the tip of my nose touches his—I smile before kissing him.

This kiss. There's something about it.

It's wispy cotton candy clouds. It's summer rain after a drought. It's the coziest blanket you reach for when you need to warm up. It's comfortable but still rich. It's your favorite song playing in the car with the windows down.

It's everything I've hoped for.

I break our kiss just so I can look into Tripp's eyes, which are more blue than gray today. He kisses my forehead, wraps an arm around my waist, and watches the sun set. I rest my head on his shoulder, taking this in. This moment. This weekend. This man.

I love this part. The idea of seeing the world you belong in, but from a significantly different perspective. Dreams feel closer, hardships feel doable, and questions get answered.

But the question really wasn't one I needed help answering.

I'm, without a doubt, in love with Tripp.

After some of the best chili and fresh apple cider donuts I've ever had, we're pulling back into The Cove. Soft lights illuminate the sign in the dark of night.  A cup of hot apple cider warms my hands. By now the stars are out, and I've missed them. Sometimes, when it's really dark and cloudless, I can see them from my patio, but the city ruins it most nights.

"Ready for an adventure?" Tripp asks. "It's your call." He looks over as he puts the car in park.

"Always."

And I mean it.

Instead of going back inside, Tripp leads me to a path on the outskirts of the bed and breakfast. I don't ask questions because I trust him and, at this point, I'd go anywhere with him. He leads us to an outdoor sitting area equipped with different chairs, a few love seats, and an outdoor fireplace. Baskets full of blankets and throw pillows feel like they're always within reach.

"Can I get you a blanket? Or twelve?" Tripp laughs as he grabs a few blankets from a basket.

I sit down at the loveseat, which is right in front of the fireplace. Tripp wraps a blanket around my shoulder, sits next to me, and then puts one across our lap.

"Thank you," I say, snuggling into the blanket. It's just the two of us out here and it's peaceful.

The crack of the flames blends with the crash of the waves. A feeling of contentment and joy washes over me. The sound has the same soothing effect as when I finally find the right arrangement of notes for a bridge I've been mulling over for a while—like a piece of the puzzle finally clicks.

I bring the cider to my lips, the steam almost like smoke when I look over my cup.

If someone would've told me I'd take a trip to a city pulled right out of a Hallmark movie to snuggle an NFL player this year, I would've never believed them.

The way this year has worked out in a completely different way than I thought, makes my smile hard to contain. There have been really steep highs and devastating lows, but I'm still here. I really thought the Super Bowl half time show would be the key highlight. The fans. The environment. Another stamp of success on my career. Instead, it's these moments with Tripp, the ones that are slow and full.

He treats me like I'm something to treasure. I've been better at being kind to myself, following Tripp's lead. I feel like I'm better at standing up for what I want when I'm with him, since he makes choosing myself easy.

"I don't know if it gets better than this." Tripp is the first to speak. His voice smooth like caramel.

"This place is beautiful. I love that you have this secret."

"*We.* We have this secret."

*We.* Swoon. I melt into his side, and he kisses the top of my head.

"From Champagne diversions to this. Who would've thought?" I joke and look up at him for his reaction.

"You *know* that was a great diversion," he says, looking down at me, the flames of the fire reflecting in his eyes.

"It really was," I agree and drink my cider, before putting the cup on the end table next to me.

"Ready for that adventure?" he asks, rubbing his hands together.

"This wasn't the adventure?" I look up to him as he stands and reaches out his hand.

"Lo, this is a patio. No." He shakes his head and pulls me to my feet. "There's the adventure."

And he points to the beach.

# Chapter 49
## Tripp

I FINALLY FEEL LIKE I've got it right. Sharing this place, this part of me, with Willow. Her hand in mine, plus the smell of the seawater, makes me feel right at home.

We run to the beach, making quick work of the distance, while her hair whips around her face. She laughs once we get to the sand, close to the water.

Get yourself a girl that will run with you, even when she doesn't know where we're going.

"What are we doing?" She breathes heavily, giggling, trying to keep her hair out of her face.

"Take off your shoes. And socks." I reach for mine and start to untie and take them off. I shove my socks in my shoes and then throw them on the sand.

"You're serious." She watches me with her hands on her hips.

"Yes! Come on. Take 'em off," I playfully plead, and I know I've won when a wide smile cracks her lips.

When we're both barefoot in the sand, I reach for her hand and take off towards the water. Unseasonably warm or not, the beach in October is a special kind of cold—the type that steals your breath and immediately wakes you up.

Tonight, I'm wide awake.

"Oh my god! It's so cold." She kicks the water with her feet and then splashes me—the water like tiny icicles.

"That's what we're doing, huh?" And before I get the last word out, she's already running in the sand, right where the water meets the beach.

I chase her, even when she tries to zig zag and throw me off.

"Baby, you forget, this is my job." She turns my way and is trying to get past me. To be fair, if I wasn't a professional athlete, she *might* be able to get by me.

I catch her and she screams. I pick her up, throw her over my shoulder, and start walking further into the water. It's an unforgiving type of cold but it doesn't beat the sound of her chuckling, losing her breath, and saying my name.

"Tripp! What are you doing?!" Her laugh is contagious and now I'm shaking with laughter. The water hits mid-calf, the farthest I planned to go, but she doesn't need to know that. I set her down in front of me, the water reaching higher up her leg.

She squeals because it's cold but uses her hand to splash me. The ocean water hits my face, and I can hear the splash of her running as she bolts for the sand.

"Catch me if you can," she yells over her shoulder. Her hair bounces, illuminated by the moonlight.

I run, and she stops right outside where the water crashes on the beach. Willow lets me catch her. I wrap my arms around her and spin around a few times. The sound of her laughter hits me. Hard. I set her down and she gets on her tiptoes to throw her arms around my neck.

Our lips meet, like they were always supposed to, and the moment is charged. Different. I've felt like I've been on the edge of something all night.

And when it clicks, I hold my breath and feel my heartbeat in my chest. Hear it in my ears. Out on the beach, the ocean at my heels, on a chilled October night, I know I love Willow.

I put both of my hands on the side of her face and kiss her like she deserves. She moans into me, her hands grasping at my shirt.

"Lo—" I say as I pull away from our kiss. Her eyes are kind and bright. Why is this so fucking scary? I know how I feel. I just have to say it. Or I could wait?

"What's wrong?" The concern in her face makes the decision for me. My sweet girl, always expecting the worst. Not tonight.

"Nothing. Absolutely nothing. Everything feels... like it should. Like I didn't know how it was supposed to feel, until you." I tuck a strand of errant hair behind her ear and she leans into my touch. "I love you. All of you." I kiss her before she can say a single word.

"You do?" she questions with a small version of her voice; the moon reflects like fire in her golden eyes.

"Of course, I do."

"Tripp," she stands still, words on the tip of her tongue. I know she's scared of them and that's okay. I can be patient. You know why?

Because she's already said them.

*Watching Willow sleep has become one of my favorite things—it quiets my busy brain. Her dark hair is splayed on my pillowcase, but it's really hers. It feels right for her to have a side of the bed. Recognizing how she's settled into my home, my life, steals my breath. I gasp and put a hand over my mouth to stifle the laughter.*

*It's not funny, not one bit. It's like my brain can't compute the way I'm watching the girl of my dreams, flutter her eyelashes and twitch her lips, while she sleeps.*

*Have I ever been in love?*

*Fuck. Is that what this is? Sweat prickles the back of my neck.*

*Willow starts to stir, moving some rogue strands of hair from her face, and purses her lips, pink and swollen from our earlier kissing. I try to be as still as possible; I don't want to wake her up.*

*She mumbles, her lips barely open, words indiscernible. Every once in a while, she'll talk in her sleep, and at first, it scared the shit out of me, but now I'm used to it.*

*Willow takes a deep breath, sighing it out. Her chest rising and falling to match.*

*But the next thing she says is clear.*

*"I love you," Willow says, wearing a smirk as she sleeps. She looks peaceful and content.*

*Meanwhile, I'm trying not to kick my feet like a fucking middle schooler.*

The way she kisses me back tells me everything I need to know. I want to give her the space to say how she feels when she's ready.

"Let's go back to the room," she says, her voice soft, mischievous.

She doesn't have to tell me more than once.

"Grab your shoes and hop on," I say, pointing to my back. She jumps on and I give her a piggyback ride back to the bed and breakfast.

We make it to the room, and I set her down outside the door. She laughs as I kiss her neck and try to open the door at the same time.

I can't stop touching her.

We're kissing from the doorway, all the way into the room, until her legs hit the bed. She takes her coat off, and I do the same. When her hands reach for the hem of her shirt, her arms crossed in front, she looks at me with eyes made of fire.

She's fucking beautiful with cheeks flushed from running on the beach. Willow bites her already swollen bottom lip and pulls her shirt up and over her head.

I step closer. She reaches, her hands like ice, for the bottom of my shirt. Doesn't matter. I want them everywhere.

"I have an idea." I say while I help her take my shirt off.

Warm water fights the coldness in my bones and there are mountains of bubbles. Willow sits in between my legs, leaning her back to my chest, and my arms wrap around her front.

"This *might* be too many bubbles." Willow laughs as she tries to get some off her face.

"Is there really a limit when you're talking about bubbles?" I ask. In all honesty, she's right. I had no idea how many to put in. Seems like there's enough for multiple very aggressive bubble baths.

"Mmm. This is perfect."

"Told you, there's no bubble limit—"

"Not just the bubbles. The drive. The Ferris wheel. The beach." She turns her head to mine, and I steal a kiss. It's sweet—full of all of the things I didn't say earlier.

*You're the first person I've considered settling down with.*

*I want to take every road trip and vacation with you.*

*There's no ocean I won't splash around in, no matter how cold, as long as you're by my side.*

*You could be my family.*

"Thanks for taking a chance on this. On me," I say, touching my head to hers.

"Here's to many more chances."

Many more.

# Chapter 50
## Willow

THE SUN SHINES BRIGHT through the windows. I'm replaying last night in my mind, over and over. Everything from the Ferris wheel, to the beach, the "I love you", the ridiculous bubble bath. I want to mentally catalog each and every detail.

Tripp has seen me naked. Touched and kissed every inch of my skin. But soaking in a bubble bath with a professional athlete, with your back to his front, is an experience. For a few fleeting moments, I wondered about the soft parts of my body. It's hard not to when you're touching a body like Tripp's, but in that moment, he leaned his head down to mine like he knew I needed the reassurance.

I never felt more loved. Accepted. Myself.

My breath hitches, thinking of Tripp telling me he loved me. The weird thing was I knew he was going to say it. I could feel it.

In the past, I'd find a way to get him to keep it to himself. Things always felt so uncertain once those words were said. Heavier. There was more at stake. It's not words themselves but what happens after—bigger conversations, expectations—and something I've never been able to get right.

This time, I wanted him to say it. The doubt still scratches the back of my mind, but it's much lighter than with anyone else before.

He currently sleeps while my arm is draped across his chest. His face is slightly turned away from mine. I pick up my head just enough to see his silhouette, his long eyelashes fluttering with sleep, and I lay back down and smile into his chest.

My phone rings, ruining the lazy moment. Tripp's eyes squint at me, and when he smirks, I could melt into a puddle on the floor.

I reach for my phone. Erik. Typically, he calls Claire or Emilie. It's rare that he calls me directly. I let the call go to voicemail and put my phone on silent. Whatever it is, I'm sure it can wait.

"Who is calling so early and disturbing the beauty sleep I desperately need?" Tripp says through closed eyes and pulls me into him, kissing my neck and jaw.

"Someone who can wait."

We stay in bed for hours, drifting in and out of sleep, because we have nowhere to be. It's satisfying and something we don't get to do often. Before it gets too late, Tripp heads downstairs to grab breakfast.

He walks in with a tray full of breakfast sandwiches, fruit, and what looks like banana pancakes. There's an espresso machine in our room he turns on like he's done it a thousand times before. Maybe he has.

When he hands me an espresso and watches me about to dig into some pancakes he pauses.

"Wait a minute." He pulls out his phone and takes a photo of me. I'm wrapped in a sheet, hair a wreck, eyes thick with sleep, and a bite of pancake almost in my mouth. "This is a morning I want to remember."

I let him take the photo, with no resistance. You know why? Because the way he looks at me makes me feel whole.

Later that morning, I see he's using that picture as his phone wallpaper.

It might be windy, but the sun is bright while we walk along the beach. It's one of those fall days where the air is a touch warmer than expected. The sounds of the waves crashing and hitting the sand are the perfect soundtrack as Tripp holds my hand and we walk along a piece of the coast. We wanted to spend some time on the beach before we headed back to New York.

I look over at Tripp and can't help but grin. This moment is telling me something I already know—I love him. I don't know if I can say it yet. I close my eyes, the sun hits my face, as I take in everything about this.

The stakes would be the highest. I'd have something, too much, to lose. Part of me wants to jump on him, wrap my legs around his waist, and scream I love him while we're on this beach. The other part wants me to deal with these feelings later.

The latter wins.

"See that, over there?" Tripp asks, pointing ahead.

At first, all I see is a dull white structure. Then I realize: it's a lighthouse.

"I used to take all my friends here, sort of my secret place. It's been empty for years but the town keeps it in good enough shape. It's for all of us."

The idea of an entire town banding behind this lighthouse warms my heart.

We walk to the lighthouse, our steps a bit quicker now that we have a destination in mind.

Tripp opens the weather-beaten front door like he's coming back home. We walk into the interior, lit by the sunshine. For something that's been abandoned, it's in great shape.

As we walk up the narrow staircase, the steps creak and groan under our weight. They're painted black and are riddled with dust and sand.

Tripp leads and steps into the opening at the top. It's mostly windows so his expression is illuminated by the sun. He's in awe.

He spins, taking in the room, like he probably has done a hundred times before.

"We lucked out. No clouds. Lots of sun. This is one of my favorite places." He looks to me and then to the windows.

The view is incredible. It's miles and miles of rocky coastline and endless blue water, and with the sun high in the sky, it's almost like parts of the ocean are glittering.

"Now I get to experience it with one of my favorite people," he almost whispers as he pulls me close to him.

His hands reach for me, moving from the sides of my face and settling on the nape of my neck. Tripp puts his nose to mine, his thumbs caressing my jaw. When the air around us crackles and sparks, I realize I'm holding my breath like I don't want to disturb a single thing.

This is one of those moments that you'll recall with daydreaming eyes and a full heart. Being here, in this snapshot of time, in this place, makes me feel complete. Almost like I've never been more myself with another human than I am with Tripp. It's startling. My stomach drops.

"Tripp—"

But then he kisses me. His lips tell secrets of need. Want. Urgency.

His hands reach into my hair and he kisses me like I'm the air he needs to breathe. I part my lips, letting his tongue touch mine. I push myself into him, wanting to touch as much of him as possible. That's when I feel his erection touching the fabric of my maxi dress.

I can't hold back the wicked groan that escapes my mouth. Tipping my head back, I give Tripp more access to me, and let my hips push further into him.

He nips and kisses up and down my neck. His hands reach down and grab my ass, causing me to stand up straight.

"Fuck, Lo. See what you do to me" He looks down to his dick, hard in his jeans. His hands knead and grab my ass in a way that makes it hard to think.

"I know the feeling," I say, breathy and quick. The ache in my low belly throbs with desire, craving him.

My hands find his stomach, muscles flexing strong and firm. When my fingers walk a path, low and intentional, to the top of his jeans, Tripp puts his own head back. The way he gives himself to me, and the pleasure I know I can give him, is another thing I crave.

I slowly undo the button, pull down the zipper and dance my fingers down until I'm gripping his shaft. I slowly stroke, up and down, tilting my head and tossing my wind-blown hair to one side. I feel the bead of moisture at the tip and can't help but bite my lip.

His hips move with and against me to get the pressure and placement he needs. He moves faster, using one hand to grab my shoulder to help with some leverage.

"Stop. You have to stop. Or I'm going to come," he says while leaning back. Pulling his dick from my hands.

"Isn't that the point?" I grin.

"No, because I want to fuck you, Lo. *That's* how I want to come." He pulls my dress up until my pink lace panties are exposed. He loops his fingers in and takes them off.

"These are soaking wet," he says, holding my panties, like they're a badge of honor.

After my panties are off, he stops, his eyes taking me in. I don't run or cover myself, I let him see me. All of me.

"Oh, Lo. Let me see that dripping pussy." He takes a finger and swipes to test my wetness. "Is this all for me?" he asks, painfully slow.

"Yes," I say like I'm pleading for help.

He pulls his jeans further down, his dick springing from his briefs. I'm two seconds away from laying down on this sandy floor until he picks me up, letting my legs wrap around him. He gently pushes my back against one of the beams.

His cock is so close to my entrance it's infuriating. He uses his strength to basically hold me up, just right against the beam, so he can thrust into me. This is the angle I didn't know I needed. He's tender at first and then picks up the pace, the beam is unforgiving, but it doesn't matter. I spur him on with moans and calling his name.

My hands reach inside the neck of his shirt, finding the backs of his shoulders. I dig in, scratching as the pleasure builds. The anticipation is killing me. It feels like I've been on the edge since that first kiss.

When Tripp's eyes catch mine, he slows for a second. I lean forward and kiss him. My hands pull his hair and wrap around his neck as I move my hips on his cock, my clit finding friction.

"Look at my dream girl, going for it." He almost growls.

I pick up the pace, each thrust has the beam pressing into me, but it's the perfect blend of bliss and being slightly uncomfortable.

I tilt my hips, just enough, to get exactly what I'm looking for.

"I'm going to…" I try to get the words out in time, but I don't. My orgasm rips through me. One hand stays on his shoulder while the other reaches back for the relentless beam. My pussy clamps around Tripp's length and it's almost too much, with my vision going hazy.

"Unravel for me, Lo," Tripp's voice says like gravel as I shake and tremble. He holds me up, strong and in control, while taking the lead, still fucking me. I'm still riding the edge of my own when I feel his full cock fill me up with more than his length. His orgasm is drawn out and strong, with his breathing quick and ragged. I ride out every last twitch and shock with Tripp inside me.

When we're both spent, Tripp slowly sets me down. The moment is tender, with him helping me clean up, and kissing me like he can't quit. My body, and soul, are sated at this point, and I wish it was always just the two of us.

I look around, making sure there's not a soul on the beach. I then start to giggle.

"What's funny?" Tripp asks, wearing his own half smile.

"Just haven't done anything like that before. Sex in a public place. Sex against a wooden beam. Sex with someone with muscles like yours that give me just what I want," I say.

What I don't say is I want to do anything and everything under the sun with him. I want to walk every coast, hand in hand. No one knows me like him.

I'm trying to make sense of this. How this thing between Tripp and I has grown into what it is. I've never shown myself to someone like this. Raw. Open.

"I love hearing that. I want to do everything with you," Tripp says the words like he steals them from me.

I couldn't be happier.

# **Chapter 51**
## Tripp

THANKSGIVING IS ONE OF my all-time favorite holidays. Not really all that surprising since it's an entire day focused on football and food.

I'm done with my team commitments for the day and I'm itching to get home, to my full apartment.

I open my door and it's buzzing with energy. There's hustle and bustle and plates and platters of food. Willow's parents are here, plus Emilie and my mom.

"The thing about pie is you have to be patient," my mom says from the kitchen. I already know she's rolling out crust for her pecan pie with caramelized bananas. I don't remember her making anything else for dessert.

"I've never made pie crust," Willow says. The sounds of them in the kitchen, on Thanksgiving morning, is fucking wholesome.

I shut the door.

"Tripp!" Lo practically skips to meet me at the door. It never gets old. Her parents follow behind. "These are my parents, Kathy and Alan. Mom and Dad, this is Tripp."

"Finally! We've been dying to meet you," Kathy says while pulling me into a tight hug. "You can call me, Kath. How was your meeting? Are you hungry? What do you need?" Willow and her dad both shake their heads when Kath asks questions before I can even give her an answer.

"Give the man some room to breathe, and he better be hungry. We've got food for twenty here," Alan says. I consider myself confident but I'm borderline shaking when her dad gives me his hand. I shake it and then he claps me on the back.

I don't know a lot about having a dad. Especially a good one.

"You've been having a hell of a season. Even at this weird new NFL team," Alan says.

"Dad! It's not weird," Willow shouts from the kitchen.

"A team materializing out of thin air is weird. It's not Tripp's fault. He didn't do it." Her dad throws his hands up and you can tell this is how they bicker back and forth.

"When you put it that way, you're right, it is a little weird," I agree with him and catch Willow grinning at me while she works with my mom in the kitchen. There's a lump in my throat. "I'm going to take a quick shower and change. Be back in a minute."

I walk into my bedroom, taking my shirt off, before I get into the master suite. I hear the bedroom door lightly click shut.

"MVP. Everything okay?" Willow asks as she puts her hand on my chest.

"Yes, it's fine," I get out without my voice cracking. I'm legit about to cry.

"That line doesn't work on me. Sorry." She shrugs while keeping her hand on me.

"It's stupid. Nothing is wrong, everything is right. I've never had a family to do holidays with. Seeing your parents here with my mom and you. It's just... something I've wanted for a long time." I wipe the tear from my eye before it can fall.

Willow puts her hands on my bare chest. "That's one of the most wholesome things I've ever heard."

"I'm thankful for you. For today. All of it." I kiss the top of her head. I hold her and we move back and forth for a few seconds.

"You deserve all of this. I hope you know that." Willow looks up at me and there are tears in her golden eyes, threatening to spill. "I think you've waited long enough. Get in the shower and let's do Thanksgiving." She pokes me in the chest and walks out.

DINNER WAS DELICIOUS. MOM and Willow pulled out all the stops which makes me wonder what they'll do next year.

Now, we're all in the living room, blankets on laps and after-dinner cocktails in hand. Football is on and it feels like we've been doing this forever. This truly is the Thanksgiving I wanted my whole life.

"How bad does it hurt to get hit by that guy?" Alan points at the TV where one of the best cornerbacks in the league is celebrating a broken-up touchdown.

"Worse than you think." I laugh and take a sip of my old fashioned.

Alan is a massive NFL fan, and he's been asking me some of the best questions. He wants to know all the ins and outs of plays, coverages, and any dirt I have on players he clearly doesn't like.

"I can't believe you have to get up after that and do it again," Kath chimes in.

"Me either," my mom and I chime in at the same exact time.

"Do you know if he's single?" Emilie quips and the room breaks into laughter. I don't spend a ton of time with Lo's assistant but whenever she's around it's a good time.

"I'm so excited to get back and see a game in a few weeks!" Kath says, rubbing her hands together.

Kath and Alan couldn't stay the whole weekend, but I promised them tickets whenever they wanted them. Sounds like they're planning to come the week before Christmas and stay for a while at Willow's place. We haven't fully planned the details, but I think we'll host Christmas at Willow's this year.

*We'll* host. I don't care if this makes me a sucker or not, because I want every single holiday with this woman and everyone that comes with it.

Willow's phone rings from the kitchen. She lets it go to voicemail. It continues to ring a second time.

"Who is calling you on Thanksgiving?" Alan scoffs while not taking his eyes off the football game.

Willow gets up, grabs her phone, and stands in the kitchen, her brows furrowed. She sighs and puts her head back before Emilie meets her in there.

"The balls on this man to call you on a holiday." Emilie comes back, with more Rose in her wine glass, and an eye-roll that I don't want to be on the receiving end of.

"Who is she talking about, sweetie?" Kath asks.

"It's Erik." Her brows are scrunched like she's trying to put the pieces together.

I know she's been dodging his calls since their latest meeting when they tried planning a tour she specifically didn't ask for. They've been trying to get her to come in for a planning session, but she keeps telling them to send over preliminary ideas to show they've shifted to her direction.

I'm fucking proud of my girl for standing strong. I know being in limbo bothers her, but she does it, nonetheless.

When her phone rings for a third time, this time with a video call, Willow answers it and walks to the bedroom—I follow because I'm a little nosy.

"Erik, are you kidding with this? What do you want?!" she says to the phone screen.

"Don't be mad. I promise, it's good news. I wouldn't bother you if it wasn't."

I don't care what kind of news he has. Calling on a holiday? Questionable. I know they've been at odds. I'm fucking proud of Willow for saying it how it is, right off the bat.

She gives him this look that screams "you would, and you know it."

"I mean, I may have done that in the past, but I do have good news."

"I'm listening," she says, sitting on the edge of the bed. Her eyes glance to me and then next to her. I follow her unspoken instruction and sit by her.

"Are you out of town? Where are you?" he asks, confused by her background. Nosy prick.

"I'm at Tripps. We just wrapped up dinner with our *families*." She enunciates and smirks at him. "Say hi to Tripp." She turns the phone so I'm looking at Erik. I've never met him but have heard enough about him.

"Oh, wow! Hey, man. HUGE FAN. I'm hoping to get out to a game soon. Been a fan since you started."

Before I can respond, Willow turns the phone back to her.

"Erik, don't lie. I know you have a Detroit Lions tattoo." She sells him out so fast I can't help but laugh. Not with Erik, but at him. He won't know the difference.

"That was a dare, and you know it!" His voice is low like he's a little embarrassed. I love it.

"Let's get to that good news." I have no interest in having this guy kiss my ass on Thanksgiving.

"You got it. Willow, we reconsidered the tour start date as well as the venues. Aiming for something smaller, that will make almost zero dollars—"

"Erik." Her voice is clipped.

"I'm kidding." He laughs in a way that tells us he wasn't. "We've managed to get a better split, more 1000-2000 person venues, with a start date in April. I emailed you the new proposed tour date list. There are even some open dates, gaps, in case you wanted to pick some of the venues yourself."

Wow. He might've actually come through. I know this is much closer to what she wanted.

"Really? You mean it?"

"I mean it. It took some convincing on my end, but we think the marketing plan will lead to more sales, across more units, and have some ideas for new revenue streams surrounding the tour. All with your approval, of course."

"I'll review the list and let you know." She doesn't let her excitement come through. Don't think she wants to give him the satisfaction.

"Let's aim to have the music mixed by the first week of January. Sooner is better but we want to give you some time to put the final touches on it."

This man is being accommodating. I bet it came down to the fact that she could actually hold this album until her contract with them ran out. Money talks.

"That's doable. Thanks, Erik." She hangs up the phone and then wraps her arms around me.

Now that Erik is gone, she squeals into me, shaking us on the bed with her kicking feet.

"I'm fucking proud of you. Holding out isn't easy."

"Thank you. I feel like I can finally breathe again."

"Okay, we should get back out there."

"Another minute. I want to be proud of you. Just the two of us," I say.

Willow melts into my chest.

"Thanks for being proud of me."

"Always." I squeeze her into me.

"I love you, Tripp." Her voice is sweet, small, and sincere.

My heart stops. The moment slows. It's the first time she's said those three words, when she wasn't asleep. I knew she meant in other ways like how she looks at me, or kisses, but never with her mouth, not like this.

"I know you've been waiting for me to say that, and I've felt it for a while. I just, I don't know, all of the stuff that comes after? I've never been able to get right." Her eyes are pinched with worry.

"You don't need to do that, apologize for waiting until you were ready," I say. "Plus, you kind of told me you loved me first." She tilts her head in confusion.

"What do you mean?" she asks, slow and deliberate.

"Well, remember how I said you talk in your sleep? One night, you told me you loved me."

Willow's cheeks flush pink and she rolls her eyes before letting out a laugh. "Of course, I did that. You didn't say anything..." She locks her eyes on mine.

"Of course not. There's no reason to rush any of this, and I knew you'd say it when you were ready."

"Giving me an awful lot of credit, MVP," Willow says, raising her eyebrows.

"Why wouldn't I?"

She stops and the room is silent, only sounds from the living room are muffled and present. I can almost hear my heart beat in my ears.

"This, this right here, is why I love you," Willow says while putting a hand on the side of my face and putting her lips close to mine.

I can't hold her tight enough.

# Chapter 52
## Willow

TODAY, I AM THANKFUL for indoor stadiums. It's a snowy November day in New York, the wind whipping your face, and I can't wait to be tucked into the suite, watching Tripp hopefully get a win. I bribed him with a live version of any song, his pick, from my new album, if he scored a touchdown.

Mom and Dad left early this morning. I rode with them to the airport as they gushed about how Thanksgiving was perfect. My parents can't get enough of Tripp, or Wendy, if we're being honest. Watching our moms plan holidays and things to do the next time we're together was the sweetest thing.

My parents never had a strong connection with Dexter. It wasn't that they didn't like him, but they never went out of their way to make plans. During this short visit, Tripp even took my dad to the Cosmos practice facility, just the two of them, because he knew my dad would love it. Dexter would never.

And you know what? That's okay. I learned a lot from my relationship with Dexter, and others before. It may have been a bunch of what not to do or things I couldn't settle for, but learning, nonetheless. Plus, this whole path brought me to Tripp.

Needless to say, it's a resounding "yes" from my parents, not that I had any doubts.

Something Wendy and I have sort of made "our thing" is putting together game-day outfits. She comes shopping, sometimes Emilie joins, and we find a way to tie Tripp's team or team colors into what I'm wearing.

I love getting excited about something, even as trivial as game-day details. It's fun when other people join in on something as simple as picking out an outfit.

Today, I'm wearing a white Cosmos jersey, obviously #17, black leather skirt, and custom thigh-high boots. They are Cosmos blue, with Swarovski crystals, and Tripp's number on the side. You may not notice his number if you weren't looking for it, but I know it's there, which makes it perfect.

Our suite is packed with friends and family of some of Tripp's teammates. Everyone, as always, has been so kind and welcoming. There was even a young fan, probably about nine years old, and when she saw me in the hallway she started screaming one of my songs. I made sure to go back and take some pictures with her. I live for moments like that.

"Look who it is!" Erik says as he enters the suite. He followed through on his end of the bargain, getting my tour closer to what I wanted, so I had a ticket for him. He told me he only needed one.

"Glad you could make it," I say, giving him a friendly hug.

"Go Cosmos!" he shouts in the suite and everyone starts to clap for him. The man loves attention.

"It's going to be a good game, I can feel it," I say, tipping my drink in a cheers to Erik. He heads to the bar to get his own. People clap and cheer their drinks in response.

I love the few minutes before the national anthem. The stadium radiates energy, fans feed into the atmosphere, no matter where they're sitting.

I find Tripp on the sideline and I wait for him. He turns to the suite, finds me, and I put my hands on my chest. He copies me. We started doing it after our weekend getaway to his hometown. I know people make fun of us, but I don't care. Not even a little bit.

It's him saying he loves me, in front of his team, in front of the whole stadium.

They do their best to catch our moment on the Jumbotron. When people see it, they go wild. It feels like this is the first time I'm on the right side of public opinion when it comes to a boyfriend. It doesn't really matter, but I love hearing people cheer for us during this sweet moment.

My heart races as the game kicks off.

The Cosmos are unstoppable. Today is their day. The offense is completely in sync and the defense is quick all over the field, not allowing a single point from the opposing team.

It's the third quarter and the team is up by twenty-one points. Tripp has a ton of catches, but no touchdown yet. I know it's eating at him because he wants to be the first person who hears a live version of a new track.

Tripp is lined up on the outside of the formation, and he runs a slant route, one of his favorites. We've been going over football terms and play calls in length, as of late. He's only a couple strides in but I have a feeling he's going to get open.

And he does. The quarterback sees him right away, throwing a pass which Tripp catches, in stride, right in the end zone. It feels like the entire suite, maybe the stadium, is holding their breath.

Touchdown!

Before we can scream in celebration, a defensive player tackles Tripp. A late hit. That will be a penalty and 15 yards.

Instead of jubilation, the tone is different. It's a collective groan, anger at the late hit. The player who delivered the hit stands over Tripp. Goosebumps ripple down my neck and arms. Something isn't right.

He's awkwardly on his stomach, one arm underneath him and the other to his side. He's going to pop up any minute or roll to his back. Tripp says sometimes you get hit and lose your breath.

He doesn't do either of those things.

When the medical team sprints to the field and his teammates move everyone away from where he is in the end zone, that's when it clicks.

Something is terribly wrong.

Tripp isn't moving.

The suite is too quiet. Wendy stands next to me and squeezes my hand so hard it hurts. We try to get a better look at what's happening, but we can't see anything. The people around him are quick and meticulous. I'm frozen. This doesn't make sense in my brain. Tripp gets hit all the time; he pops right back up.

All the players are kneeling. Not just Tripp's team but both. There's nothing on the Jumbotron.

Then I see an ambulance start to drive out on the field. Why is there an ambulance?

"We need to go." Seth comes up behind me, lightly putting his hand on my shoulder. He speaks softly but with clear direction on what we need to do next.

"Go where?" my voice sputters and cracks.

"Willow, they're taking him to the hospital. Emilie, grab their things." He points to me and Wendy.

Wendy lets out this sound. It's horrific. A low groan, her teeth and lips almost pressed together, as she cries "no". Over and over. The type of sound that hits my bones. She almost loses her balance and Erik is there to help keep her up.

"Come on, let's go," Erik says. Trying to get Wendy and me to move. It clicks.

They're putting him in an ambulance. He's going to the hospital.

Tripp isn't moving.

# Chapter 53
## Willow

There are clouds painted on the ceiling of the hospital waiting room. Motivational quotes hang on the wall. It's a slap in the face to anyone who is trying to cope, for any reason, in here. I hate those stupid fucking clouds.

Everything is on top of each other: machines beeping and whirring, people talking in the hallways, phones ringing. I don't know what's worse, the overwhelming hospital sounds or the crowd after Tripp's hit.

*Tripp's hit.* Is this a thing now? This moment. How long will it stay? How bad is it? Tears fall down my cheeks and I wipe them away as fast as I can.

Seth and the security detail were able to get us into a semi-secluded area. They stand near the entrance and in the hallway. It's smaller than the general waiting room but still meant for the same nervousness and anxiety. Mountains of questions. Piles of fear.

The press couldn't even let us get in here without taking our photo. Tears running down Wendy's face. Disrespectful. Infuriating.

I sit in a chair where all I can think of is how many people got bad news while sitting here. How many people had their worlds changed as they gripped the arms?

"Willow, you're digging into your own arm," Emilie quietly points out. She lightly puts her hand on top of mine, so I'll stop. She's right. There are scratch and nail marks on my arm. Emilie holds my hand.

This all feels too big and like I can't do anything to move the needle. It's like I'm on a boat, and there are these massive waves, and no matter how many I get through, they don't stop coming. My efforts are helpless.

I look over at Wendy, whose leg shakes as she continuously taps it on the floor. She rests her elbows on her knees, moving her whole body, while she picks at her nails.

Erik is here too. He helped get us through the stadium and into our car. He came with us here but I'm not sure if it was necessarily on purpose since there's no way to get a car here without being mauled by the media. Some of Tripp's coaching staff started to trickle in. This depressing room is a weird combination of people.

There's no way to get comfortable. Sitting. Standing. I pace the room, wrapping my arms around myself. The sound of my boots snap on the vinyl floor. Crystals catch the fluorescent lights serving as another reminder of how wrong this day went.

We've been waiting for an update. It feels like it's been forever. My phone tells me it's been just over an hour. How is that possible?

It feels like my world crumbles each minute I don't know what's going on. My brain replays the hit. Over. And over. And over. The way his body was limp. Still.

Too still.

He's strong. Built for this.

Right?

SECONDS DRAG INTO MINUTES and lag into hours. People are either still or unable to stop moving; there's no in between.

The anxiety and panic pressing on my chest has made me numb. It all hurts but it's like I can't feel anything at all. Emilie still holds my hand, rubbing the top when I'm gripping it too tight.

A new voice breaks the heavy silence in the room, "I'm guessing we're all here for Tripp Owens?" A doctor comes into our waiting room, clipboard in hand.

"Yes. I'm his mother. What's going on?" Wendy shoots out of her seat and is in front of the doctor.

"Can we speak openly in here?" He looks around at the odd assortment of people. Wendy looks at me for reassurance and I nod yes. It's not like this won't be all over the news in a few hours. She nods for the doctor to continue.

"Tripp suffered a severe concussion. He lost consciousness on the field, not sure the total time, but I'd call it significant. We're still running some tests, but it's difficult because he's been in and out of consciousness since he's arrived."

"What does that mean?" Wendy asks, voice quick.

"It means, I know you've been in here for too long without an update but I don't really have one for you." The doctor drops the clipboard and his arms to his side.

The whole room deflates. I'm standing but then it's like I stumbled. Someone says, "thank you" but all I hear is Emilie. She's holding on to me, lowering us into the chairs.

"Shhh, Willow. It's okay. You're okay. Tripp is going to be okay." She rubs small circles on my back, as I sob into her chest.

# Chapter 54
## Willow

I LOOK AT THE clock, it feels like a fucking traitor with how slow it moves. I know I should be hungry, but I feel empty and full at the same time. My brain just adds up the time since I've seen Tripp, since he's been at the hospital.

Finally, the doctor returns. Everyone is on their feet, waiting for an update.

"Tripp is awake and stable," he says, pausing. Sighs and "thank gods" fill the room. I step closer to the doctor, not wanting to miss a single word while Wendy wraps the man in a hug.

Emilie comes up next to me and is rubbing my back. When it clicks that Tripp is okay, I turn and put my head on her shoulder.

The doctor awkwardly pats Wendy on the shoulder before she lets him go.

"He also has some sort of shoulder injury. We'll do a full work up to see what's what after he's had time to rest. There's no rush," the doctor says, crossing his arms.

"Can we see him?" Wendy asks.

"You can but we need to be gentle," he makes eye contact with everyone in the room. "Tripp needs rest from bright lights, loud sounds, and shouldn't be overly stimulated. One person at a time."

Wendy's hand finds mine. She's obviously going to see him first. She hugs me and whispers in my ear, "I'll be right back." She follows the doctor out. I finally feel like I can breathe. I slump back into one of the terrible chairs and move my shoulders away from my ears.

Emilie hands me a bottle of water—she truly thinks of everything. I open the bottle and drink half of it.

"He's awake. He's going to be okay. Try to relax a little before you see him," she says while sitting down next to me.

Her suggestion feels impossible.

Minutes crawl the slowest they ever have in my life. My body feels like it's living in slow motion. Wendy comes back, looking relieved, her cheeks red with tears. She smiles at me and nods, indicating it's my turn.

I make quick work of the hallway but stop right before the door. I'm trying to mentally prepare myself. I don't know what to expect.

My fists are balled up, knuckles white, as I try to steady my breathing. I shake my hands and stretch my neck from side to side. Deep breaths in and out. In and out. My heart feels like it could run out of my body.

After stalling long enough, I open the door and walk in.

There he is.

Tripp is in a hospital bed, his arm in a sling, and connected with wires and machines. His bed is up at an angle, so he's kind of sitting up, but his face is expressionless, and his eyes are closed.

When he hears my boots, these stupid fucking boots, he opens his eyes. It takes him a second to register but then he gives me a dim version of the bright smile I'm used to.

A wave of relief hits me hard enough that I have to stop. I'm awkwardly standing in the middle of Tripp's hospital room.

"Lo. You came." His voice sounds small but still like Tripp.

Surprisingly, I still have tears to cry.

# **Chapter 55**

## Tripp

"BABY, COME HERE," I say, patting the side of the bed with my good arm. Or shoulder. Who knows at this point?

Willow looks like she's been through it. Her skin, usually bright and full of life, is pale and blotchy from crying.

She walks towards me. Slow. Hesitant.

"I don't want to hurt you." She pauses at the edge.

"You won't," I say, trying to reassure her.

Before she attempts to get in next to me, she stops to take off her boots. Her Cosmo blue boots which make my stomach flip. Seeing her in anything team related drives me wild.

"Those boots," I say.

"I know, I know. They're so impractical and I thought it'd be fun but then we were here and they're loud and I didn't have anything else to wear. Why would I bring a pair of shoes? I didn't think—"

"Lo. Take a breath." She's spiraling. I'm sure I don't look great, but I can't look that bad. Can I?

She tries to take a breath and ends up sobbing into her hands. Still at the edge of the bed, I wish I could go to her. When she finally catches her breath, she gently lays in space next to me, careful not to jostle me.

"I was so scared. You weren't moving," she cries into my chest. I hold one of her hands with the arm closest to her. The good one. Will I now have a good and bad arm moving forward? The thought is fleeting.

"Shhh." I try to calm her down. "I'm okay. You're okay. We're both okay."

"You shouldn't be the one doing this. I should be the one telling you these things," she cries.

"Baby, I don't think there's a manual on injury protocol. You being here is enough. I promise. Let's stay like this for a while." I know she needs time to process this. As do I.

I don't remember it. It was like I made a catch, blinked, and then in a span of five seconds, I was in a hospital bed. According to the doctors, I was knocked out cold, and then was in and out of consciousness from when they took me from the field to the hospital.

When I came to and was there long enough to remember, it was too much to take in. Lights flashing in and out. Jersey being cut off. Equipment being thrown to the floor. Doctors trying to get my attention.

*Tripp, can you hear us?*

*Are you with us, Tripp?*

I couldn't answer. It's like I knew I wanted to but then it was black. And then I was somewhere else, different people, and it was too bright.

*Tripp, can you squeeze my hand?*

*What's the date, Tripp?*

When I told them my name, birthday, and stat line for the whole year, everyone relaxed a little. I followed up with the score of the game before I got smoked and they even laughed. I knew I had a concussion, but I was with it. At least at the moment.

Everyone relaxed a bit, but I wasn't off the hook. The tests were extensive. Doctors were cautious.

They tell me I've been in and out of consciousness. I look at the clock and it's fucking startling. Like, how did this happen.

The one mistake I made was asking to see the hit. It was like I couldn't believe it happened. The doctor said it might help me understand.

I watched it once. A late hit which left me completely limp and on display for an entire stadium. Now, I can't stop thinking about it. Hearing it. The sound of the hit. The commentator. The gasp of everyone seeing it in real time.

Even though it was hours ago, it feels like the hit plays on replay in my mind. I'm afraid it won't stop. It wasn't just me but the cut to my mom and Willow. Their faces. Pale. Holding hands. Trying to see what they could from the suite.

That hurt in a way I didn't expect.

I can't believe that was me. I looked like I was dead. Per the doctors, I will probably never be able to fill in the blanks. So, it's a piece of my life I'll never see or get back. It doesn't make sense.

Willow squeezes my hand.

"What hurts?" she asks, her voice level.

"I feel weird. My head feels heavy, but I wouldn't say it hurts. I know my shoulder is fucked up, but I can't necessarily feel it yet."

"It's okay to feel weird," she says, putting her hand gently on my chest. I think she's feeling for a heartbeat.

"This is the first time I've ever really been hurt. In the NFL at least."

"Yeah?"

"Would not recommend."

That gets her to laugh, for a short second, before her face gets all serious.

"You know you can be real with me. It's me and you. I'm going to ask again. How do you feel?"

How does she know what I need before I ask for it? She wants me to go past the surface. I'm afraid to say what's hiding there. I take a deep breath, exhaling all the way out, before I try to put it into words.

"I... I feel like... everything is different. This is a turning point." And when my voice cracks, I know there's no use trying to hide. "Today was the scariest day of my life." She takes her fingertips and lightly wipes the tears from my eyes. "I woke up and kept thinking, 'can I move my toes. Do I feel them? What about my fingers?' I fucking hate that I had to do that." I stop to catch my breath.

"I can't imagine. Even though I saw it, I couldn't imagine being you."

"I've always been ridiculously terrified of who I am without football. What do I do when it's over? And this is the first thing that has scared me more than that." Saying the words is hard but eye opening.

"You're still going to be Tripp Owens." Her hand taps my chest.

"Will you love me even if I'm just a normal Tripp Owens?" Her lips are pressed together like she's trying to put two and two together. "If I'm not the Tripp Owens in the NFL?"

"Of course. You don't even need to ask that."

"I do need to ask it. Because I'm thinking about it."

Her eyes go wide, matching my typical reaction whenever I think about my time being up in the NFL.

"I'm thinking about doing the scariest thing I've ever wondered about... because I think today was worse. Seeing my mom. Seeing you. Seeing the clip."

"I didn't mean to come in here like that. I tried to get myself together but—"

"Don't you apologize for caring about me. I can't say I wouldn't have done the same thing you did. I don't know what I would've done." My thoughts drift to the equivalent of seeing Willow getting hurt at a concert. Very unlikely but my stomach flips at the hypothetical thought. "You asked me how I felt... and I feel like, I'm not sure I can play football anymore. Who knows, this shoulder might be trashed, anyway."

She gives me the space to keep going.

"I need you to keep this secret. This is the first time I've ever said the words out loud. They scare me. Hearing them out loud? Brutal."

"You don't even need to ask. I'm a vault." She puts her hand on her heart. "You are stuck with me. I don't want to go anywhere unless it's with you. I will support you, no matter what you decide. Whether that's today, tomorrow, next season, or years down the road."

"Years?"

"Years." She kisses my cheek. "I love you, Tripp Owens. I'm not going anywhere."

# **Chapter 56**
## Tripp

Fucking finally.

Back in my own bed. I fall on top of the comforter and even though it's the middle of the day, I'm a different type of exhausted.

The worst part about staying two nights in the hospital is the bed situation. I don't know if I actually feel better or if it's the fact I'm back in my apartment, with my sheets.

Seems like I'm out of the woods with the concussion. I'll have a follow up appointment next week. But if everything goes as it has, there shouldn't be any long-term impacts. Unless I get another one, but that's another thought for another day.

Didn't get so lucky with the shoulder. Based on the tests, doctors are estimating a grade 2 tear. It could need surgery but no one has a strong opinion at this time. I'm on the injury report for this week and will not be doing any sort of physical activity. It's been a decade since I've not been allowed to do anything. It's weird.

"Tripp. Do you need anything before I go?" She says as she stands in the doorway.

Willow has a meeting with her label to start wrapping up the album. She's been by my side for the last two days. Between her and my mom, I was never alone, which kept my slow-moving brain busy.

I sit up. "No. I'm all good. Are you going to come back or stay at your place tonight?" I fish for her plans. I feel like I've asked so much of her the last few days. I hate it. But I need it. Can't imagine doing this without her.

"Coming back," she says while walking towards me and kisses me on the lips. Her hands touch the side of my face.

"There's a key card on the table, take it with you. And you know what, why don't you keep it?" It's hard to keep my tone casual. I could throw up.

"Keep it? Are you sick of your building security calling you for permission to let me up, Tripp Owens?" Her lips pull into a sly grin. The way her eyes catch mine tell me it was the right move.

"No, I want you to have it." It's hard to pretend like you're being nonchalant when you're internally hating yourself for sounding like a fucking sap. "Only if you want it."

"Of course, I want it. I want anything tied to you." She kisses me again. "I'll be back in a few hours. I'll have my phone on if you need me."

"Go finish your next album of the year."

The door locks behind Willow and it's the first time I've been alone in days. Gone is the parade of doctors, sports specialists, nurses, team doctors, teammates, coaching staff, and anyone else to distract me. Nothing but my beaten-up brain and my thoughts.

I sprawl out on my bed and stare at the ceiling fan. It oscillates and is oddly soothing after a while. Consistent. No variation.

What am I going to do? I think about putting my equipment back on. Pads. Jersey. Helmet. A cold sweat breaks out over my forehead and my mouth feels like it's full of sand.

Did I really tell Willow I was thinking about walking away from football? Why did I do that? Is that something I should consider?

I shouldn't have said it out loud. It made it real. It's right there in front of me like something I can grab.

I'm going to have a panic attack. I don't want to run from it. Part of me thinks I need to feel it. The spiral. The pull. Before it even starts, I know this is something I'll keep to myself.

My chest rises and falls too fast. Breaths are hard to find and even more difficult to hold on to. I'd usually put my head between my knees at this point, but I don't. I stare at the fan. The blades cutting through the same air I'm trying to pull in.

I pinch the skin on my arm to prove to my brain that I'm here—this is real. I touch my chest to feel my heart beating. My good hand touches my face, feels the too-fast breath.

Can I go back to the game? Can I step back on a field? What if the answer is no?

I've never been more ill equipped to think about this. My brain is healing and I'm contemplating major life decisions. It feels like it steps through thick mud.

I welcome the panic and weight of something impossible. There are no winners here. And it feels like the air in the room goes from hazy to crystal clear. There it is.

In this moment, I know there's no way I can win.

"BABY, LET'S GET YOU under the blankets," Willow says. I look at the clock. I must've fallen asleep.

"No. I don't want to." I don't know why I argue.

"You know you'll feel better under the blankets." She pulls the comforter out from underneath me and up to my chest.

I know I should ask about her meeting. I don't have it in me.

"Lo. Don't leave me in here," I say, the edge of the panic attack still in my grasp. I reach for one of her shoulders.

"I'm not leaving. I'm going to put my pajamas on, and I'll be back," she says as she touches the hand I reached with.

My heart races like it doesn't believe her. But I do. I know she'll do what she says because this woman has never let me down.

I force my eyes to stay open until she slides into bed. Immediately, I feel better knowing she's here. With me.

"Do you need anything? It looks like you didn't eat dinner or anything."

"No. Nothing." I turn my head and look at her while she lies on her side. Since my shoulder injury, I've only been able to sleep on my back.

Willow turns the light off on her side of the bed, gets situated under the down comforter, and holds my hand. She draws soft small circles on it until I fall asleep.

# **Chapter 57**
## Willow

MY DAYS HAVE BEEN nothing but Tripp and this album. If Tripp wasn't recovering from a head injury, it'd be quite amazing.

We're taking a break from mixing songs, which are almost done. Next, we're tracking the last of the new songs left to be recorded.

"I mean, it makes sense he's bummed. That was terrifying," Emilie says as we find an empty lounge area to regroup before the next hours of work. "The press has been brutal. I'll never understand the need to show the clip on repeat." She shakes her cup full of iced coffee, mixing it together.

"I'm not sure bummed is the right word. I saw it once and never need to see it again."

"You're doing the right things. Being there. Keeping an eye on him." She tucks a red curl behind her ears.

"I know. Just want him to feel better. Anytime someone from the coaching staff calls or tries to come by for something, it's like he's on the edge of panic mode. He's short. Agitated easily."

"That has to be fairly normal, right? This was a major injury."

"That's what my research says. Concussions are weird. People have a wide variety of physical and mental symptoms afterward."

Emilie nods in understanding. "Have any of his teammates or friends come by? Maybe he needs something that isn't so... formal?"

"I don't think so. I don't know if they've ever been to his place. Like, Tripp does things with them during the week, and after games, but don't think people swing by his place a lot."

"Men are weird like that. I have Zack's number. We could call him and see if he's busy."

"Zack, huh?" I am not surprised. Emilie and Zack gravitate towards each other anytime we're in the same vicinity.

"We're friends." Her cheeks blush.

"Uh huh." I sip my warm lemon water, a go-to when I'm recording. "Thank you for taking this assistant position. Most of this year has been wild and you've made it easier."

"Someone's gotta pick up the designer pieces for the popstar," she jokes as she takes a drink of her iced coffee.

I lightly push her shoulder. "You know what I mean."

"I do. And I hope you'll need an assistant like me for a long time." She pretends to rub money in between her hands. This is one of the reasons I love working with her. She's intentional, thoughtful, and surprises me with jokes during borderline questionable times.

There's something about a bridge that makes me feel like I've got something. Something for the fans but specifically something for me. Especially this song because I wrote the bridge first. It came to me while Tripp and I were driving back from Golden Cove, but pieces of it flooded my brain after we were on the beach.

We saved this song for the end because I knew it'd keep me excited throughout the day to get to it. Find a musician who doesn't have a favorite track or two on an album and I'll show you a liar.

The click track fills my headphones. We're doing the first take of the bridge, one of my favorite pieces I've written for this album.

*You're the coast I'm mapping*
*Every cliff, beach, and bay*
*You look at me like*
*It's worth finding our way*
*I want to mark each rock*
*the grains of sand*
*Explore the hidden coves*
*Where your secrets stand*

We do a few re-records but not many. I know I nailed it and would probably be content with any of the takes I did. It felt right. Easy.

After I record the whole song, two more times, we're done for the day. They have everything they need for the whole album. Issues could come up when they're mixing or mastering, but the bulk of the work is done. It feels good.

"Willow—"

"I know, I know. You love the bridge!" I clap my hands together and jump up and down in excitement.

"I do, but that's not it." Her brows are creased and the warm demeanor I know is nowhere to be found. "Have you seen this?" She gives me her phone.

***No Tripping Here – Tripp Owens to Announce Retirement***

I scan the article and immediately know something isn't quite right. Quotes like "Sources close to Owens" and "An anonymous teammate" are what make up the entire piece. There isn't a single line attributed to Tripp, his team, or the Cosmos.

"This isn't true. I have to go."

"Everything okay over here?" Erik comes over just as I'm about to make a break for the door.

"Yeah, I forgot about a dinner thing tonight. Have to get going." I tell the white lie because I don't want to draw a single ounce of attention to the article that's going to be or is already on everyone's social media feed.

"Get out of here then. Good work today. We'll be in touch after we get closer to finalizing the tracks," Erik says as I'm halfway out the door.

# **Chapter 58**
## Tripp

MY HEAD COACH IS calling me. Probably to check in.

"Is there something you want to share?" he asks, his voice clear and to the point.

"No, not particularly. Is there something *you* want to share?"

"This isn't a joke, Tripp. If you're thinking about retiring, it'd be nice if you had those conversations with us before anyone else."

Retiring? The only person I even uttered the thought to was Willow.

"I'm not exactly following…"

"We've been fielding calls asking to comment on your pending retirement."

"This is the first I've heard about it," I say.

"You didn't tell anyone that retirement was a serious option for you?"

I don't answer. I can't answer. My fingers tingle as I hold the phone too tight.

"Listen. I know that hit scared the shit out of you. It should've. My advice to you is to not make any decisions without some space from it. And once something like this comes out, the team would be stupid not to put themselves in the best position to win."

"What does that mean?"

"It means the front office can't unread this. It puts doubt in their mind. Their minds will be open, even if it's just a crack, on the roster for next season. I'm not saying it's right and not that they're actively looking but I want to be straight with you."

Fuck me. This is not happening.

"No, I appreciate it." And I do. I don't think there are many coaches who operate like mine. Straight to the point even when he doesn't have to.

"I'd try to figure out the leak."

No. No. No.

There's nothing to figure out. The only person I told was Willow. Right? Fuck. My brain is fuzzy. It's like a haze covers parts of my memories.

Who else was in the room? No one. Couldn't be. I was terrified to say those words out loud. I would've never done it if anyone was in there.

"Definitely. Thanks for calling, Coach. I haven't made any decisions, and I won't until I'm ready. I promise you'll be the first one I talk to."

"You have to do what's best for you. I hope it's being a starter for this team next year, and a few more after. Call me if you need anything, ok?"

The line goes dead. I stare at the phone in my hand. Tears cloud my vision. Mostly out of frustration but I'd be lying to myself if this doesn't hurt. Willow didn't keep my secret. My coach basically told me this could jeopardize my future with the team.

*Nothing. Nothing. Nothing. You have nothing.* My own brain bullies me. I try to breathe through it, but it hurts to breathe in all the way.

Football is a massive question mark, Willow is a hard no, and my shoulder fucking hurts.  I pace. I walk the same short space from my kitchen to the living room.

This isn't happening. There's no fucking way. The wave of dread envelops me. Alarms are going off and I'm starting to hyperventilate. There was a reason I never took this risk, trusting another person, because most of them prove me they shouldn't be trusted. Why the fuck did I think Willow would be different?

Did she really tell someone? One of my deepest darkest secrets. Did she share my most vulnerable moment?

Before I can plan my next move, the door opens.

Willow.

"Tripp, did you—"

"Who did you tell?" I turn to her too fast.

"No one," she responds with no hesitation.

"I can't believe this. You're the only one I told." I look at my phone on the end table. Texts are coming in. My mom is calling.

"Tripp. You have to believe me. I didn't tell anyone. You know me." She taps her hand on her chest, right over her heart.

I thought I did. There's no other explanation for this though. My brain is trying to sift through the mud. Everything is murky.

"There's no other way this got out. It was only me and you in that room." An angry tear falls down my cheek. "I kept all your secrets and followed your rules. I did what I was supposed to, and you couldn't do this one fucking thing for me?!" I know I'm yelling, and I don't care.

"Please, take a breath. Let's sit." Willow gestures to the couch. When I don't move, and continue pacing, she asks the burning question. "Tripp, are you going to retire?"

"I don't know if it's my choice any more. The Cosmos are on alert. They think one of their best players is turning into mush and leaving them behind."

"If it's not true, put out a statement. Things like this always blow over."

She doesn't understand. *Why isn't she listening to me?*

"I can't put out a statement! I have no idea what I'm going to do. Plus, my coach called. Basically told me this put the thought in the team's mind that they may need another wide receiver next year." I've never been one to yell but I don't feel like she gets it. I pace back and forth. Small steps.

"They wouldn't do that..." she says.

"You don't know anything if you think that. I'm here, in this apartment, because of a random move I never saw coming. Quit being so fucking naïve."

"Don't talk to me like that."

"Willow. You fucked this up! I thought I was going to have time to think through this major life decision and now I have to make it while everyone analyzes every fucking thing I do, say, or breathe."

"I didn't tell anyone. And don't be mad at me that you have to make a call on something difficult. The decision was always there. Before me."

"Before you, all of this, no one would've cared what I did." All the training sessions I skipped, hours I drove, and late nights roar back to me. All of the things I gave up so I could see Willow, comfortably, when we were early in this. "After everything I gave up. Changed. All the things I did to make this work for you. You couldn't do this one thing for me."

"Sure, the press followed me and immediately found you. It wasn't you spraying Champagne, winning a Super Bowl, interacting with paparazzi and drunk fans. It was all me."

"Maybe you need this. The constant attention. The press feeding into your every move." My words are razor sharp and the look on her face tells me everything I need to know.

Everything hurts. It hurts to think. Hurts to feel. Hurts to be in this room right now with someone I thought I could trust.

This is over.

"Seems like you need the attention. Attention I can't give you." I don't want to look at her, but I do. My skin is hot, and my pulse is in my ears.

"Just say it, Tripp."

"I want you to leave.

"I can't believe this. Nice way to treat someone you supposedly love."

"You're one to talk. Put the key on the counter before you leave. You won't be needing it."

The words hit her, and I swear I see her stumble back by their force. Her mouth is open, before pressing it into a tight line. She shakes her head back and forth and crosses her arms.

"Try not to scream about my hometown on your way out. If you can help yourself." I can't even look her way.

"You're going to regret this." She slams the key on the counter and the door shuts a few seconds after.

Willow's gone.

# Chapter 59
## Willow

THE PATIO ISN'T MEANT for December, but I don't care. I brush the snow off the furniture, light the fireplace, and grab all the blankets.

I'm bundled up in cold-weather gear like I'm going to play outside, how you do when you're a kid. In reality, I'm preparing to sulk; catalog the broken pieces.

I silently cried the whole way home. Seth didn't ask me a single question and I didn't divulge anything. I texted Emilie and let her know I wanted to be alone tonight; she has a key for the SoHo apartment and will stay there instead.

As I sit on the patio, snowflakes fall, heavy and wet. The cold seeps through my layers but it's almost like I need it. The external match for my internal turmoil. I pull my knees to my chest and sit. Staring at the flames.

The crackling of the fire offers a comforting backdrop to my thoughts, but it's not enough to quiet the questions swirling in my mind. Why does Tripp think I would betray his trust? Why would he believe I would reveal something so personal and sensitive?

Doubt creeps in. Maybe I said something without realizing it? Maybe my words were misconstrued? No, that can't be it. I *know* I didn't say anything. I didn't utter a single word of that conversation to Tripp, let alone anyone else. I know he said those things coming from a place of fear and I'd never share that with anyone. My heart cracks because he thinks I did. He sees me as a person capable of doing something so awful.

No matter how I look at it, I can't figure it out. Maybe Tripp told someone else? Ugh. I don't buy it. He didn't even tell his mom, the person who has been by his side through it all.

How could he think I would do that to him? That's what cuts me. The sharpest knife. This whole time I was worried about trusting Tripp but I never thought about if he trusted me.

The way he looked at me. The way he spoke. Gone was the sweet version of Tripp and replaced with someone who thought I did something terrible.

Everything hurts.

I gave him all I had. It still wasn't enough.

When will it be enough?

I glance at my phone. The screen is covered in notifications. They don't stop coming in. I text my parents, letting them know I'll call them tomorrow and everything is fine. They might know it's a lie, but I need some space to think through this.

I turn my phone off.

And then I think about Wendy. What do I do about Wendy? I feel empty. The severity of the situation reaches my bones and everything aches.

The flames dance before me, casting flickering shadows on the snow-covered ground. I wish they could show the truth as easily as they light up the patio.

And then it clicks: I was so concerned about trusting Tripp and I didn't consider if he trusted me.

As the night wears on, I find myself lost in a maze of what-ifs, unable to find a way out. I wrap the blankets around me, tight, trying to block the chill from both the wind and recent events.

# **Chapter 60**
## Tripp

IT'S BEEN THREE DAYS since Willow left. The first day, I did nothing besides stare at the ceiling, frozen with the severity of the decision I needed to make. I convinced my mom I was alright, even if it wasn't true, but I wanted some time by myself. I'm surprised she didn't come over here; sometimes she finds it hard to listen to my requests.

The second day, I started it off with a mediocre panic attack. Felt like even my subconscious is too exhausted to go all in on a panic response.

I went to an appointment for my shoulder. I wore a look that said, "don't fucking ask me about anything you've read or heard" and it worked. I knew I was being borderline insufferable and irritable, but it's all I had.

The shoulder isn't as bad as originally thought. Per the doctors, I could rehab it without surgery, or do surgery in the off season. Seems like I could even play at the end of this season if we make the playoffs.

Another fucking decision to make. I want someone to tell me what to do.

Today, my mom's coming over. She gave me all the space she could muster but that's run out. I had lunch delivered and am trying to get everything set up. Doing things with one working arm is more difficult than I thought it'd be.

I know the headlines haven't quit. It's been made worse because I refuse to give a statement until I know what I want to do.

What do I want?

I want things to go back to how they were before the game. I want how Willow and I were before.

She hasn't tried to get a hold of me. I haven't reached out either. At this point, I don't have anything to say.

Is this how relationships end? You have a soul-crushing fight and then you're trying to remember the last time you kissed? Or the last time you heard their laugh in your bed? How can all of these things turn into a list of "last times?"

My mom knocks before coming in. She takes one look at me before her smile falls and is replaced with concern.

"Tripp, what's wrong?"

"A lot." I give her an honest answer.

"Have you been sleeping? Eating?"

"A little."

She stands in front of me and puts her hands, cold from the winter, on the sides of my face.

"Tell me everything," she says while she leads me to the couch.

I do. It feels like reaching into my chest and pulling out pieces of me for everyone to see. I tell her about Willow, the call with coach, my terror in making this decision, and then some.

"First things first, you can't do this. Hold on to all these things. You don't need to tell me everything, but you need to tell someone." She's such a good listener, letting me ramble without a single interruption for who knows how long. "Football isn't an option forever. It's never been."

"I just want someone to tell me what to do. A coach, a doctor, a psychic. I'll take anyone at this point."

"No one can make this decision besides you. I know that's not what you want to hear but it's you that has to live with the results."

"I know. I feel like I've only ever had this one thing. I've been trying to answer who I am, without it, for years. There's no answer. I'm a shell." My voice trails off at the end as I try to find the words.

"I did the same thing when you moved out and went to college. I didn't have practice clothes or jerseys to wash. Dinners to make. You've always been much more than who you are on the field. I'm sad you don't see it."

"I almost saw it..." My voice fades because I can't bring myself to be this pathetic. I don't have it in me to tell her that I'd thought about trading football for a life with Willow. I don't say it because it's embarrassing and it's also not a possibility.

"I find it hard to believe you told Willow this deeply personal thing and she told someone. Especially after you confronted her."

"I know, but if not her, then who? It doesn't make sense."

"You act like you're not a professional athlete who fights with the press on a regular basis. Who knows?" My mom throws her hands in the air before resting them on her lap.

"Even if she did, isn't this sort of what you wanted? Pressure? You still have a decision to make but this time you'll do it without anyone in your corner."

Fuck. Is she on to something?

"Everything happened so fast. Coach called and she walked in right after. My body hurts from not doing anything. All the frustration and fear built on top of each other." I try to get my words out, but my voice is shaky.

"You've always been impulsive." My mom leans back in her seat, crossing her arms, and letting out a laugh. "All of this is up to you and you know I'll support you forever. If I'm being honest, I'm sad about Willow. Watching you two together, was..." She stops because her voice cracks. "It was really something." She can't hide her tears.

She cries. I cry. We remember there's lunch and move to the kitchen. We don't bring Willow up again, or me playing or not playing. We talk about the things that barely matter.

I thought my mom would give me more direction. The woman seems to have an answer for everything.

But all I have is more questions than answers.

# Chapter 61
## Willow

IT'S BEEN TWO WEEKS–FOURTEEN days–and not a word from Tripp. He hasn't addressed the retirement rumor but has decided against having surgery this season. He's doing rehab for his shoulder in the hope he'll still be able to play this season (or at least that's what the article said).

I'm torturing myself by keeping up on his progress. It hurts. I could stop but I won't.

Tabloids are starting to speculate we've broken up. This is the longest we've gone without being seen in public. To be fair, I've not been anywhere besides my home, with Emilie.

We hashed out the Tripp fight the best I could without telling her his secret. Even now, I want to keep it. It may have been out of spite, but it was important to me. Emilie knew I wasn't giving her everything, but she didn't press me.

Since I technically wrapped the album already, I didn't have a creative project to throw myself into. This led me to write an obscene number of songs during the last week.

I've been known to pour myself into writing when things are bad. I have no idea if they're any good, or if they're just cathartic for the time being. The only way to know is to keep going.

I'm in my home studio, getting ready to record some piano, while I figure out the bones of these new songs. Before I start a new project, I always clean up any rogue files so things don't get lost. Sometimes I have to go back and find something so minuscule and the least I can do is keep them in the right place.

There are only a few files, and they're short, so I play them back. A few verse melodies I didn't end up using, a half-written song I scrapped. The last one is the most interesting. It's Tripp and me, talking; I must've accidentally recorded when we were hanging out in here.

The night comes back to me. It was the first cold night in October before we went to Golden Cove. With a cloudless sky, we'd be able to see the stars, which meant a perfect hot tub night. I remember it because I almost told him I loved him twice. Had to catch myself before the words spilled out before I was ready to hear them.

The file is almost done playing and there's only a few seconds left. At this point, I've gone back upstairs to grab brownies out of the oven. Tripp talked about how he hadn't had one in forever, so I pulled out one of my favorite recipes and made them from scratch.

On the recording, Tripp takes a deep breath and sighs. And then, when it's just him in the studio, he says, "Willow, the only girl I've thought about marrying." He laughs and then I hear his footsteps scurry up the stairs.

I cover my hand with my mouth. This is the sweetest, most tender thing I've ever heard someone say about me. Not only the words he said, but how he said them. How I almost spilled my guts to him after this, because of the way he was looking at me. Now, I know what he was thinking.

The way this hurts. I want to call him and tell him I found it. I heard it. And that if he can go back to how we were, I'd do it. I have the phone in my hand, but I can't bring myself to call him. I know this isn't about me. Part of it, maybe, but Tripp has things to figure out.

I'm feeling everything and now's a perfect time to put a voice to the words I've written. I pull out my journal, sit at the piano, and start putting riffs together. A few tears fall and hit the keys, and I know my voice sounds horrific, but it's the only thing I can do to make myself feel better.

A MEETING WITH ERIK and the label is what pulls me out of my music cave. Apparently, there's something we need to discuss.

"An opportunity has come up, one that has your name all over it. There's a unique type of tour about to be announced and they're looking for someone big. The main artist wants two headliners. Each artist plays a short set of their own discography but then the main event is a collaboration set. Doing duets of each other's music."

Wow. That sounds different.

"She doesn't hate it. Keep going." Claire looks from me to Erik.

"Claire. Chill out." She makes me laugh. I know she did it because I need a laugh. "She's right. I'm intrigued. Who is the artist?"

Erik puts his hands on the table, starting a fake drumroll. He looks around the table for everyone to join in. Everyone plays along, except Claire. Not surprising.

"Asher Wilde."

"You're lying." It's the no-filtered reaction. Asher Wilde is one of the biggest musicians of my time. He's older than me and hasn't had new music or a tour in at least five years. He's been off the grid.

"I am not lying."

"What's the catch, Ricky?" Claire asks.

"The catch is that they want music from the most recent toured album of Willow's. She'll be able to play new stuff. Really, creative control would be with Asher and Willow. The other is the timing. We'd have to cut the current tour we're planning short to prepare."

"How big are they thinking?" I ask.

"Massive. Stadium tours. All over the world. Spanning almost two years. We think it has the chance to be the most memorable tour, ever. They want the whole thing: full-stage design, high-dollar tickets and experiences, and the ridiculous costume budget. It would mean a much smaller rendition of the tour we're currently planning."

I can't have both. I can have part of what I was hoping for with the new album, but not both.

"How did this come up?" Claire asks.

"Asher had someone slated and they backed out."

"Why and who was it?"

"Don't know but their loss is our gain."

"When do you need an answer?" I ask the room.

"I can get you three days. They want to move fast and get things rolling. I have all the proposed dates and locations here." He holds up a folder. "And, if you agree to it, we're going to need a contract extension. You'll sign for both on the same day."

Three days. That's barely any time. Doesn't surprise me they'd put the contract on top of it. They don't want to get screwed out of the revenue. This thing, whoever does it, will be legendary.

"Okay." I reach for the folder. "I can give you an answer in three days. Now, the new album, how is it coming?"

As expected, everything is going smoothly. The songs are all being mastered and getting to their final version. I'm still playing around with album titles which is something that drives the label mad. I love to keep it secret, if I know it, up until the last minute. Or I want to give myself the time and freedom to find something that fits perfectly. The perfect title hasn't hit me yet, but I know it will. It always does.

"Asher Wilde. Didn't see that coming," Claire says when we're buckled into our car, Seth driving.

"He's like, one of your idols, right?" Emilie asks.

"To be fair, he's almost everyone's idol. He's an icon," I reply.

I've waited to open the folder until it is only my team. I look at the dates and locations. They weren't joking. This is three US legs, plus substantial international dates. There are chunks of tour where I wouldn't see my house for weeks. Claire peers over my shoulder.

"This is bruuuuutal. But probably an opportunity of a lifetime," Claire says, scanning the list of dates.

"Can I see?" Emilie asks. I pass her the folder. Her eyes go wide when she sees what we're talking about.

"Thoughts?" I ask her.

"Really? You want to know what I think?"

"Of course."

"Well, on one hand it sounded like the exact opposite of what you were trying to do, but on the other, it sounds like a once in a lifetime opportunity." She flips through the rest of the pages. "Honestly, it might be a nice Tripp distraction."

Both of those things have crossed my mind.

"There's no way you're dating someone with *this* schedule." I appreciate her honest reaction. She's right. There's no way I'd be able to see Tripp but that doesn't even need to be a consideration.

"Tripp wants nothing to do with me so that shouldn't be a problem," I say, feeling sorry for myself a little bit.

"He hasn't called?" Claire asks. She rarely wants to get into the details of my personal life.

"No. He hasn't. I haven't. It feels over." I reach for the folder, mostly so I have something to do with my hands.

No one else says anything the whole way home.

# **Chapter 62**
## Tripp

I'M BACK AT THE practice facility and it feels so good. I've been medically cleared, from my concussion, to resume normal activity, both from an independent and our team doctor. I'm thankful the team doesn't mess around with concussion protocol.

I do feel pretty good. My shoulder has even started improving quite a bit. Amazing what rest will do to your body. I'm not going to be able to play this week but it's noticeably better.

Being around the guys immediately lifts my mood, well, almost all the guys.

"You look like shit," Zack says, his eyes checking me over.

"It's good to see you too," I respond, shaking his shoulder with my good hand. His dark blonde hair flops back and forth.

"Your skin, it's like, not the right color. Do you have a fever?" Zack uses the back of his hand to touch my forehead and I don't pull away. Instead, I roll my eyes.

"No. It's just been a rough... however long it's been." I try to reassure him with a small smile.

"I thought Willow would do a better job taking care of you." The sound of her name has me go rigid. It's like lemon juice in an open cut you forgot about.

"Ah, fuck. What happened?!" Zack's shoulders slump when he reads my face.

Before I can say something, or nothing, a coordinator lets me know that my head coach wants to see me. I give Zack a look that says we'll talk about it later, even though I don't mean it.

"Coach, you wanted to see me?" I pop my head into Coach's office. He's watching film. I swear, this man is always watching film.

"Tripp Owens. Always great to have ya at the facility. Close the door. Have a seat."

Why do I feel like I'm about to be in trouble?

"I'm medically cleared from the concussion, but the shoulder isn't ready," I say.

"No. How are you feeling?" He leans forward.

I slowly take in a breath. "I'm feeling much better. Being back here helps." When he doesn't say anything, I have a feeling he wants me to keep going. "I'm hoping to play this season. If we can hold the playoff spot, for sure. I know you want to know about the retirement rumor, but in all transparency, I haven't decided. The thing I'm focusing on now is coming back, this season, and seeing how that goes."

"You don't owe me anything when it comes to that decision. I'm here if you ever want to talk, just you and me. I was a player who once had to make the same decision and it's one of the hardest ones."

"How did you know?"

"Well, unlike you, I had an injury-riddled career. I was successful but my body was banged up from what felt like the very start. One day, it was harder and harder to make it to the facility. My body was taking longer to recover. I felt the itch to do something else, even if I didn't know what it was. And ultimately, I wanted to go out on my own. This next part sounds like complete bullshit, but it's not. You'll just know."

"Really?"

"Really. There's a difference between knowing and following through. Lots of guys know they should hang up the cleats but keep playing because they can. I could've kept playing but the risk was too great."

"That's helpful. I appreciate you checking on me. This is obviously a setback, but it currently feels good to try and get back this year. I'm still seeing my sports psychologist and we've had quite a bit to talk about."

"You're a smart guy, Tripp. You'll figure it out. There's lots of good things after playing. Families. Time for other activities. I promise it's not all bad."

"Thanks, Coach."

"I'll want to sit in on your shoulder examination before game day. I know you won't play but I'd like to see where you're at. "

I nod in agreement and stand to leave.

*Families.*

I don't have one of those. I mean, I have my mom, but lots of guys retire to spend more time with their wives and kids. I don't have either. I never seriously thought about kids. My lack of dating history always made it feel more of a hypothetical than anything possible.

Focusing on my shoulder and getting back to the team has been keeping my mind busy. I try not to spend every moment thinking about Willow. I'm still upset, more disappointed than angry, but it's a lot to sort through. My mood ebbs and flows throughout the day and I spend more time staring at my phone than I'd admit.

Thinking about calling her. Not calling her. How she hasn't called me. Wondering if she's staring at her phone the same way.

There have been times I have almost given in.

But I know I won't.

# Chapter 63
## Willow

I HAVE A PAPER calendar for the two years the tour would span spread out on my table. I'm handwriting in all the locations so I can see it out of a list. I could probably find an app to do this but there's something soothing about doing it by hand.

Today is the deadline; Erik's waiting for my answer. I'm leaning toward doing it, even though it's the exact opposite of what I was looking for. But it's Asher Wilde. I don't know if he'll be putting out any new music after this. Honestly, it's the perfect example of a once-in-a-lifetime opportunity.

When we were planning out the original tour, I did want to leave the door open on me being around for Tripp's season. I never said it out loud to anyone, but I had such a great time at the games and couldn't imagine missing out on almost all of them.

Things have definitely changed.

Someone knocks on the door. I look out and see it's Seth.

"Hate to bother you. Do you have a minute?" he asks.

"You're not bothering me. Come on in." I wave him in, and we sit at the table, covered in calendars and markers. A surprise Seth pop-in is pretty rare.

"Is everything okay?" I ask.

"It's hard to answer that. What's all this?" He points to the table.

"The tour the label proposed. It's massive. The one I have to decide on today."

"Wow. Looks extensive."

"That's a good word for it. I'm sure you didn't swing by to watch me write things down on massive calendars. What's going on?"

"You know I hate meddling, right? Meaning, you know I'd rather be anywhere else but here."

"Yes. I do," I say. I know he means it. He'd rather be tackling a stalker compared to getting into whatever he's about to.

"I realized we haven't been to Tripp's place. I also saw the news about him potentially retiring. This news, paired with your conversation after the label meeting. I know I couldn't keep this to myself."

"Keep what to yourself?" What in the world is going on?

"Tripp is mad because he thinks you told someone about something... *sensitive*, correct?"

Oh my god. Did Seth overhear and tell someone? I can't believe this. This might actually be my fault.

"Yes," I say warily. When Seth doesn't say anything, I jump to the conclusion hanging out in the middle of the room.

"Tell me it wasn't you. Tell me you didn't tell someone Tripp said that. Because—"

"Willow. Absolutely not. No. Never."

A wave of relief hits me. My clenched jaw relaxes. The nails digging into my thighs relent.

"But I know who did." He takes a breath that spans what feels like a lifetime. "Erik. It was Erik," Seth says but my brain can't connect the words to what this means.

"What do you mean it was Erik?"

"The doctors came by at some point when you were in Tripp's room. I wanted to make sure you had privacy, so I pulled them to the side, or around the corner of the room. I could still see you, and I wasn't too far away. I told the doctors we'd call for them when you were out of there or took a break. When I walked back to the room, I found Erik slinking around."

"Slinking around?"

"Legit standing as close to the door entrance as he could, ear pressed to the door. He was definitely listening in. It was only for maybe 30 seconds or so, but I take it that he had impeccable timing."

"How do you know he heard what was leaked?"

"Because he literally muttered the word *retirement*, like a dumbass, before I snuck up on him and grabbed him by the back of his shirt. Plus, he found a way to leave right after. I followed him out to the parking lot and heard him talking to someone about tour timing and something was *about to go his way.*"

No way. I can't believe it. Erik.

"I hate that I'm doing this. But I like Tripp. Out of everyone you've dated, this guy is someone who cares about your safety. He's thinking about your comfort level. I made him jump through so many hoops in the beginning—" he pauses when I shoot him a side-eye "—but it's my own way of kind of weeding out the losers."

I truly can't even find the words.

"If you and Tripp aren't going to work, that's fine. But for it to be over because of that sleaze ball, Erik? No way. That can't be it."

It's like this haze, clouding my vision, is finally lifting. My brain can make sense of what happened, from start to finish. It still hurts that Tripp thought I'd divulge that kind of information, but I can understand how it didn't make sense any other way.

"Seth. You might be a hopeless romantic, you know that right?"

"No, I'm not. And don't tell a soul," he says, pointing at me. "Are you mad?"

"Livid. But not at you. I'm thankful you told me. I truly had no idea how this got out and now it's starting to make sense."

Something isn't right with this Asher Wilde tour. All I can think about is how Erik wanted to do the tour right at the start of the football season, which would've taken me out for all of it. I didn't tell him that was one of the reasons I didn't want to do it, but it was.

"I can't believe Erik did that."

"I can," Emilie says while she's walking down the stairs, shaking her phone at me and Seth. "I don't mean to eavesdrop, but you need to see this."

***Willow Announces Major Tour with Asher Wilde.*** This is the headline that shows on her phone. The bogus article also talks about me signing a massive contract extension.

"Can I meddle one more time?" Seth asks, his eyebrow raised, clearly devising a plan. "Let's go to the label. We'll pick up Claire on the way. Surprise that little bastard before he has a chance to do anything."

"I love it. We should do that." Emilie is pointing at Seth, enthusiastically.

I think he's right. If I try to call, there's going to be some bullshit, runaround explanation.

"Let's go." I grab my coat and Emilie has the door open, putting her shoes on as we leave.

Do I FEEL BAD that I told a little white lie to Erik's assistant? Yes. I told her Erik called and asked me to come down for an urgent meeting. I need to keep going because I can't lose my nerve. Seth is even marching down with us. He wants to stay close because according to him, he "doesn't trust that rat bastard".

While Emilie looks laser focused, Claire looks like she could spit fire. I asked her to stay back unless I tap her in. She called my lawyer on the way and confirmed what I was 99% sure of. I can withhold this album, the tour, all of it.

I walk right into the meeting like I belong there.

"Mind if we join you?" I ask. Erik's face is priceless. He's surprised and not in a good way.

"Did we have a meeting?" Erik looks at his phone. When no one answers him, he tries to smooth things out. "Sure, have a seat. We always have time for you."

What a snake.

"First, I decided on the Asher Wilde tour. It's going to be a no for me. I know this will be difficult since you already made the announcement but, what can ya do?" I shrug my shoulders in the most nonchalant way.

"Lo—"

"Don't you dare call me that and do *not* interrupt. Second, I'm not signing a contract extension. As a matter of fact, my lawyer is currently looking into terminating our contract early. But no matter, if I have to wait to put this music out, I will." I pretend to look at my nails, giving him a break to let that soak in. "I will not do another thing that is tied to you. Third, you should be ashamed of yourself. I know what you did. You took something someone very close to me told me in confidence and you leaked it. To try and get what you wanted from me. You are a disgusting excuse for a human."

"What are you talking about?" Erik stands and asks, like he has no idea what's going on.

"If you try to gaslight me right now, I will take every detail of this to the press. I'll air this whole thing out and sign my name. You know what you did. Don't make me say it."

"Maybe I do want you to say it? Maybe you've got it wrong?" He fucking baits and gaslights me at the same time.

"Ricky, do yourself a favor and shut the fuck up," Claire says through gritted teeth.

"You are a walking piece of garbage," Emilie says in disgust.

Erik's eyes go from Claire, to Emilie, and back to me. He tries to soften and give me this sweet smile. I wish there was a cornerback here to smoke Erik. Knock that smug look off his face.

"Are you really not going to do the Asher Wilde tour? That seems foolish."

"No, Ricky. What seems foolish is saying I agreed to do it when I didn't. Also, I bet if we called his team, we'd hear how this was your idea and how you approached them, right? You are despicable. You knew I was hurting... a hurt you caused and tried to use it to your advantage. Not like I haven't made this label millions of dollars."

"You don't know what you're talking about," Erik says, almost in a growl, and puts his hands in his pocket. The rest of the people at the table look like they'd rather combust than be in here.

"I do." And before I can keep going, Seth leans his head in the doorway.

"Remember me?" He waves and smiles at Erik. It's one of the best mic-drop moments Seth will probably ever have in his life and I'm thankful to witness it.

"Is this true, Erik?" One of the big wigs walks into the conference room. I couldn't have asked for better timing. I don't know where she came from, but I am so happy to see her.

"They have no idea what they're talking about," he says but it's no use.

"Quit talking. Get in my office right now." She points out the doorway.

"I'm in the middle of a meeting," he tries to reason with her.

"Not anymore you're not," she says in a way that reminds me of Claire.

"Willow, let me get to the bottom of this. I'll call you, personally." The exec says to me with eyes that plead an apology.

I watch Erik speed walk out of the room, shooting daggers with his eyes the whole way.

"Seth. Claire. Emilie. I need a favor if you're up for it."

I have a plan and I'll need some help pulling it off.

# Chapter 64
## Tripp

WILLOW IS GOING ON a huge world tour. The news hits me like a punch to the gut. The fact that I heard someone talking about it at practice, asking me about the details, because they thought I knew. While there's been speculation about our breakup, no one has confirmed anything. It's not something anyone asked me as soon as I made it back to practice.

I have so many questions. What about the other album she fought for? The small-scale tour she stood her ground for? Is this it? Am I only going to know her through shitty tabloids and hearsay?

Maybe I'll call her? Fuck. I don't know.

It's game day and I'm dressed in a jersey, joggers, and still have the sling. It feels bizarre to be here and not suited up, since I've never missed a game due to injury. For the last game, I stayed home instead of traveling. I don't like it, but I have realized something. I do *want* to be back out there.

It's the first time I felt good about trying to play this season. I think I tricked myself into thinking it was the right decision, but right now, on the sideline, I feel it.

I turn to see the suite. My mom sees me and waves. I told her she didn't need to come, and she was adamant about supporting me, even though I won't be doing anything.

My heart drops when I remember the last time I looked at the suite before the game. Lo and I had this ritual. The memory stings.

WE'RE UP 24-7 AND the second quarter is running out. Coach comes over and puts his arm around me.

"Hey, need you to stay out here for half time. They're doing some PR shit and I thought you'd be perfect for it. They'll tell you what to do. Don't sweat it."

"You got it, Coach." I have no idea what it could be but I'm not one to argue. Especially when I'm trying to stay in the organization's good graces.

The quarter ends and the team goes into the locker room. I stay out, like I was asked, with a few members of the coaching staff and assistants.

The announcer's voice fills the stadium, "For today's halftime festivities, we have a special guest. Please direct your attention to the fifty-yard line."

I'm sitting on a bench near our end-zone. I look to the fifty to see someone walking out. Not someone. Willow. With a guitar.

The crowd goes absolutely wild. I can feel the screams to my bones.

Willow waves to everyone up until she hits her mark, where a microphone stands. She's wearing my jersey with a yellow peony pinned to it.

A lump forms in my throat. I'm trying to make sense of what's happening. I thought I'd be mad, seeing her next, but there's no anger to be found. It's almost like relief.

"Wondering if you'd mind if I play you a song? From my new album? One that I've never played live for anyone before. Would that be okay?"

I don't know if I've been anywhere louder. This game is sold-out, and people didn't anticipate a Willow half-time performance. My heart races, watching her start playing the guitar.

"I wrote this song after one of the best weekends of my life. The kind of weekend you wish you could re-live over and over again." The clapping is so loud I'm amazed we can hear Willow over it. "This song is called Our Secret Cove." Willow starts playing the guitar.

I'm mesmerized from the first note. The first word. The song is about our weekend getaway. I try to hold on to each line, each verse, but my mind is tripping over itself. Why is she here? How is she doing this? How did my coach know?

I close my eyes and try to take this in.

*Our silhouettes on the sand*
*Under the moon*
*Beneath the skylight*
*Hearts intertwined*
*You feel the rush as we stand*
*Only truth, me and you*
*There's no better life*
*You look at me that way*
*Falling more in love with you*
*Uncovering something new*
*Nothing more that I want, than I need*
*So we'll dive right in*
*On shores, we'll rush in, pour ourselves holy*
*You're everything*

She goes from the chorus to the next verse, and I'm in awe. Tears silently roll down my cheeks. I know they're going to show shots of this later and I don't care. The melody takes me back to that weekend. Us running through the freezing water on the beach. The moonlight sparkling in her eyes as I told her I loved her. Mountains of bubbles. The feeling of getting this thing right.

Willow finishes the song, her voice strong and clear. The crowd erupts into a deafening roar, and I stand to join them. I try to clap but having one arm in a sling makes this much harder. They show Willow on the Jumbotron, wiping tears from her eyes, wearing a smile that could light some of the darkest places.

Before I can talk myself out of it, I'm walking towards her. She sees me and walks in my direction. The second the crowd knows what's happening, the whole place goes feral. I truly couldn't hear myself think.

We finally meet and I wrap her up in a hug with my one arm. She puts her hands around my stomach and puts her head on my chest. She then reaches up to whisper in my ear.

"Tripp. I'm so sorry. I figured it out—"

And I kiss her because I can't help myself. I don't let her say another word.

"I can't believe you did this," I say.

"I had to find a way to say I was sorry. I played my hand knowing it may not work. I was terrified I would come out and you would go back to the locker-room."

The screams from the crowd rattle my bones, make my ears ring. I hold Willow's hand with my good one.

"Let's find somewhere we can talk," I say as I lead her back to the team tunnel.

Fritz stands right at the entrance and stops me.

"Equipment room is free. I grabbed everything they might need and set it outside the door. That's also where a decently angry security guard seems to be camping out."

It has to be Seth. I thank Fritz with a smile before heading towards the equipment area.

I close the door and Willow is already pacing. Her dark hair is in loose curls, pinned back with a Cosmos blue hair clip, including the team logo.

"Tripp, I am so sorry. It was Erik." Her words trample each other.

Erik. Huh? Now, that's someone I wouldn't have guessed. It's like the final missing piece to a puzzle, clicking into place.

"The slime-ball was hanging outside your hospital room and Seth got him to leave, but it was too late, and this whole thing is a mess, and—"

"Willow, breathe." I interrupt her and tap next to me, wanting her to sit. She takes a breath and sits next to me.

"You aren't the only one who needs to hand out an apology. I'm sorry. For all of it." My voice cracks with joy and relief. I'm thankful for the opportunity to tell her how I feel.

"I'm sorry I didn't believe you. I'm sorry I didn't call. I thought about it so many times. I'm sorry I made you leave your key." I catch my breath and place my hand on hers. "I'm sorry for the way I spoke to you, in my apartment. It plays over and over in my head and I'll never forgive myself." I can't even look at her right now.

"Yes. You will. Tripp." She tilts my chin up, speaking while holding my eyes with hers, her eyes golden with compassion.

"I just want more time," I say, my voice small.

"We'll figure it out. We have lots of time."

"But what about the tour with Asher Wilde?"

"Nope. That was an Erik special and I turned it down. I don't want to miss a whole season of you playing the game you love."

"What?" I don't know if I'm following.

"I'm sorry that someone in my corner did this to you, to us. You didn't deserve that," she says. I don't know what to say so she keeps going. "You and me. My life is better with you in it. I don't need a tour that keeps me from you for months at a time. I can tour on my, or our, timeline. I've earned that."

"Our timeline?" I smirk at her because I love hearing her fucking say that.

"It's your play to call, but that's what I'd prefer." She's reserved and fidgety.

"Our timeline. Our call. I'm in."

And I kiss her for each *I'm sorry, I missed you,* and *I love you* that I haven't had a chance to say.

# **Chapter 65**
## Willow



"We can't be late to the fucking Super Bowl, Willow!" Emilie screams at me from the guest bedroom in Tripp's penthouse apartment. I roll my eyes as I delicately put my pink lipstick on.

"We're not going to be late. We're already in the city!"

The Super Bowl is being played at one of the other New York stadiums. Even though it's not a home game for the Cosmos, it sort of is.

"Did you check the line for the game? Has it moved at all?" I ask Emilie about the betting line. I want to know what Vegas thinks about the matchup: the Seattle Serpents versus the Upstate Cosmos. The NFL couldn't have asked for a better storybook ending to this season.

The Upstate Cosmos stole a playoff spot with some late season magic, which gave Tripp the chance to play again this year. Not only has Tripp played every playoff game, but he's scored at least one touchdown in each. His obsession with training really paid off when it came to rehab. There's still a substantial risk of him injuring the same shoulder, but he wants to play, and I'm there to support him every step of the way.

Every day, I am proud of him.

"The line is -1.5, Seattle!" my dad yells from the living room.

"I can't believe they're still banking on Tripp not being 100%. Can't wait for them to eat those bets!" Emilie yells loud enough for everyone to hear and they clap in response.

My parents, and Wendy, are also hanging out at Tripp's before the game. Tripp stayed at the team hotel last night, even though it's practically a home game, and it's been great spending time with everyone. I've never had a core group like this.

Yesterday, I had my settlement meeting with the label. While they fired Erik, for other complaints other than mine, we still decided that going our separate ways was best. We've been great for each other during the last decade, but I'm ready to move to a smaller, female-owned label.

*True Blue Records.*

My own.

Emilie is the one who asked me about it, all nonchalant, like it was a stupid question. I've learned so much about the industry and I'm happy to grow a small label for other artists who need to be heard. It's in the early stages now, but I will be releasing my new album under that label. Plus, I paid Emilie a massive advance to ensure she's always involved, one way or another.

I stand in front of the mirror in Tripp's bedroom, or our bedroom I guess you could say. After my grand gesture at the game, Tripp and I exchanged keys. We rarely spend nights apart and try to do what's best for both of our schedules and careers. He's my biggest fan and I try doing the same for him.

My outfit, courtesy of the trifecta (Mom, Wendy, and Emilie), is a custom Tripp Owen's jersey, but sewed into a dress. It tapers in at the waist and flows out, hitting mid-thigh. I paired the dress with shimmery tights, because how often are those appropriate? Tonight is the perfect occasion. The jersey is white which means my thigh-high boots are Cosmos blue.

No one knows about the special lingerie set I have on underneath the jersey. I called Emilie's friend with the boutique in the city and she made me the most beautiful black lace set, with Tripp's number in the center of the bra.

My heart is full as I stand in Tripp's jersey, hearing the sounds of my parents in the living room. Emilie's laugh carries and I know she's doing her pre-game handshake with Wendy.

THERE'S EIGHT SECONDS ON the clock, it's fourth and 9, and the Cosmos are down by five points. It doesn't matter that it's fourth down because this is it—there's only time for a single play. The Cosmos have to get a play off before the nine seconds are over, but it technically could go longer than nine seconds. The suite is stressed, considering there have been seven lead changes throughout the game.

I see the personnel coming in for the final play and notice something. Zack. For some reason, the long snapper is on the field for an offensive play.

Emilie squeezes my hand when she sees Zack on the field, her wide eyes finding mine.

We know this can only mean one thing. A trick play.

There's no air to breathe. My lungs no longer function. I squeeze Emilie's hands, probably too tight, she just pulls me closer to her.

The offense lines up, the referee blows the whistle, and the play clock starts to tick.

*Nine.*

The ball is snapped to the quarterback.

*Eight.*

He tries to scan the coverage down field, locking in on the right corner.

*Seven.*

The defense moves to the right, reading the quarterback's eyes.

*Six.*

Someone gets free to the right of the quarterback.

*Five.*

The quarterback pitches the ball. To Zack.

*Four.*

Zack hops back, like he's going to pass the ball. There's no way he's going to throw it, right?

*Three*

The quarterback blocks for Zack, giving him the second he needs.

*Two.*

Zack passes the ball. WHY DOES ZACK PASS THE BALL?

*One.*

The ball sails to the left corner of the end-zone

*Zero.*

Tripp catches the touchdown!

Game over.

Cosmos win!

Cosmos blue confetti falls on the field, thick and glittering. Seth and his team follow close to Wendy and me while we look for Tripp.

The Upstate Cosmos are the first NFL expansion team to win the Super Bowl—it's unbelievable. My voice is hoarse from screaming, my heart beats too fast, and a smile is plastered to my face.

Wendy sees Tripp and starts to jog. He swallows her up in a hug. They spin a little and I see her face in complete awe of the game, her son. Wendy's facial expression is what most of us are feeling.

I give them a minute because they deserve it. Seeing them embraced like this, makes me so happy for them, especially since it was never easy.

My hand sits on my chest, soaking in this moment, and I'm not the only one. Cameras click and reporters try to get a word with Tripp and Wendy.

Then, Tripp sees me. His eyes, which I swear are Cosmos blue right now, make my heart stop. I can feel my mouth pull into a jubilant smile as Tripp steps towards me.

He reaches for my waist and picks me up. I laugh and put my hands on his shoulders before I kiss him. This kiss is full of promise, pride, love, and certainty. He sets me down and wraps his arms around my low back.

"I can't believe that happened! I'm still shaking!" I say to him before kissing him again, leaving pink on his lips.

"Me either because I can't believe Coach let us call that play." Tripp laughs, one that reaches his eyes and his bones. He puts his head in the crook of my neck and kisses up and down.

"I love you so much. Having you here on this field, confetti in your hair, is a fucking dream I didn't know I had." He kisses me in between words.

"I love you to the cove and back," I say with a wink. "Think you'll be named MVP for the second year in a row?"

"Doesn't matter. You're the only prize I need," Tripp says while dipping me for a dramatic kiss.

Cameras flash and click, and we hear *awwww* coming from people in the background.

This is the moment. The one where I know, no matter whether we win, lose, or draw, on our own, we're always winners together.

# Epilogue
## Tripp



The sea of cellphones always catches me off guard, no matter how many times I see it. After clearing security, it's nothing but lenses from any and every angle—not paparazzi but Willow's fans instead.

With a maximum occupancy of only 800 people, tonight's venue is special. Excitement and pure joy rolls off every person as I walk by. *All for Willow. My dream girl. Believe me, I totally get it.*

As I make my way to my spot, near the side of the stage, I stop as people ask for selfies. It's easy to say yes when they're so damn kind and thankful to be there. The Upstate Cosmos fans are incredible but there's something next level when it comes to Willow's loyal fanbase.

"Hold up, Tripp!" Zack yells. I turn back—he's taking his own photos with groups of fans. He's been begging me to bring him to a concert and this is the first one that aligned with our schedules.

Ever since Zack nailed the trick play to win the Super Bowl, he's become a household name. It's not that people didn't know him before but now it's like a switch, from "some" to "almost all". Rumor has it there's a jump in kids wanting to play his position—long snapper—instead of the traditional quarter back or wide receiver. That's pretty fucking cool.

He's one of the good ones. I love seeing him get the attention and recognition he deserves. Except for now, when he's slowing us down. And letting someone whisper in his ear?

I squint, make sure I'm seeing things correctly. Zack has always been a magnet for this type of attention. A short blonde, wearing an Upstate Cosmos shirt, laughs as he says something to her. "Zack, you coming?" I ask.

The blonde, hands Zack her phone and he types something in, probably his number. She pouts as he waves and turns back to me.

"Do you know her?" It wouldn't be the first time Zack arranged to meet someone while we were out.

"Not yet," he raises his eyebrows. "But hoping to later." He shakes my shoulder with his hand, and I can't help but roll my eyes. I've never been one to casually hookup with anyone, so maybe I just don't get it, but Zack has had quite the roster ever since we won the Super Bowl.

According to him, he carries multiple condoms with him at all times. At least he's being safe.

Stage lights flicker, indicating there's only a few minutes before the show starts, before they land on Willow's piano—her two guitars next to it. My stomach flips, the butterflies making their pre-show appearance.

Tonight is Willow's tenth tour date, and I know what to expect logistically, but it's like my brain can't comprehend some of the details.

How I'll never need a concert ticket, because I have a reserved spot, at every venue. How the tour sold out in a single day. How people show up wearing Cosmos gear and they're excited to see me even though I'm just a fan like everyone else.

*How she's mine.*

I'm so fucking proud of her. The new album, "A Love Letter to The Coast", is at the top of the charts, going on week six. The accomplishment is even sweeter since it's under her own label: True Blue Records.

She wanted to keep the tour timeline the same, which meant breaking things off with her original label and diving into this side of the business much sooner than was probably recommended.

"Wow, she looks good," Zack says, his voice trailing off.

I follow his eyes and see an enthusiastic Emilie waving. She's off to the side of the stage—where our seats are. "Don't you dare," I say, my finger pointing at him.

"I would never…" he says, with a smirk, one that tells me not to believe a thing he just said.

"Cutting it close," Emilie yells, pointing at a fake watch on her wrist.

Zack breaks away from the mass group of people trying to get his photo, right off the barricade for our spot for the night. "We're right here! Not going to miss anything."

I shake my head, smiling through the interaction, as Emilie puts a hand on her hip, shifting her weight. Her hazel eyes throw friendly daggers at Zack. It's the four of us, more often than not, and every once in a while, Zack and Emilie bicker like they've known each other their whole lives.

Emilie feels like one of Willow's limbs at this point. Willow asked Emilie to have her hands in the new label; she single handedly found all of the venues and organized the small tour, the one of Willow's dreams, on a tight schedule.

She's killing it but no one's surprised.

The security guard waves us through, his eyes quickly checking our VIP passes hanging around our neck.

"What are the odds Willow invites me on stage tonight?" Zack asks, scoping out the stage and crowd from our seats.

"Zero," Emilie and I answer, and half laugh, at the same time. Zack whips his head, looking between Emilie and I before waving us off with a hand.

Emilie pulls me in for a hug, "Have fun," she says.

"You on the other hand, don't have too much fun." She points at Zack and winks, before she heads backstage.

For the first few shows, I watched from backstage. Honestly, I'm not picky and would be happy being anywhere in the vicinity, but Willow never forgets that I was a fan before I was her boyfriend. She proposed this side section for friends and family and she was right. Seeing her show this way lets me take in all of Willow with the audience experience.

*It's fucking intoxicating.*

The lights go down and the crowd starts to cheer. It's like you could reach out and grab hold of the energy.  I clap right alongside them.

Willow takes one step on the stage and the entire place erupts. Even though this is a much smaller venue, the sound is deafening, and the smile feels like it's glued on my face.

"Holy shit!" Zack says, close to my ear so I can hear him. "I have goosebumps." He shows me his forearm.

"Told you!" I yell over the crowd noise.

Willow stands at the front of the stage, waving and blowing kisses to the crowd—this is how she always starts. Tonight, she's wearing a flowy blue dress, that's ridiculously close to Cosmos colors. It's tighter on the top, with sheer sleeves, her dark hair pinned back from her face. In addition to the intimate venues, she's only working with up-and-coming designers for her concert wardrobe. You won't find her in anything designer but she does a shoutout for each designer at the end of the show, helping other creatives with more visibility.

She walks back to the piano, and finds me, our pre-show tradition. Willow places a hand on her heart and I do the same thing back to her. When she looks at me, fuck, it's like I can do anything.

"If I didn't love you guys, this would be impossible to watch. You know that, right?" Zack bumps his shoulder into mine before giving Willow a wave.

"Welcome to the Coastline Tour!" Willow says into the microphone, while playing a few notes on the piano. The noise of the crowd, even louder than before, feels like it reaches my bones.

"We may not be on the coast tonight but hope the music takes you somewhere special." She smiles and I feel like everyone can see her golden eyes sparkling, no matter where they're sitting.

"Speaking of special, I want to give a shout out to someone who means the world to me." She shifts from the crowd until she's looking at me, playing a melody I know all too well. "Today, Tripp Owens signed a three-year contract extension with the Upstate Cosmos!" She picks her hands off the keys to clap, all while looking at me.

After winning another Super Bowl, no MVP this time, it was clear I still wanted to play. My time in the league isn't over. My shoulder injury rehabbed like a dream and I know I'm lucky. There's not many guys who could've made it back in the same season. But I did. And I couldn't have done it without the woman derailing the start of her concert to give me praise.

Zack claps my back before hooting and hollering with the rest of the crowd. I look out and see fans clapping and jumping up and down, finding me. Willow's fans knowing when I'm at a concert, or cheering me on like this, will never get old. I wave, trying to show them how thankful I am.

"If you don't mind—" Willow's fingers dance on the piano. "I'd like to switch up the setlist a bit more than usual. Starting with a song that I felt like I was trying to write my whole life, but was only able to finish it recently. The pieces fell into place on a cold October night, on the beach."

The crowd screams, knowing what song is coming next. Tears cloud my vision.

"I hope I'm able to write a thousand more love songs, just like this one, but for now, this is called Our Secret Cove." Willow locks her eyes on mine, for a few long seconds, and I can't move.

I knew it was coming, the piano melody engrained in my DNA, but I still must look up to blink the tears away.

Willow mouths, "I love you," before her hands dance on the keys, playing a song I've heard a thousand times. I'll never get sick of it.

Of her. This life. How lucky I am.

Because sometimes, you fall in love with the girl of your dreams.

And she loves you back.

# Acknowledgments

I almost didn't publish this book. Now, I'm sitting here, looking at the acknowledgments, trying not to cry. This book taught me how important it is to have the right people in my corner. I'm so thankful for everyone who showed up, giving me their time, energy, and space.

Erik, who is *much* cooler than the fictional Erik in this book, for letting me use his name. Here's to a real one! I owe you a drink.

Anna, for collaborating with me on *Our Secret Cove*. Having a custom song for this book means the world to me and your voice is such a perfect fit. Thank you!

Wendy, for being my second mom for what feels like my whole life. Thank you for always cheering me on.

Adah, Grace, Rachel, Megan, Ambar, and Kendra, for being the ultimate hype team. This book had a rough start and the imposter syndrome raged. Thanks for encouraging me to tell this story and give a voice to Willow and Tripp. I'm pretty sure I cried to all of you, at some point, and I'll never forget your kindness.

Stephanie and Rose, for being the best beta readers I could've asked for. Your feedback helped this book be the best it could be while making me feel like Willow and Tripp were more than worthwhile. When I think back to this whole experience, you're one of the brightest parts.

Keona for being the best PA/beta reader/hype girl. I'll never forget when you called *A Lodge Affair* one of your "soul books".

Kaitlyn, Dani, Allison (Glam Fam Murderinos), for letting me ramble about sports romance, obscure genres, booktok drama, and ultimately being proud of me.

Chels, Ryan, and FJ, for always asking about my writing projects. But, mostly Fritz for loving me the way he does.

Carly, for all of the writing sprints and cheering me on. I don't think I deserve a beautiful butterfly like you, but I'm so thankful.

Liz, for knowing me better than I sometimes know myself. Thanks for your honest feedback and challenging me to be a better writer. Here's to doing things I thought I'd never do with a best friend I found on the internet.

Robby, my lovely husband, for giving me inspiration for writing someone like Tripp. I'll never forget when you'd bring flowers to the gymnastics gym, when I was coaching, just because. Love you to the moon.

***Listen to "Our Secret Cove", the official song for***
**Your Play to Call**

# LISTEN TO "OUR SECRET COVE"
# OFFICIAL SONG FROM YOUR PLAY TO CALL

Our silhouettes on the sand
Under the moon
Beneath the twilight
Our hearts intertwined
Feel the rush as we stand
Only truth, Me and you
Me and you, There's no better life

When you look at me that way
I'm falling more in love with you
Uncovering something new

Nothing more that I want
That I need
So we'll dive right in
On shores we'll rush in
Pour ourselves holy
Cause you're everything

RACHEL LABERGE is the author of YOUR PLAY TO CALL. When she's not reading or writing, she's probably thinking about donuts, sour candy, or looking for her next hyperfixation. She lives in Michigan with her husband (Roberto), her two Frenchies (Rafa and Ruby), and cat (Riley).

You can connect with her on Instagram, TikTok, and Threads **@rachellabergeauthor** (no 'R' name required).

Want to be first in line for updates and bonus content? Sign up for Rachel's newsletter at rachellaberge.com.

***Other books by Rachel LaBerge***
*A Lodge Affair*
*A Love Letter to Those Who Left Me Behind*